Penghu
Moon in the Well

井月澎湖

Penghu
Moon in the Well

井月澎湖

A Novel Centered on the Lives of Two
Penghu Families During the Colonial Years
in Taiwan

澎湖兩大家族的興衰糾葛
見証歷史的台灣小說

Louise Lee Hsiu

李秀

To order additional copies of this book, contact:
Xlibris Corporation
1-888-795-4274
www.Xlibris.com
Orders@Xlibris.com
104248

CONTENTS

A sketch map of Penghu

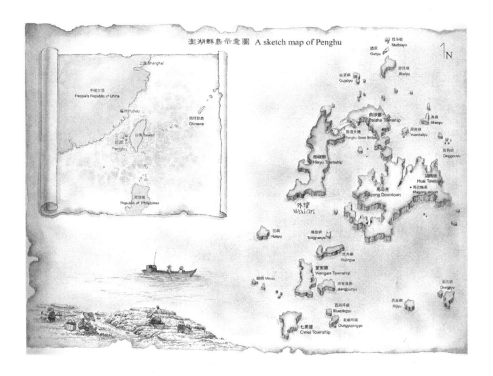

Copy from Penghu, Love at First Sight
Published by Penghu County Government

In memory of my parents and

survivors of the Japanese

occupation of Taiwan

紀念 先父母 以及

台灣被日本殖民的苦難時代

Pondering my future with Father beside my mother's grave.

Forever writing about family relationships will become my future.

和父親在母親墳旁沉思；書寫親情將是我永遠的主題

Photograph by 李成在 *(author's third oldest brother)*

The writer needs an address,

Very badly needs an address

That is his (or her) roots.

—Isaac Bashevis Singer

作家首要任務就是尋根

—以撒辛格

The Relationships of Characters

In Taiwan, in formal situations, each person is introduced by his or her family name preceding his or her given name. For example, if we look at the name Lee Zi-Shan, Lee is the family name and Zi-Shan is the given name. Family members are addressed by their given names only in informal or family situations.

Lee Family

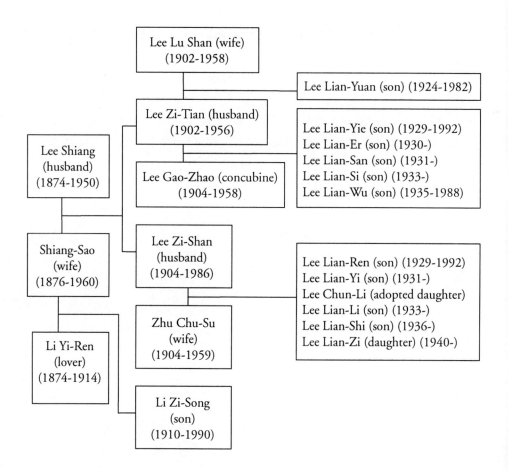

Lee Lu Shan (wife)
(1902-1958)

Lee Lian-Yuan (son) (1924-1982)

Lee Zi-Tian (husband)
(1902-1956)

Lee Lian-Yie (son) (1929-1992)
Lee Lian-Er (son) (1930-)
Lee Lian-San (son) (1931-)
Lee Lian-Si (son) (1933-)
Lee Lian-Wu (son) (1935-1988)

Lee Shiang
(husband)
(1874-1950)

Lee Gao-Zhao (concubine)
(1904-1958)

Lee Zi-Shan
(husband)
(1904-1986)

Lee Lian-Ren (son) (1929-1992)
Lee Lian-Yi (son) (1931-)
Lee Chun-Li (adopted daughter)
Lee Lian-Li (son) (1933-)
Lee Lian-Shi (son) (1936-)
Lee Lian-Zi (daughter) (1940-)

Shiang-Sao
(wife)
(1876-1960)

Zhu Chu-Su
(wife)
(1904-1959)

Li Yi-Ren
(lover)
(1874-1914)

Li Zi-Song
(son)
(1910-1990)

Zhu Family

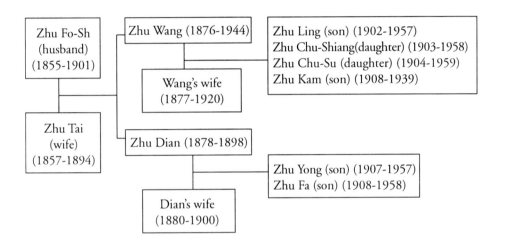

Preface

The Service of the Leaves

In each place in the world, there are always some fascinating sights to visit. They might be a series of mountains, historical monuments or wonderful lakes. Every country is proud of their features, and everyone is interested in talking about them. In my home country, the Penghu Islands offer a rich diversity of spectacular geological scenes and landscapes. Not only are there many special spots and symbols of interest that attract a great number of tourists, but for me there is a personal connection with my parents who spent their childhood there. However, no portrait of these sights is complete without mentioning the special landforms and maritime aspects of the Penghu Islands.

The Penghu Islands consist of nearly sixty islands and are located between Taiwan and mainland China. Most of the islands are low and flattopped and surrounded by steep cliffs. Because the Penghu Islands are volcanic, composed of basalt magma and sea alluvium eroded over the years, these elements have shaped the currently magnificent outlook. Moreover, the Penghu Islands have been a strategic hub for navigation in East Asia, a vital source of fish for European countries since ancient times, and a stopover for the Chinese on their voyages to the far seas and their migrations to new lands.

For example, Hsiyu is a small island located on the west side of Penghu. Fishing and mining are the major industries here. The surrounding sea is concentrated with squid, lobster, colorful fishes, and mussels. Once, Europeans called Hsiyu the Island of the Fisherman. In addition, Penghu and Italy are the world's two largest agate-producing areas, and Hsiyu's agate has been recognized worldwide as being the best because of its colors and fine quality. Searching for agate along the seashore is my favorite activity because it reminds me of all the delightful family times there when I was young.

Waian, the township where my parents were born, is located to the south of the Hsiyu. A lighthouse was built in 1778. It was the first lighthouse in Taiwan and was built to guide the boats between mainland China and Taiwan. It was my favorite place, so as a teenager, I would often watch the ocean's movements, reading them like a book that recalled happy memories of my parents when my mother was still alive.

Additionally, it is easy to discover a lot of chrysanthemums throughout this area. This flower thrives in a climate of strong seasonal winds and a scarcity of rainfall. Its vitality symbolizes the inhabitants' spirit of fortitude and endeavor. It also seems to be a symbol of my parents' life; hence, I always walk along paths, looking for this flower whenever I come back to Penghu from Taiwan or Canada.

Is it possible to find a place where the special geological landscape, colorful kinds of fishes, and varieties of scenery are combined in such wonderful harmony? Of course, different people have different opinions about the same sights. I don't know if it is because Penghu is my home country, but I am convinced that Penghu has some of the most fascinating sights I have ever seen, and there I feel connected to my family. If you visit Penghu, you will also fall in love with this land. A Swiss man, who is my son's friend, said that he has visited many types of seashore of different countries, but Hsiyu's coastal beach is a truly memorable place for him.

I adore my parents timelessly. Even though they passed away many decades ago, whenever I see them in my mind, I feel strong emotions. And so I wrote the novel *Penghu Moon in the Well* to honor my parents. This book has won two literary awards in Taiwan, and it has even been read over a period of two months by a Kaohsiung radio station.

The novel begins in Waian, the place of my parents' birth, and then shifts to Kaohsiung when my parents move there. In 1895, China's Ch'ing Dynasty was forced to sign the Treaty of Shimonoseki (馬關條約), ceding Taiwan and Penghu to Japan, and so this historic event forms the background of *Penghu Moon in the Well*. In this novel, I describe Lee Shiang, who embodies my grandfather whose son Lee Zi-Shan is, in fact, the embodiment of my father. The novel highlights the lives of two Penghu families as a testimony to the colonial years in Taiwan. The Lee family represents my father's relatives, and my mother's relatives are presented as members of the Zhu family.

The noted Taiwanese critic Dr. Ye (葉石濤) said that this novel is outstanding because of the following features:

It fully reflects the historical time, social movement of each stage of Taiwan from the end of the Ch'ing dynasty (1895) to the 1980's. It presents the details of daily public life and the distress of the people in Penghu under the rule of a foreign nation—Japan. The local history of Penghu Islands is the epitome of the whole historical situation of Taiwan.

It complains about the misery of women's lives in Penghu because of the human rights that Taiwanese women were deprived of under feudalism.

The details about the people's faith in the Goddess Mazu and other kinds of religious activities are vividly portrayed; it is like a scroll of folk illustrations of Taiwan.

This novel is also an example of oceanic literature. Surrounded by the sea, the Penghu people's survival depends on the kindness of the sea; cultivation of the land is secondary. Their lives are inseparable from the coastal ecology.

Excellent command of the mother tongue is important in accurately portraying the true nature of Taiwanese culture.

The reality of Taiwan as a multiracial society is highlighted. There are various kinds of racial backgrounds in the novel. The portrayals of the characters are vivid and full of contrasting personalities; the novel interlocks lives of complicated lightness and darkness.

I very much appreciate Dr. Ye's analysis of my novel.

Once, a reporter asked me if writing was my mission. I have been writing for many years, but the thought of a mission never crossed my mind. I just think that emotions are inextinguishable and that they control our lives. From parental love, the love between friends, to romantic love, it's the most basic of human instincts. In fact, I have continued to adore my parents very much even after their deaths—I depended on them so much while they were alive. My writing has always focused on family love, and this novel is my greatest tribute to this subject.

I worked on this novel, *Penghu Moon in the Well,* for about four years. This included a lot of historical research. Now Penghu is no longer just an abstract noun. She specifically touches my mind to remind me where my blood relationships began. I do appreciate the Taiwanese poet who gave me access to his library of history books, enabling me to verify the historical background of *Penghu Moon in the Well*. I immigrated to Vancouver over ten years ago, and now I have translated *Penghu Moon in the Well* into English to open up the story of my home country to more people. It took me two years to do this; I am grateful to Canadian writer Barbara Ladouceur, who edited this translation for me. In addition, I've also translated into English a series of essays about family love, a book of children's poems, and a book of poetry written by a Taiwanese poet.

I strongly agree with the advice "Writing in the mother language is a good way to solve homesickness in a foreign country." Thus I translated my children's poems from Chinese to Taiwanese, my mother language. I always say, "I come from Taiwan, my hometown is Penghu." My friends and relatives in Taiwan asked me if I miss my home country. Of course I do, but instead of responding to my country's summons to come home, I work hard on projects that will introduce my beloved homeland to the Western world.

I hope that the story of my adored ancestors can show in some way my beautiful home country, the Penghu Islands, which lay like pearls reflected in the sparkling Taiwan Strait. Furthermore, when I know something is magnificent, the first thing I have to do is share it with my friends everywhere so that the knowledge of this beautiful thing can spread everywhere around the world. To paraphrase the words of the poet Tagore about God's message to the ocean, the service of the fruit is precious; the service of the flowers is sweet, but let my service be the service of the leaves in the shade of humble devotion.

Louise Lee Hsiu
December 2011
Vancouver Canada

Preface in Chinese

讓我奉獻一些濃蔭給您

「井月澎湖」英文版序文

世界上每個地方，總會有迷人的景點值得觀光。它們也許是一系列的山、豐富的歷史紀念館或是美妙亮麗的湖畔。每個國家都爲他們特有的景觀感到驕傲，並且大家都很樂意的談論著。而我的家鄉「澎湖群島」，她的地質地形豐沛多變，是一處面海的窗，美得令人讚嘆，不但是造物者的神奇圖騰，對我來說，更是與雙親連接的根點，因爲這個澎湃的大自然所在，充溢著父母的形影。如果沒有深入描繪她特殊的地貌和異乎尋常的海事驚豔，你是無法探觸到這塊大地雕塑的神奇。

澎湖群島位於臺灣和中國大陸之間，由六十幾個島嶼組成，多數島嶼低平且被峭壁所環繞，由於澎湖列島係由一系列的火山形成，多年來又被腐蝕的玄武岩漿和海沖積層的元素，而塑造成當前壯觀的外型。另外，澎湖海島的地位，遠古時代就扮演東亞航海的重要戰略中心、歐洲國家漁類源頭以及中國人遷移至另外一個新大陸的中繼站。

例如，西嶼鄉(Hsiyu)位於澎湖西邊一個小海島，以捕漁業和採礦業爲主。主要出產烏賊、龍蝦、五顏六色的魚和淡菜，被歐洲人稱爲「漁夫的海島」。澎湖和意大利是世界兩大瑪瑙生產區域，但西嶼瑪瑙顏色美好、質量佳，更稱冠世界。而我，一個澎湖子女，喜愛搜尋玩耍沿海瑪瑙的活動，感覺這樣可以貼近對先祖的記憶。

外垵(Waian)位於西嶼鄉最南邊的小鎮，就是父母出生的血跡所在。 早在1778年的第一個引導臺灣和中國大陸之間海上船隻的燈塔就建造在此，我渴望在這片臨海的大地奔跳、讀海，似乎這樣我才能真實的捕捉少女快樂的記憶，因爲那時父母健在。另外澎湖又有「菊島」之稱，燈塔週圍遍地菊花，整片黃色花浪，不畏猛烈季風候和降雨量的缺乏，生長於痛瘠瘠薄土地，她照樣盛開迎風招展，象徵著島民剛毅、打拼的生命力，也似乎是父母早年生活的標誌。因此更是我成年後每次不論自臺灣或溫哥華回鄉最愛留連的地方。

有什麼地方能尋到如此巧奪天工的地質，五彩繽紛的魚種，一座被漁船依靠有如曠野裏的島嶼，她不時擲出鏗鏘迷人的韻腳？當然，不同的人對相同地方會有不同的觀感，是否她是我的故鄉而我有特殊的鍾愛？但我深信，從來沒有一個地方的景觀如此的扣人心弦、叫人肅然起敬！如果你有心想親近她，你會愛上她的。我兒子一個瑞士朋友他說，雖然他走過世界很多海灘，但西嶼沙灘令他驚奇和難忘。

從小對父母的依賴和害怕他們突然消失，我是懷著這種心態而長大。事實上，他們真的離我而遠去，而今既使他們過世幾十年，午夜夢迴尋不著慈顏依然叫人惆悵心悸。爲懷念他們，早期於臺灣出版一本長篇小說並獲兩種獎項(吳濁流文學獎及高雄市文藝獎)，也曾被廣播電臺盜播兩個月之久的「井月澎湖」。

這本小說的劇情是從雙親出生地「外垵」開始，到他們移民至臺灣「高雄」，作一個生活歷史的結合；從馬關條約的簽訂，到日本入侵澎湖、臺灣作爲小說背景。自描述李祥(祖父的化身) 爲起點，到李子山(父親的化身)過世，傳遞澎湖李家和許家的興衰糾葛，見証殖民時代的悲歡歲月。其實書中李家(Lee family) 是我父親的家族，許家(Zhu family) 是我母親的家族。

著名評論家葉石濤先生曾評論 *井月澎湖* 是傑出的歷史小說，它有六大特色：

1. 充分反應臺灣各階段歷史的時代、社會的變遷，從清末到1980年代。透過民眾日常生活的細微末節反映異族統治下澎湖民眾的愁苦。澎湖列島地方史是臺灣整體歷史情境的縮影。
2. 透過澎湖婦女悲慘的生涯來控訴封建制度下臺灣婦女無人權的生活狀況。
3. 民眾的媽祖信仰及各種宗教活動均刻劃入微，是一卷臺灣民俗圖繪。
4. 這本小說也是海洋文學，描繪四面環海的澎湖人以海維生，和海岸生態是密不可分，但耕種是次要。
5. 善用母語，表示本土性的重要。
6. 注意到臺灣是多種族社會，小說人物具多種族背景。人物刻劃栩栩如生，給小說帶來複雜的光和暗交錯的表現。

感謝葉老的評語，他可以探觸到本書所表達的重點，更感動他說到我心坎深處。

曾有記者問我寫作有否使命感？寫這麼多年，從來沒有想過使命感，只是感到人類千古不滅的情感，一直主宰我們的生活。從友情、愛情，到親情，始終是人性底層最掙扎課題。而我執著親情，對雙親近乎病態的依賴，十本著作幾乎以親情為主軸，「井月澎湖」更是發揮到淋漓盡致。

從感念父母到追尋父祖的澎湖，可說是投入文學書寫始終不離的主題，經歷四個寒暑，此刻澎湖已不再是抽象名詞，而是具體感受家族綿延的顛沛，我的血緣如此真實生活在那口歷史井月之中。感激台灣詩人無葉豐富的歷史書庫讓我應用，使本書更具歷史真實。如今移居溫哥華十多年佔英文語言的地利方便，我又花了兩年時間將之譯成英文，讓更多種族了解我的故鄉；感謝加拿大作家Barbara Ladouceur為本書的英文編輯；此外我也將自己一系列親情文章、童詩、臺灣詩人的作品翻成英文，有些刊在當地報紙和入選北美詩刊，並獲讀者回應。我欣賞這種說法:「在異鄉寫自己的母語，可消除思鄉的痛苦」，於是我又將童詩翻成臺語文。「I come from Taiwan; my hometown is Penghu」是我的口頭禪。親友問我住在溫哥華會不會想念家鄉，我就是這樣努力用功來回應家鄉的呼喚。

期望我的文學，幫我展現對祖先的崇敬，以及我美麗的家園澎湖像珍珠鑲映臺灣海峽之中閃閃發光。當我知道某事是壯觀美好，第一件事想做的是分享朋友，進而傳播至更遠的國度。我知道果實的奉獻是珍貴的，花的奉獻是甜蜜的，讓我姑且做一片葉子的義務，謙卑地奉獻一些濃蔭給您!

李秀 寫於加拿大 溫哥華

Foreword

Penghu Moon in the Well

I have never been to Taiwan, never had the desire to visit there. I just thought of it as a small island nation situated beside gigantic China. And when I visualized it, I merely saw a country filled with countless factories because so many products come from Taiwan. I did not see anything picturesque or beautiful about it. But then I read *Penghu Moon in the Well*, and Louise Lee Hsiu opened my eyes to the epic history and amazing landscapes of Taiwan that I had remained totally ignorant of all my life.

All I knew was that, once upon a time, Taiwan was part of China until the communists took over China and Chiang Kai-shek fled to Taiwan where he formed a separate government. But there is so much more to Taiwanese history, and I have learned about it in the most memorable way—through the experiences of individuals, rich and poor, young and old, good and bad, male and female. This novel teems with the exciting historical events that shaped Taiwan's destiny. But more importantly, we get to know the generations of little girls and boys, young men and women, old women and men who struggle to keep their families alive and together, often in the midst of financial ruin and dangerous situations created by wars that go on and on between Taiwan and Japan.

Because the unfolding saga of Penghu parallels the domestic saga of two families, Hsiu uncovers many personal and political layers of Taiwan's history and culture, which proves to be much more multifaceted than I ever imagined. From the humble fishing village of Waian on Penghu Island to the bustling Taiwanese seaport of Kaohsiung, members of the Lee and Zhu families grow up, fall in love, have children, love and protect their children who then grow up to love and protect their parents until they finally have to bury their elders and carry on their families' legacies, passing on their parents' teaching to their own children—a never-ending universal pattern of lives that takes place over and over throughout the world.

Reading Hsiu's poetic descriptions of individual emotions that are reflected by surrounding fields, shores, seas, and stars as well as the sun and the moon, we can't help but relate to the different forms of love and hate between parents and children, husband and wives, sisters and brothers, and among friends, enemies, and strangers. Hsiu's novel affirms that we are all connected, for better or for worse, forever and ever. We travel in a never-ending circle because we want to return home to the source, to the light at the end of the tunnel.

We take this journey with four generations of two families, and in the process, we learn that Taiwan has a much longer, more complicated history than having simply broken away from China. And we now know that Taiwan is much more than a small island filled with factories. Namely, there are the lovely Penghu Islands—over sixty of them. Through the author's eyes, we see their haunting beauty and long to go there; we especially would like to visit the Penghu Islands with Louise Lee Hsiu to watch and read the ocean's movements with her and follow her along paths lined with chrysanthemums, symbols of fortitude and endeavor, which is essentially what this endlessly enlightening novel is all about.

Barbara Ladouceur

介紹「井月澎湖」英文版

by Barbara Ladouceur

中譯者: 李 秀 (Translated by Louise Lee Hsiu)

台灣！我從未到過，也從未想要去參觀。它給我印象僅是龐大中國旁邊一個小島國家而已。有許多產品來自台灣，想像中，充其量台灣只是一個佈滿工廠的地方，更遑論有美麗如畫的事物了。但是，當我讀到李秀小說「井月澎湖」，她史詩般的撰述台灣、澎湖迷人的景物，確確實實改觀我對台灣有限的認知。

根據所知，台灣曾是中國一部分，直到共產黨接管中國，蔣介石流亡到台灣另組一個政府。實際並非如此，透過在地人的生活經驗，我隱約知道那裡人的貧窮和富有、年輕和年老、好和壞、男和女的一些印象。然而李秀這本小說讓我大開眼界，它不僅充滿了精采的史實，更重要的，透過她扣人心弦的描繪，讓我們更詳悉世代真實的事跡。台灣的男女老少，在被日本殖民物質缺乏和危險的戰爭年代，他們如何努力、掙扎在台灣和日本之間，相互緊密的生活，並堅持維護家庭的連結。

李秀藉著澎湖兩個家族，發展出兩條平行線所延伸的事端，開始揭露比我想像更豐富的個人經驗和台灣政治文化的層面。從澎湖群島的小漁村—外垵，到一個繁忙的台灣海港城市—高雄，李家和許家成員，在這之間長大成人、墜入愛河、養育孩子以及保護雙

28

親，直到最後埋葬長輩和繼續他們的家產，再尋著前輩的腳步教養子女 ... 等等。一個永無止盡的生活榜樣，就這樣在這個世間不斷的前進、輪迴。

欣賞李秀詩意般獨持的描寫，由環繞視野的反射，能感受到各式各樣的曠野、濱岸線、海洋、星星、甚至太陽和月亮。也許不能真正觸及，可是由她寫自已家族強烈情感的表述，可以完全叫人體悟到不同的形式，反映在父母孩子、丈夫妻子、姐妹兄弟、朋友敵人和陌生者之間的愛恨情愁。她的小說肯定了人類全部被聯繫在同甘共苦之中，成為一個永無休止的旅行，因為人們終竟要回鄉、歸根、尋到隧道盡頭之光為止。

在閱讀這部小說的歷程，我跟著兩個家族、四個世代來造訪台灣、澎湖。過程中，學習到台灣原來有她更深長、更豐富的歷史背景，因而打破僅從中國方面而來的簡陋介紹。現在更知道，台灣並非我先前的刻板印象，只是一個充滿許多工廠的小島而已。也就是說至少那裡有一個可愛的澎湖群島，週圍還環繞著六十幾個小島。透過作者的眼睛，我們看到台灣、澎湖那縈繞在心頭的澎湃美麗，進而渴望到那塊天地去翱遊。特別隨著李秀的足跡去尋訪，那海洋的脈動，遁著遍野的菊花小道，去感受台灣、澎湖人，如何善用堅韌的毅力生活在那塊土地上。基本上，這就是作者所要撰述的理念，因此這本書給我們無限的啟發和學習。

Prologue

Summer 1996

Nearly three hours after the ship, *Tai-Peng-Lun,* leaves Kaohsiung, Lian-Zi wanders on the deck, her hair flying loose against the sea wind. Surf and wind play a dignified yet miserable march as she nears her destination, Penghu, which is the place of her parents' birth.

Lian-Zi thinks about where she is. The Penghu Islands are located in the Taiwan Strait; the China coastal current, a branch of the Japan current and the South China Sea monsoon current come together in the surrounding seas. Long ago, ships took people from Penghu to Taiwan to find a better living. During the early twentieth century, they would bravely sail across the black waters to their destination. The black waters were aptly named because they had a strong undertow at the bottom of the sea so that boats sailing on them could easily drift off course. Ships often met typhoons or storm tides, giving the whole sea the aspect of a cemetery. Thus immigrants had to cross over such dangerous black waters to reach Taiwan safely.

Sailing for many hours, *Tai-Peng-Lun* noses her way through the winding channel, nearing the Port of Magong in Penghu in the stifling heat of the storm. The ship keeps on her course, shaking the passengers in their beds and the goods stored below; faster and faster she speeds over the tossing sea, still troubled by the sway of the monsoons.

The moment she arrives at her destination, Lian-Zi cannot stop her tears as she sees her homeland for the first time in ten years. If you look at her face, you can't distinguish if you see seawater or tears. Indeed, whenever she thinks about her parents, she cannot stand up to the heavy wind and rain. She hears some rustling of things behind her sad heart, yet she cannot see them. She asks herself, "What is going on? Is love a wildfire that burns out the loving heartstrings?"

The sound of receding footsteps echoes through the passage of time. Now vaguely, now clearly, they run through the million glories and disgraces of the Penghu Islands; traces of her ancestor memories are left to the winds in the cracks and pockmarks of old houses and walls. And Lian-Zi keeps waiting, listening quietly to the heartbeats of ancient times. Now she seems to clearly hear the anxious voice of her grandma Shiang-Sao, calling her father's name, Zi-Shan.

井

月

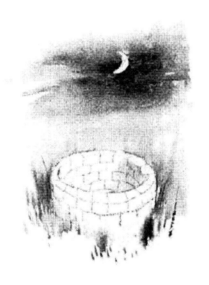

PART ONE

Moon in the Well
(1894-1922)

1-1

A Life of Garbage

Autumn 1909

"Zi-Shan! You must go to the trash place to pick up some fish gills, scales, and fish intestines," Shiang-Sao ordered her son. Mother and son cherished the things that others discarded. With the fishy smell mixed into the meal, it would be much easier to swallow the rotten potatoes.

When he heard his mom's order, eight-year-old Zi-Shan quickly put down a cow-dung chip he'd found and grabbed a worn-out jar before running to the Waian's fish marketplace. He usually picked up whatever he wanted from the trash, but today he could not find anything to take. Did he come too late after the workers already took the fishy wastes to the garbage? He ran back home disappointedly.

"It doesn't matter! We can wash the fish parts from the garbage. You can still pick some up. Go!" Shiang-Sao said.

Although Zi-Shan felt uncomfortable culling from bloody, sloppy, and muddy fish parts, he still had to grab the jar again to go to that fishy, smelly location after looking into his mother's encouraging eyes.

While Zi-Shan bent his knees to look for fish parts in a pile of trash, he heard a hospitable sound from Mr. Dong,

"My lad, I will give you a whole fish later. You don't need to do this insufferable job."

The poor child felt grateful as he looked up at this charitable grown-up. Then he waited for other grown-ups to silently finish their work in the corner of the temple. Of course, his eyes stared excitedly at Mr. Dong, who was generously offering to help him.

The other grown-ups were four huge square-built seamen and several masked women dealing with fish parts together, ripping the fish open with their long knives, spreading them flat, salting and counting them in front of the temple. After their shore-net fishing activities, they reeked of fish pickle and bilge water.

He carried the fish from Mr. Dong very carefully. He wanted to tell Mom immediately that they had a real fish to eat. When he arrived at his beloved but needy home, he yelled out, "Mom! Mom!" He didn't get his dear mom's answer, but he heard a neighbour's voice instead.

"Your mother went to a field behind the house to pick peanuts, and she also wants you to go there to help her."

"Thank you for telling me this. I am going there right away."

For twenty minutes he ran toward the north hill until he saw his mom bowing her back to search for peanuts in the vast field. Through the thickly veiled windy sky openings, splendid silver and ruby rays of light broke through and pierced the clouds like skylights in a dome.

In opposition to the noise of the heavy wind, he yelled at his mother, "Mom, we have a big and true fish!" He quickly leaped over the stone walls that surrounded the fields to provide protection against the wind.

"You are coming too late to help me. You see, the sun is setting soon," his mother said accusingly.

"Mom, Mr. Dong gave us a real fish," he said again, but this exciting event didn't bring her joy, only tears instead.

"I will put it in salt. Let you enjoy it slowly, okay?" She kept silent for a while, and then she said, "We are going home now."

He wanted them to leave soon, yet he suddenly noticed how pale and drawn Mother looked. He said timidly, "Did the garden master scold you for picking the peanuts like this?"

"Shut up!" his mother yelled at him. However, she saw that she had scared the child, so she softly explained away the child's fears. "If we don't pick them up in time, the seeds will germinate. To avoid waste, we have to pick them quickly."

Seeing only a handful of peanuts in Mother's basket, he knew that the garden master had plowed the field very thoroughly. The Penghu farm produce was limited, owing to small amounts of rainfall, strong dry monsoons, and salty soil. Thus the peanuts were a valuable produce.

The hours passed excitedly and hungrily as Zi-Shan helped his mom pick while in the infinitely empty regions beyond, the light slowly changed till it grew less unreal. Feeling starved and cold, Zi-Shan urged his mom to let them go home early. Here, there were no trees, but the gaillardia weeds were everywhere; yet the region lacked materials to use as fuel. The residents collected cow dung to dry as fuel; this was called cow fuel.

In this area, architecture was very simple. Material was obtained from local sources by piling up stones or using clay to build a wall. Whenever *laoku* (rock) houses or clay houses were built, they were located in the north and faced the south. The layout was used in order to have shelter from the wind and be able to relax in a cool place in the summer. The house was built to connect with cowsheds, pigpens, wells, and warehouses. Roads were arranged to pass in the front and back of the house, with lanes on both sides. From any height, the open sea could be seen. Shiang-Sao and Zi-Shan passed through this small fishing village, which was beaten about by the winds the whole year round as they blew through the different *laoku*, clay, or brick houses. The fierce wind swayed Shiang-Sao and Zi-Shan all the way home.

When they reached a *laoku* house, Shiang-Sao said to her son, "My dear, you go home to eat something now. I am going to Mr. Wong's place to deal with something. I will come back quickly."

Shiang-Sao came back tired after a few minutes. She ate nothing, just drank a little water and lay down for a rest.

"Why are you not eating?" Zi-Shan demanded.

"I will go to downtown Magong by early ship tomorrow morning," replied his mother with a sad air.

"Going to faraway places and needing to travel two hours by ship, to do what?" Tears welled up in Zi-Shan's eyes. In his whole life, his mother had never left him for more than one day alone. How could she stay on her tiny feet during the long journey as huge sea waves rocked the boat?

"Tears! Look what you're doing!" Mother was teasing him, and with perhaps a hint of sadness, she added, "Remember, a real man doesn't cry easily."

He bedded down and grasped his brother's pillow, secretly bursting into tears. He dared not roll over. He feared that if he did, his mother would hear his sniffling. His brother, Zi-Tian, was put up for adoption around two years ago because his mother was too poor to raise more than one child. Zi-Shan was not only sorry for his brother, he also worried about his mother's safety. And with the heavy weight of depression, he tossed about in his sleep for a while and tearfully drifted into dreamland.

On a gloomy moonbeam, he was forced by a strong power to fly to the eastside wharf. He saw that many people began to arrive at this Waian seashore from all points of the vast area. Like birds flocking to a call, they assembled circularly on the cruiser, and from the clearly empty corners of the horizon, others appeared on every side. A crowd of people got off from the ship's deck, one by one. Meanwhile, a strong man held two bags of fish in his hand and walked up to him, smiling. "Papa!" he blurted without thinking. Mom said that he was only four months old when his father went to Taiwan to live. After that he never saw him. Listen! This kindly soul was calling his name, "Zi-Shan!" Yes, he undoubtedly was his dear father. He wanted to touch him, but he could not get through the crowd to the place where his papa stood. Even though he yelled out anxiously, no sound came out. Finally, he put forth all his strength to reach his papa. Instead, he woke himself up.

Zi-Shan opened his heavy eyelids. Morning, the real morning light was coming. Night had passed. He knew his mother had already gone because her straw hat had disappeared. In his mother's absence, he needed to do some of her work, such as going to the seashore to pick up more seashells. He wanted to give her a delightful surprise when she came back home.

In the large intertidal zones around the Penghu Islands, especially in the nearby waters of the Waian fishing village, there were a variety of sea snails, clams, and other seashells. Zi-Shan prepared a big jar to be able to collect more. He gave Mother his word that he would never cross the eastern seashore where there were three big rocks to stand on while he picked seashells because this was a dangerous zone full of fast-moving water. In fact, as long as his feet were firmly balanced on the rocks, there would be no danger, he thought. However, he finally fell into the ocean while jumping between two of the rocks. Even though he desperately tried to reach safety, he rapidly lost his breath.

The sales action on the seashore of Magong was suddenly disturbed by a deep moan that came from the corner where street vendors were doing business.

"I cannot get my breath," gasped Shiang-Sao. She then told her business partner, Mr. Wong, that she had a severe pain in her chest. She felt a little weak. But she made one more effort. "Don't worry about me, I will be fine soon."

"Take it easy! Don't rush! Maybe you are not used to yelling like this." Mr. Wong bent down to get Shiang-Sao's attention, and then he continued to yell out, "Come here! Fresh fish is here! Only three cents for one big bag." The experienced vendor was hawking to draw a crowd.

Shiang-Sao had figured out that if they sold two boxes of fish, she would earn fifteen cents. While she had enough capital to do her own business, she could also earn double the money with Mr. Wong. And then both she and her child, Zi-Shan, would have a better living.

The fish selling was going well, but in the middle of this busy time, she heard a loud shout with the whistling from Japanese police growing louder every moment; and then she saw Mr. Wong, who was carrying the boxes, spring up and frantically rush to a long narrow alley.

"Dammit! We could do this before, but we cannot do this now. Why?" Mr. Wong yelled both furious and scared. "Japanese cops are really too much."

Once in Waian, Shiang-Sao also saw those police, who used to wear yellow uniforms and round hats, but they didn't create such unhappy events. Villagers always kept at a respectable distance from these foreign people. However, she experienced great fright this time. She immediately worried about her son's safety. What was he doing while she wasn't at home? To speak the truth, she was anxious about selling work like this so far away from her son, but she hoped to, someday, earn a decent living from it.

Japan imposed bans on everything in this colony. The residents really didn't know where to turn to adjust. Seeking some advice, Mr. Wong went to a foreman to discuss how to manage his business in the future. Meanwhile, Shiang-Sao was anxiously waiting for the ship to take her home to Waian, which made it impossible to focus on the men's discussion of trade problems with the Japanese police. She longed to return home as soon as possible.

When she was on deck, she looked around her with anxious eyes over the familiar circle of the sea. Looking at the waters, she felt a great anguish, full of an unknown mystery that froze her deep soul. Her mind filled with images of her poor child with his soft eyes and clever little figure; at the thought of embracing him again, tears began to fall heavily and swiftly down her cheeks, and then sobs rent her chest. She just couldn't understand why.

"Alas! Shiang-Sao, hurry!" When she left the ship, she saw someone wringing his hands and saying "God help you! God help you!" in a voice of despair. "Your son drowned in the sea. Fortunately, he was rescued by a Chinese man, but he is still in a coma now." These deafening words were like a sword bloodlessly piercing her heart.

"The nose bleeding has stopped, the fever has shaken off. Don't worry!" The Chinese man, Li Yi-Ren, said this in a slight Fuzhou accent as he tried to sound optimistic, and then he reassured her again, "He isn't destined to die. It's fortunate that I paid more attention to watching him because of his red trousers." The red trousers were actually Shiang-Sao's old clothes that she had sewn into trousers for her son just one month ago.

Thank God! She prostrated herself before this man who was both strange and familiar and the savior of her life. Facing this man, Shiang-Sao felt that she was reunited with her family.

1-2

Li Yi-Ren

In February 1910, Waian Island was buffeted by strong northeasterly monsoons. The winds carried a lot of salt from the ocean. The damp freshness of the air was more intense than a dry chill; when breathing it, one tasted the flavor of brine. All was calm and darkness except for the sound of winds in the early morning moments of this small fishing village.

The hurricane of the first lunar month penetrated into the ruined gate of the backyard. Shiang-Sao carefully lit matches in the kitchen, but they were blown out immediately by the winds. She stood up on shaky legs, heavy with pregnancy, to tighten the door to avoid letting the strong gale into the house. In fact, she not only kept the winds outside, but she also blocked away the glimmer of the early morning sun. The room was in complete darkness.

"I should have some light to make breakfast for the Lunar New Year festival," murmured Shiang-Sao, now a little troubled. She walked in the dark to seek a match again and to build a fire. She poked the fire in the stove, set the food on the table, and then sat down to wipe away her tears, which she couldn't distinguish as happy or sad tears. After that, she went around and cleaned the room.

At last she halted before a so-called gods hall. A wooden statuette of the goddess Mazu was fastened on a bracket against the wall partition in a place of honor. This patron saint of their family was rather antiquated and made very simply several years ago by her husband, Lee Shiang, who had left her and his sons to go to Taiwan after he finished the statue.

She looked at the statue. There was a rumor that Lee Shiang also had a woman in Taiwan. Gray days followed one another, but Lee Shiang appeared no more, and the mother and two sons lived on in their loneliness. With the colonial age, their daily existence became harder and more expensive. Finally, their neighbor Lu Han, whose family had no son and only one daughter, adopted their elder son, Lee Zi-Tian. Even though Shiang-Sao lessened the burden of providing enough bread and butter, she had a long cry when her dear son was given away to another family.

"I should stop thinking about these sad things on a festival day," she said to herself. She looked at the little bits of rich foods on the table to honor her ancestors, and she was happy because she hadn't had this contented feeling for a long time; not until she met Li Yi-Ren, who had rescued her beloved son Zi-Shan from the sea several months ago. Since then she had not only been in a romantic relationship with Li Yi-Ren but she had also been struggling in her mind about this affair.

When a couple lived together secretly, such love as theirs was like Penghu's cacti. Even though all cacti have thorns, they can nourish the starving mother and son. No! She knew she should stop herself from continuing this warm but immoral relationship with Yi-Ren. But how else could she manage? Although she had tried to abort her pregnancy repeatedly, the baby still grew day by day. Despite all her efforts, she couldn't stop rumors about her in this small fishing village, but she still used all her energy to do so. Was she to be forever condemned as the secret wife of a foreigner, facing unfriendly eyes every day and passing her whole life in painful anxiety here?

However, the happiness of her life with Yi-Ren defeated the malicious rumors. In fact, Yi-Ren carried into her world a life that flourished, wiping away the failure of her previous life; moreover, her son, Zi-Shan, who had an irresponsible father, now had a loving stepdad in Yi-Ren, who didn't care about the rumors. Still she was deeply troubled by her happiness, for it seemed something too unhoped for, as unstable as a joyful dream. But she wanted a labor of love and a baby, and in fact, she had no more energy to care whatever the rumors were. She should just go on living.

Even though war could destroy many human beings, the Sino-Japanese War brought Shiang-Sao great satisfaction because it brought Li Yi-Ren into her life. This was the period of Japanese occupation. To begin with, Li Yi-Ren was a Chinese soldier who was transferred to the Western Fortress of Penghu in the year 1895. After Yi-Ren served as a guard at the Western Fortress for one year, Taiwan and Penghu, together, formed one Japanese colony. Thus Shiang-Sao and Li Yi-Ren came to meet each other on this small fishing island.

Near the end of the Sino-Japanese War in 1895, there was an unusually heavy rain. In the midst of the storm, a bullet hurtled through the air. Its whine broke the silence of the village—a shrill, continuous sound and a kind of prolonged zing. There was a farmer working among the fresh guava fields. Zhu Wang stopped his farmwork to listen to what was going on. Through the curtain of both salt and freshwater hitting his face, he saw two wounded soldiers walking toward him.

"Master, my friend got a serious wound. Please give me a hand," pleaded the more slender man who was Li Yi-Ren.

On this day, the military of China's Ch'ing dynasty was badly defeated with only slight resistance. After that, the Japanese army took only three days to occupy the whole of Penghu Island. On April

17, twenty-four days after the Japanese army occupied Penghu, Li Hung-Chang and Itou Hakubun signed the Shimonoseki Treaty; and China ceded Taiwan and Penghu to Japan.

The people of Penghu still worked hard, and the sky of the fishing village rained saltwater after the fall of the island. It was true, a typhoon could bring disaster even as it moistened the drought; likewise, death belonged to life just as much as birth did. Similarly, when Li Hung-Chang signed the Shimonoseki Treaty, he sparked a good romantic relationship between Shiang-Sao and Li Yi-Ren. Since she was with Li Yi-Ren, she and her son didn't go hungry anymore.

On this New Year's Day, the morning rays of the sun following the sound of firecrackers came at last; as in the days when time began, they seemed to divide light from the darkness. It could be seen that night had finally passed, and the vague glimmer gave Shiang-Sao hope for better days.

After she had placed festival foods on the worship table, Shiang-Sao sat down in the dressing room, finally taking a rest after her housework. She began to comb her hair, coiling it in the shape of a snail shell on the back of her head. She picked out a Sunday suit that was a birthday gift from Li Yi-Ren and put it on to welcome the New Year and new days.

"Wake up! There is a lot of food to eat today. Be quick!" she yelled in excitement to her son. Zi-Shan jumped out of bed. He looked out the window, and Mother smiled at him from the kitchen door across the courtyard. It was bright outside, and the wind still went on with its fearful din. Uncle Yi-Ren, who happened to be passing by, came into their home. Zi-Shan did not really like this uncle, but he took delight in the happiness of his mother. In fact, he was an obedient child. He and Mother relied upon each other for life.

1-3

Zhu's Family Affair

One morning in the spring of 1897, having helped Li Yi-Ren to look after his wounded friend for several months, Zhu Wang, whose sunburned face was the picture of a farmer, was having breakfast as usual. When he finished his meal to walk outside, his grave dark eyes looked intently into the distance as though he was expecting to find some change in their fruit garden. To the left of the Temple of Kind Navigation, the road led along a steep slope from which the native guava trees growing below reared their topmost branches.

Away, over the crests of the guava trees, he saw his father Zhu Fo-Sh walking like a huge lofty tree under the guava trees. He seemed to be taking a relaxing stroll after his meal. Far below lay the peaceful, dignified red-topped temple, almost entirely surrounded by green trees. Even though this was a public area, Zhu Wang and his father planted a lot of guava trees in there.

Before very long, a short man, who was the head of this small village, advanced toward his home. When this man had almost come up to him, Zhu Wang waved and cried out in a loud voice, "Good morning, Mr. Leader! How are you doing?"

"Congratulations! Your father got an award from the Japanese government. You know, the Penghu area has nine scholars, and our village has only one person—your papa—to get this honor. Zhu Fo-Sh really brings glory to Waian."

Zhu Wang read the paper Mr. Leader gave him.

> *The Japanese established the present government's policy on excellent people in Taiwan and Penghu to promote Japanization and set up an award to honour these loyal subjects.*
>
> *The date: Meiji 30 [1897] on February 12.*
> *Recipient of award: Zhu Fo-Sh.*

Zhu Fo-Sh, over seventy years old, was the only scholar in Waian fishing village. He not only taught at a private school but he was also an excellent calligrapher. He had created calligraphic masterpieces in his neighborhood wherever there was a doorframe, window, or kitchen.

In the prime of Zhu Fo-Sh's life, his Dutch blood impelled him to trace his ancestors. He used his inventive and investigative talents to discover the background of Penghu and Zhu's family. In doing so, he learned more about his family history.

> *In the early seventeenth century, pirates, smugglers, the Japanese, the Spanish, and the Dutch from the southeastern bank of China gathered in the Taiwan Strait to pursue trading advantages at sea. The flames of war continually broke out in the waters around Taiwan. Penghu, located in a strategic position in Eastern Asia, became a coveted prize for foreign powers. Hence, wars broke out every year.*
>
> *For example, in the late fifteenth century, progress in navigational techniques allowed Spain and Portugal to spread their power to Southeast Asia. In the year AD 1582, the Netherlands became independent from Spain and established the Dutch East India Company to compete*

with the English for the ocean-trading business, aggressively developing eastern Asian markets and hoping to do business with the Ming dynasty and Japan. In July 1604, Dutch fleets led by Wijbrand van Warwijck met a hurricane near the Chinese bank of Kuanchou and changed direction to anchor in Magong City, Penghu.

In the meantime, an exotic love developed between a Dutch soldier and a Penghu woman. Unfortunately, a half year after they met, this soldier was ordered to leave Penghu because the Ming Dynasty sent Shen Yu-Jung to negotiate with the Dutch and ordered Wijbland Va Nwaerwijck to retreat on the emperor's edict.

Six months later, this Penghu woman went into labor, feeling exhausted both mentally and physically as she gave birth to her baby alone after her lover had left her, never to return. This infant was Zhu's ancestor.

Zhu Fo-Sh liked the feeling of tragic romance in this love story. However, he felt very serious about the idea of the main character of this love story being his forefather.

So then, in the course of his life, he had a great many concerns for whatever passed from mouth to mouth about their family history. He often talked with his children to teach them about their family tree.

"The Penghu archipelago is the only county of Taiwan which is made of volcanic lava that hardened into basalt. The geological and topographical landscapes differ tremendously from those of the island of Taiwan. Even though Penghu is the home of basalt houses with rich and diversified structures, it is too difficult to run a farm." As often as not, Zhu Fo-Sh confided to his children, Zhu Wang and Zhu Dian, "Luckily, our pomegranate garden actually has good soil that is sheltered and protected by our ancestors. You need to imprint this point on your mind."

"While the others have to dig out salty water, our well is both cool and delicious. It is really wonderful," said Zhu Dian, supporting his father's words.

On the other hand, the elder brother, Zhu Wang, had opposite ideas and he answered with the first thing that came into his head, "But the water is not always sufficient to support our family. When we haven't been paying attention, our water has often been stolen."

"To help or benefit others by giving them the things they need—," Zhu Fo-Sh hadn't yet finished his argument when he was interrupted by angry Zhu Wang.

"I don't think so. Don't you remember? If somebody hadn't stolen our well water and spoiled our fruit garden, my mother would not have passed away so quickly."

"You know," Zhu Fo-Sh said, "I can tell you a way you can relax. Nowadays, living is a difficult matter. There are no choices. If someone is suffering from starvation, then they would do anything, even steal. We should understand the situation."

"It is said that Taiwan is a good place to make more money. We can sell some land here and then go there," said Zhu Dian enthusiastically.

"Nonsense! I never want to sell my family property even if I am starving to death," said the venerable old man. He scolded his sons for the absurd notion and stood up to defend his own way of thinking. Zhu Fo-Sh went on with his explanation, looking like he was teaching in private school. "People in olden times bravely sailed across the black waters to settle on this Chrysanthemum Island, which in addition to suffering from a lack of water, was an infertile and windy place. Therefore, we can feel the difficulties of Penghu's residents in their livelihoods more than Taiwan. It is true, being a Penghu person means having to work very hard to make just a little money." He breathed a sigh of sadness and kept silent for a while. "Fortunately, we have ancestors to protect us from harm. We are much better off than others."

The genealogy of the Zhu family had been a harmonious lineage until a fierce rivalry began between the wives of Zhu Wang and Zhu Dian. These sisters-in-laws' squabbles resulted in Zhu Fo-Sh becoming very depressed because he considered family togetherness to be very important.

Even though he had one motto—"A loving atmosphere in the home is the foundation for life"—to encourage people, he still couldn't deal with his own family affairs. Moreover, he needed to follow the rules of foreigners in his own land. Although he had Dutch ancestry, he was recognized as an "excellent resident" by a foreign country—Japan. Not only did he get deeply frustrated but he was also confused. What on earth was this world coming to?

He had received an honorable medal from the Japanese government, which gave him a moment's joy. But he was no longer the scholar of old, purposeful of gait and steady in his resounding voice. All that had vanished before the double suffering from the weakening of nation and kin.

An example was seeing the Japanese police frighten Penghu's people because the Japanese established many laws different from the Penghu legal system in order to promote Japanization. Furthermore, he knew his daughters-in-law constantly fought over even trifling matters.

He had become like a homesick boy gradually losing his values, such as compassion, joy, loving-kindness, and equanimity; he hardly spoke except to answer an occasional question in a fragile way. Were all the world's phenomena and ideas unreal, like a dream, like magic, or like a fleeting image?

He had grown pale and bent over more than ever, as if the fountain of death had already touched him and he swam in its downfallen water. Then one autumn night, he never returned. His spirit completely disappeared from melancholy Waian Island as if only his body remained in the house, yet his soul had merged with the furious clamor of this world.

1-4

Reluctance

In Waian, towards the end of October in 1898, on an already chilly day, Zhu Wang's wife was looking for a pumpkin in the farm field to prepare the sacrificial offering to her father-in-law. She was wearing the traditional outfit for local women. Because of the strong dry, sandy wind, women who worked outside needed to use a cloth to cover their face with only their eyes showing.

All of a sudden, she realized something was missing.

"Has a thief been here? Who stole the pumpkin?" she rolled her eyes at the woman who was her sister-in-law, Zhu Dian's wife.

"Damn, you rotten bitch. How dare you ask me such a question?" said Zhu Dian's wife with a peevish toss of her head.

"Oh hell! I never said who the thief was," Wang's wife answered her jeeringly. "Does someone have a guilty conscience here?"

"Your eyes looked at me pointedly." Dian's wife was much put out by the attitude of Wang's wife. "Obviously, you are blaming me for this."

"There's something strange about that. Why can't I see whatever I want to see?"

"Nonsense! You make trouble out of nothing."

"You should be ashamed of yourself!"

Their bitter fight became so loud it resulted in an explosion of anger from the Zhu brothers, who were in their father's home, concerning themselves with matters of consequence for their father's funeral. They were taken aback by the war between the sisters-in-law.

"Oh, shut up! I don't want to hear your voices anymore," Zhu Wang yelled at them. "Why, oh, why can't you maintain a peaceful condition for the family's sorrow?"

Zhu Dian was also not happy. He said to these two women, "Your squabbles disgust me!"

"If it wasn't for your father's funeral, I would never come here," Zhu Dian's wife retorted.

She and her sister-in-law looked at each other in disgust, and then they moved themselves individually toward the kitchen to prepare the food for the last rites of their father-in-law.

Zhu Fo-Sh, this old man who had passed away, had tried to maintain the togetherness of the clan-built family when he was alive. Actually, this family tradition had been handed down through the centuries and remained practically unchanged until his generation. He was disappointed that his daughters-in-law couldn't tolerate each other and chose to live separate lives to avoid seeing each other. There was nothing for it but to face the deathblow; indeed, now he didn't need to face this difficult matter at all because he had already left the noisy world forever.

This family's life was like crossing a sea where they traveled in the same narrow ship. In death, Zhu Fo-Sh reached the shore and went to a different world.

Even though their father's death was over, his children would still need to continue their struggle for honor to prove their worth. They would, in fact, face even worse problems under a Japanese colony.

Everlasting night or everlasting day, one couldn't say what it was; the island sun, which pointed to no exceptional time, remained fixed as if presiding over the fading honor of dead things. It appeared as a little circle, being almost without essence and vastly enlarged by a shifting halo.

Wang and Dian leaned against each other on the seashore after their father's funeral.

"Brother, I need to go to Taiwan again," said Dian.

Being a businessman, Dian traveled often between Penghu and Taiwan. He realized countryfolk's subtle differences under the colonization of a foreign country. Some of them, such as the Arabs, were the kind of people who had to humble themselves to the strict police of Japan. Dian couldn't live with the shame of these folks. Some of them, on the other hand, rose against the aggressors. Twelve Tigers Society was an example of such a brave group. Lee Shiang, villager of Waian and a neighbor of Dian, was one of the Tigers. Dian adored Shiang for his brave character.

"I want to visit my hero, Lee Shiang," said Dian again. "I'm preparing to join the group of Tigers to resist the Japanese colony when I arrive in Taiwan this time."

"Is there any information he can give?" asked Wang.

"Yes, I have a friend who knows him."

"I wonder about Lee Shiang, who is Shiang-Sao's husband and Zi-Shan's father," Wang added an instant later. "He is an irresponsible husband and father, I guess."

"Every family has some sort of trouble. We cannot judge this case. There seem to be some misunderstandings," replied Dian. "Anyway, I will give him a piece of advice and induce him to come back to Waian to take care of his family."

"You need to be careful in Taiwan when you join this group of anti-Japanese rebels," said Wang anxiously. "I wonder if they have strong weapons to oppose the Japanese army, such as powerful guns."

"There's no knowing what may happen. However, it is us, the Taiwanese from the land of the free and the home of the brave, who should be contributing to the country."

"Additionally, I also worry about the relationship between our wives. As you know, there has been no love between the sisters-in-law for a long time." Wang could not say anything more. His words were choked by helplessness.

"Brother, I hope you will take care of them for me while I stay in Taiwan."

"Sure, I will."

Then they began their lives in different places. Dian went to Taiwan to join the group of Tigers, and Wang still lived in their hometown to take care of the family property.

Penghu had no high mountains to ward off the strong winter winds blowing from the northeast. In the summer, the flat terrain could not capture the moisture from the southwestern monsoon winds; thus, Penghu only had an annual precipitation of 1,000 millimeters.

More sad months followed until it was early July, humid and hot intemperate weather. Outdoors, the southwestern monsoon winds had again risen. Wang had just come from his fruit garden where he saw the guava fade for want of water. He was embittered by frustrations.

Meanwhile, the other victim of separation, Dian, in Taiwan with the Twelve Tigers group, opposed the Japanese army with knives and axes. *Hiss!* Again the whine broke the silence of the air—a shrill continuous roar, a kind of prolonged zing that gave one a strong feeling that the pellets buzzing by might sting fatally.

For the first time in his life, Dian heard that sound. The Japanese bullets that came toward his people had a different voice from the knives or axes held by the Taiwanese. *Split! Bang!* Again and yet again! The bullets fell in steady showers now. There were no longer enough Tigers to fight the enemies.

"The Japanese!" shouted the Tiger members with the same brave spirit.

At this moment, Dian came out grandly; his family would have been proud to see him as such a warrior. Indeed, his fierce emotions arose from the Japanese-scorched land policy that had injured and oppressed his wife's hometown, village of Xiao Lung, which was the first place that the Japanese attacked in Taiwan. The result of this cruel event was that none of the Tiger members would give up.

However, this time they found that there were too many enemies, and two of them were springing up from the long, tall grass. In a moment of supreme indecision, the Taiwanese, hit by the rain of Japanese bullets, almost gave in to an impulse to retreat, which would certainly have meant death to them all; but Dian continued to advance, tightening his knife to deal with them bravely.

Even though he was full of energy, he suddenly felt a sharp rap upon his breast and, in a flash, immediately understood what it was even before sensing any suffering; he turned toward the others following and tried to cry out to his hero, Lee Shiang, "I think I've done my best!" In the great breath that he inhaled to refill his lungs with air, he felt the air rush in through a hole in his chest with an awful whoosh, like the sound of his heart breaking. At that time, his mouth filled with blood.

"My son, you must rouse yourself," said Shiang anxiously, holding Dian in his arms as they hid behind a tree. A sharp pain shot through Dian, which rapidly grew worse until it became cruel and unspeakable. He wanted to say something to Shiang, but before he could say a word, he fell heavily to the earth of blood and thunder.

1-5

The Water Lights

It was the time of the Ghost Festival on the fifteenth day of the seventh lunar month. In the temple of the Noble Wun, the god received the most sacrifices in the temple. He was a representative for all the gods who protected the village of Waian by repelling evil spirits, and for that fete day, there was an altar every year. Colorful streamers were erected on top of the bamboo, and lights were hung everywhere in the front yard of the temple. It presented an attractive notice to all ghosts that there was a festival with sacrifices to them.

According to folklore, the gates of hell open during this time of the year—the seventh month on the lunar calendar—allowing its dwellers to come to the human world to feast. Generation after generation was passing on a message that there were many different kinds of hungry ghosts. If these ghosts received sacrifices, the people would be settled down and safe. Otherwise, the ghosts would all present the same unseemly behavior to bother and bring misfortune to people.

Fate and belief blended in the fishing village; each fishing boat was a bead of sweat rolling on the ocean's cheek. In fact, the work of fishermen was a dangerous and unpredictable activity. The temple represented the spiritual dependency of fishermen, burning incense sticks and paper money and setting off firecrackers to honor their ancestors and appease wandering spirits

Belief was a process, and ceremonies were acts of humbleness that constructed bridges between mortals and immortals. The whole temple was full of incense and candles lit in order to not only ask the gods to guard residents' safety but also to appease specters to avoid trouble.

This day it was not only the adults that were busy taking care of the offerings to gods and spirits but also the younger people that were active as bees buzzing around to help family get the work done quickly.

Zhu Chu-Su was a girl of eighteen with a rare fair complexion in this village of Waian where most people were darker skinned. Her rather short profile was quite noble, her nose continuing the line of her brow with perfect rectitude as in a Dutch statue. Though she appeared to be soft and pliable, she had inherited the great self-respect and strength of character of her ancestor, the brave Dutch pilot. Yet the expression in her eyes was both constant and tender.

She was the youngest daughter of Zhu Wang, the master of the guava garden, who much preferred land to sea—a rare feature in an island of fisherman. Still he played an important part in organizing the festival in this land of fishermen. He explained the origin of the Ghosts' Month to villagers in front of the temple. First of all, Wang cried, "Gather round me everyone, and listen carefully to what I have to say to you," and then he began his tale:

"At the beginning of the seventh month of the lunar calendar, the gates of Hades are opened wide for the souls of the departed to visit earth to enjoy themselves. That is why the seventh month is often called the Ghosts' Month." Gradually, more and more people came to Wang. He looked at them carefully, and then he continued, "It is advisable that during this month, human beings should be more careful about going outside the house, especially at nighttime, in order to avoid crossing the path of the souls of the dead, mainly hungry ghosts."

Serving those ghosts' purpose in the human world, people prayed and offered food to the hungry ghosts, fulfilling the ritual of relieving souls out of hell; those souls who were not too sinful in life had the privilege of enjoying themselves by eating the various food offerings and collecting burned paper money.

Additionally, floating over everyone was a deep, religious sentiment, a feeling of former days, with great respect for ancient idolization and the symbols that protect them and for the sanctity of the compassionate Noble Wun who was the main god, and a series of bodhisattvas. Side by side, with the perfume of incense, the lit tapers and the abundant offerings of villagers were hung all over the sacred arch. Even though each person had always lived a frugal life, he or she provided the best offerings they could to gods and ghosts.

There were many kinds of events at the temple fair. Smoke slowly fluttered in the hot air, and each face covered in copious sweat longed for shelter. At this special time, an old man in one corner told a story of bygone days that was a sutra about a Brahman woman who neglected her mother. The story of filial conduct was deeply important to many people, especially to Zhu Chu-Su. As a result, she couldn't go away when her father urged her to go home to do the housework.

In the story, the Brahman woman's response to the voice from space that prayed for her was "My mother bore me, and I should have been a better daughter. Now my mother has died because I did not take good care of her. I am extremely grieved." The voice from space replied:

> *The tree would be still, but the wind will not rest.*
> *The son and daughter would maintain them, but the parents are gone.*

Indeed, the kindness of parents was as boundless as the sky, higher than heaven and broader than the earth. The Brahman woman felt remorse and shame that she had been unable to repay such compassion, and so she cried day and night.

It was such a secret place, the land of tears. Suddenly, Chu-Su missed her own mother. She went back home in a hurry, holding her beloved mama tightly in her heart when she saw her in the kitchen.

"Mama, may you live a hundred years." She gave her mother a big hug.

"What is going on, my dear?"

"You need to live with me forever! It is a deal."

"Are you mad?" Mother said, smilingly.

At this moment, Chu-Su heard voices anxiously calling her from outside. It was Yong and Fa, who were Uncle Dian's children—her cousins.

"Is something wrong, my brothers?" she asked softly.

"My mother is sick. She always screams in pain and yells out my father's name," said the elder brother.

"How long has this been happening?"

"My father said that he would definitely come back before the ghost festival, but he still hasn't come home yet. My mom is so worried that she can't eat or sleep."

"It is too bad. Okay, I'll go with you to see your mom. Don't worry too much."

Then Chu-Su told her mother, "Mom, I'm going to Uncle's home to take a look because Aunt seems to be seriously sick."

"What a strange thing, the gruesome bitch got sick!" But even though she showed contempt for the woman who often liked to argue with her, she pushed her daughter to go and take care of her.

As far back as Chu-Su could remember, her uncle wasn't usually home because he needed to do business in Taiwan. So Uncle expected her to look after his family when he wasn't at home. She really appreciated Uncle's kindness, but she didn't admire her cruel aunt.

Chu-Su and her cousins walked up the path together to Aunt's bungalow and went in through its open door. As she entered the room, she found many clothes lying scattered on the floor. Aunt lay on the bed, loudly expressing her suffering, and there was an odor of decay in all the rooms.

"My dear . . . oh, I don't know what on earth . . . Why hasn't your uncle come home yet?" She could not say anything else. Sobbing choked her words when she saw her visitor.

"Uncle must come home soon. Don't worry too much." Chu-Su realized that she, herself, was very close to tears.

"I feel something is going to happen to him. I can't help it . . . I can't stop myself."

"Don't talk nonsense, Auntie. You should eat something. I am going home to get some food for you." Chu-Su found out later that Aunt's kitchen stove was cold.

Chu-Su was confused and overwhelmed by the many emotions she felt about her Aunt's situation. She heard a rustle of things behind the sadness of heart. Yet she couldn't see them.

When the wind was in the south, a smell came across the whole village from the place where fishes and squids were drying, but today there was only the faint edge of the odor because the entire community was perfumed in the scents of incense and offerings.

But it happened that after several events had taken place that evening, Chu-Su heard her father, who was absolutely furious at having been robbed, when he came back from the guava garden.

"Who are these bastards that always steal my fruit? Those responsible for this crime will be severely punished." And then he hastily looked for some nails and planks to punish the robbers by placing the planks on the ground, nails sticking up, to stop the thieves.

"Watch! I will teach these hungry ghosts a lesson!" he yelled as he collected what he needed. Chu-Su often heard her father complain about the disappointing results of his gardening. However, rarely had she heard her father in such a state as he was now.

Indeed, often after working diligently for a long time, there was nothing to show for it. Living and working hard every day in a colony environment was diffcult, often with little or no reward.

Then both a bitter pain and sweet joy came over Chu-Su; she was charmed at the idea of a date tonight with Zi-Shan, who lived on the east side of Waian. There was also agony at the thought of leaving everyone she knew and loved, with the vague apprehension that someone might not come back again and some trouble might happen.

A thousand noises rang in her head. Around Chu-Su was the bustle of temple events where a group of Buddhist monks prepared to put the water lights into the sea. At the appointed hour, everyone met together for the opening procession, except Zi-Shan, who had not appeared. Time passed, but he did not come, and Chu-Su felt that she should go to check on her family. Then she suddenly realized that it was for Zi-Shan's pleasure, and his alone, that she had put on her best dress. If he did not turn up at the night ceremony, the evening's enjoyment would be upsetting for her.

At last he arrived, apologizing, with important information for his sweetheart Chu-Su.

"My father is coming home from Taiwan this afternoon," he said.

"Zi-Shan! This is a happy event." Chu-Su felt shocked and excited by this news because Zi-Shan's father was rarely seen in Waian. Then she went on anxiously, "Did he meet Uncle Yi-Ren?"

"Yes! Their meeting was awful," he replied sadly.

The adults had their love affairs; the youth had their emotions. As they walked along together, she felt sympathetic respect and tenderness toward Zi-Shan; she would have liked to tell him about her family's troubles but a sudden rush of feeling came over her, and the words were stopped in her throat. She said not a word about her family.

And so they went their way, with the refreshing evening wind full of the odor of the sea, leaving the crowd of people in front of the temple yard. Their evening courtship in that mournful spot was gloomy and ominous because of Zi-Shan's mother's opposition to their relationship. His mother had a preference for another girl. Her son, Zi-Shan, on the other hand, had never loved any other girl but Chu-Su. Zi-Shan was a son of filial obedience but not when it came to his love for Chu-Su.

Toward the end of the seashore, he had been quite vexed when he remembered what his father had told him. He turned to Chu-Su and told her, "Your uncle has some trouble. This was the bad news brought by my father."

"Whatever does that mean?" she asked.

"My father came back home for your uncle this time."

"No. Can it be that my uncle has died?"

"One never knows," he said evasively.

"I want to go home." Avoiding the curious eyes of villagers and worrying about her family, Chu-Su hurried home to confirm the information about her uncle.

When she entered the house, she saw that her parents and Zi-Shan's father, Lee Shiang, were sitting in the living room to discuss some serious matters. A feeling of gloom was in the air, wrapping around everyone like a misty dark presence. It seemed like ghosts were in the room with them.

"First, we take his ashes to the temple, then I will hold a funeral for him," said Chu-Su's father heavily.

"Ashes? Whose? Is it possible that they are Uncle's?" Chu-Su asked, talking to herself in a low, flat tone.

Outside, beyond doubt, lay the sea and the night as the water lights were put into the sea one by one to save the spirits of the dead. She hoped Uncle would be able to see the water lights of his hometown and come back home.

May Buddha deliver Uncle from all evil.

1-6

Life Reflected in Well Water

Winter 1922

Outside spread the wind and night—the infinite solitude of dark fathomless winds. The northeast monsoon blew in the winter, and the transient wind speed reached more than twenty-two meters per second, which was similar to a midsize typhoon. A woodwind clock hanging on the wall pointed to two o'clock—two in the morning—and the winds pattered at the wood door.

Shiang-Sao threw her arms round her little son, Li Zi-Song, and drew him toward her tenderly as she pulled the quilt over him to protect him from the cold. Afterward she stepped into another room to take a look at her eldest son, Zi-Shan, who was sleeping deeply. There were dark clouds covering the sky, broken up only by the light signals of the western lighthouse. She looked through the window, thinking about her children having the same mother but different fathers.

Thinking of Zi-Shan's father, Lee Shiang, Shiang-Sao fell into a reverie about her childhood. When she was ten years old, Lee Shiang's parents had adopted her. In fact, they had decided to make a match of her and Lee Shiang. Touching her feet, she felt sad. Indeed, her feet had not been wrapped at a young enough age to become three inches, the required length of a woman's feet to keep up with the tradition. Because she had had to help her needy family, she had had no time to care for her feet. She could remember meeting Lee Shiang for the first time; he looked down unhappily at her feet because they were bigger than normal standard. She felt greatly afflicted by her big feet. For a long period, she lost her bearings in her embarrassment about her feet. However, she could do housework very well because of her big feet.

The family of Lee was not good to her except for her foster father. Her foster mother was very mean about money. Lee Shiang, who was called her future husband, was hard to deal with. He was her senior by three years. Yet even though she did housework day and night, she had nothing to complain about. This was her duty as an adopted daughter until her foster father was killed in a sea accident.

"What a miserable life!" she yelled in her pain as she faced her life without her kind foster father.

Now everywhere Shiang-Sao went, the world was full of sorrow as she felt her adverse fate. According to folk custom, her marriage with Lee Shiang took place within the hundred days after her foster father's death. After that day, of course, it was called a marriage. In fact, she was only a sex object for Lee Shiang even during her menstruation. She never had a desire for sex.

Her memory of nursing the baby was still fresh. Her breast milk still had been rich even six months after she gave birth to Zi-Shang. However, there was awful pain if after three or four hours her baby had not been fed. One time, they went to Magong City to visit a senior relative. Because of their baby's absence, her breast milk couldn't be sucked up. She asked Lee Shiang to help her to relieve her swelling and suffering. Unfortunately, he not only didn't help her, he also loudly scolded her in a public place,

"You are a shameless bitch!" he yelled, and then he ran away.

In the midst of her own tears, she thought about how unvalued a woman was. Her body, her breasts—Lee Shiang could use them whenever he desired. He only cared about satisfying himself, yet he couldn't relieve her suffering. During the day, as Shiang-Sao did her housework, she never complained. However, at night when Lee Shiang took her for his own pleasure, she felt deeply depressed.

Foster Mother insisted that her child not do the work of a fisherman after Foster Father was killed in the sea mishap. Thus Lee Shiang decided to go to Taiwan to find a job. Unfortunately, he left for good, and it was hard for Shiang-Sao to support her family after his mother passed away. Lee Shiang blamed her for neglecting to take care of his mother and stopped sending her money. And then he never came back home again. She didn't know what on earth this meant. If he wouldn't support her, shouldn't he at least raise his own child? "Ah! Slide into this course and take it as it comes." She always talked to herself like that.

"Mom, I want to pee," said her little son dreamily, disturbing her thinking.

She wiped her tears away with her hands, and then she pulled out the chamber pot from under the bed for him.

"How big you've grown!" she said softly and smilingly. "You should do it by yourself."

Recalling the father of her little son, the kind Chinese man Li Yi-Ren, she was filled with both sweetness and bitterness. Hot tears welled up in her eyes again. The twentieth of December came and went, over and over. How swiftly the days flew by! It was already five years since Yi-Ren passed away.

Originally, she had been an illiterate woman until Li Yi-Ren taught her some basic reading and writing skills. Now she read the words on a spirit tablet mechanically and with great difficulty:

In memory of Li Yi-Ren, Lost at sea, near the Straits of Taiwan, in the storm of December 20th, 1914.

Like a great shudder, a gust of wind rose from the sea, and at the same time, something fell on her, like Li Yi-Ren's soul surrounding her. She stood up in front of his slab and lit an incense to pray for his peacefulness. She felt cold yet remained seated on the wood bench, her head reclining against the clay wall.

When she was thoroughly exhausted, she threw herself, still dressed, upon her bed. She remained in the same position, chilled and benumbed. In her quiescent state, her eyes continued to weep; she felt the impression of a band of iron round her temples. Sometimes she called Yi-Ren's name in a low, tender voice, as if he were close to her, whispering words of love to her.

When Li Yi-Ren arrived in her life, he brought her great satisfaction and happiness, but he also caused a lot of harmful gossip from neighbors and her husband Lee Shiang. Still she now understood the wonderful relationship that was possible between the two sexes since she met Li Yi-Ren. Even though she was the so-called wife of Lee Shiang, she was actually Li Yi-Ren's wife.

While she was enjoying her life with Yi-Ren, Lee Shiang suddenly came back from Taiwan.

"You stupid bitch!" Lee Shiang yelled at her as he put his hands around her neck and tried to strangle her. She felt her heart beating like the heart of a dying bird, shot with someone's rifle.

"You don't need to be furious with her for this thing. You also have another woman in Taiwan." Li Yi-Ren stood up to protect Shiang-Sao as he bravely challenged Lee Shiang.

"How can you have the nerve to say that?" Lee Shiang shouted at Li Yi-Ren. "Go on, corrupt man. Slide down to hell. Go see your friends or maybe your mother."

One of them was a lover; one of them was a husband. There was no meeting place between them that could bring about a resolution to their dispute. Even though Lee Shiang had another woman in Taiwan, he insisted that he didn't want to divorce Shiang-Sao. Thus he still had the power to control her. It was said that his job not only brought him much wealth, but that he was a gentle person in Taiwan. However, he was a coldhearted person to her. Why did he treat her like that? Shiang-Sao complained about this.

"Don't worry too much. It is good for you to live with Li Yi-Ren, who is a nice guy, and the others have no say in the matter," said Mr. Dong, who was a charitable person in this fishing village, always backing her up whenever she was frustrated by the repeated failures in her life. So Shiang-Sao accepted and enjoyed her life with Yi-Ren; she really appreciated that Buddha had given her such great gift.

Unfortunately, after she had settled into a happy life with her lover, the King of the Sea unexpectedly took away her happiness. Li Yi-Ren was killed in a sea accident after they had been together only four years. It was a rumor that Yi-Ren owed one human being to the King of the Sea because he had saved one human's life—her beloved son, Zi-Shan—from the sea.

"It is complete nonsense," she said in a loud and raging voice.

Recently, she couldn't sleep very well, waking up at midnight and staying awake the whole night long to think of her bittersweet fate. She lifted her head to look at the sky, the moon still in the firmament. It meant that it was still a long time before sunrise as she saw nothing but the sky and the light signals of the lighthouse. However, there was more wind in the sky than there had been, and so she hoped she would soon see the daybreak.

Five o'clock in the morning. On this night as on others, with her hands clasped and her eyes wide open in the dark, she listened to the wind sweeping in a never-ending tumult over the village.

"You're tired, old woman," she said. "Tired inside."

Two months ago, she argued with Zi-Shan, who mentioned that he wanted to go to Taiwan to look for a job. He was an obedient son, so he didn't embark on the Taiwan journey. But finally, he decided to go there to make more money for a betrothal gift because he was going to marry Zhu Chu-Su, on whom his heart was set.

Zi-Shan didn't like the girl Spring who had a preference for him and not only didn't need a betrothal gift but also had one of the best figures in the village. Shiang-Sao didn't know what on earth was on this child's mind! She felt a little sad. Additionally, she could not bring herself to think that her dear son would leave her to go so far away even though he said that he would bring her to Taiwan when he settled down there.

"Ay, that's beyond the comprehension of any person. Maybe I am too old to understand young people's minds," Shiang-Sao said to herself, and then under her breath, she murmured. "Take it as it comes."

After she had been awake for three hours, she still couldn't sleep. She needed to do some housework to pass the time. She went outside, carrying a clothesbasket and finding her way by means of moonlight to the ancient well where she would wash the clothes. The well had provided for one generation after another and had been kept up until now. The well water seemed to reflect all that life was.

Her face in the light of the moon was reflected in the well, and as the wind blew over the well, her face became a variety of shapes. The moon had a diversity of shapes, such as old moon, full moon, half moon, and so on. In the same way, the life of a human being also had many shapes, such as poor, rich, happy, unhappy. But her life was an absolutely miserable shape, she decided.

Zi-Shan told her he would bring her to Taiwan to enjoy a good life one day. Did she have a happy life in her future? As her hands scrubbed the clothes, her eyes filled with tears as she sang in a barely perceptible yet deeply passionate voice. The song of *Singing to Well Moon* was a tune of Nanyue, which she had just learned from her teacher:

When the heart aches at the feel of Well Moon in the
winter wind,
Is it because of sadness?
When the heart quivers at the feel of sunshine,
Is it because of loneliness? Ah . . .
No one knows of the secret distress of my heart.
The diary is for no one but me.
No companions during my days
Except the sounds of my own song.
I will express my feelings in a song.
Ah . . . Ah . . .
The feeling in my heart
I will sing to Well Moon in the winter wind.

外埃情事

PART TWO

The Events of Waian
(1923-1928)

2-1

Secret Traps

In 1923, Penghu's wind patterns were quite different, not only from that of mainland China, but also other sea-surrounded areas. Every year, the wind was a little calmer in the spring and summer, so people only had this period to plant. The wind blew for six months of the year. It blew every day in autumn and went on until the end of winter. The residents of this area needed to overcome the difficult environment with persistence and a solid belief in the infertile and windy island. The poor fishing village of Waian was located on the west side of Penghu Island. Cultivating grass, plants, and trees was very difficult in this district except at the Zhu farm. Native guava and emerald bamboo and fruit trees surrounded their house.

Even though the shady trees were in the Zhu's private space, the villagers yearned to be able to enjoy the cool air there, especially in summertime. The result of a nice location and good feng shui was that the Zhu's neighbors longed to come here to chat together under the shade of the trees. What did feng shui mean? The direction and surroundings of a house were supposed to have an influence on the fortune of a family and their offspring. In other words, wherever there was a good feng shui house, there was a fortunate family. This so-called special house also attracted a master of feng shui to visit it. After that, he gave advice to the Zhus:

> *Although the Zhu house is great, there is something wrong in there. I feel sorry to say that, but I suppose there'll be a remedy for that. The solution to the problem requires that the house owner should henceforth practice virtuous deeds and share more interests in others.*

The master's words stimulated deep thought, but Zhu Wang neglected to follow his advice. Instead, he was absolutely furious and worried about the damage robbers had done to the farm. He didn't like adding more trouble for his family.

"It is irksome to listen to those weird ideas," Wang said aloud. He was diligent in his work every day to keep up with his ancestors' industry. Farming was rare in this fishing village, so he needed to work harder after his father and brother passed away. The meaning of his life was to fulfill his duties and be responsible. He was tall and thin, with deep wrinkles in his face. His hands had deep-creased scars from digging up poor soil when he planted and from cutting heavy tree branches. Recently, he had discovered that guava had been stolen from his garden. This trouble made it hard for him to get a good harvest from the garden. He did not like to take advantage of anybody, but he also didn't like people taking advantage of him. He just wanted to do his best for his business.

Tomb-sweeping day was one of the major festivals in Penghu. The weather was clear on April fourth. This day Zhu Wang led his wife and children toward the tomb that was set on the west of the mountain ridge. They took incense, candles, flowers, spring rolls, and other food for worshipping their ancestors.

The tiny village was gradually left far behind them. They followed the path of the stone wall to climb up the hill and walk through field after field until they reached their destination—their forebear's grave. The hill was undulated and rocky; from these heights, the open sea could be seen, and they could also feel the islands linked by waves—the Penghu archipelago displayed its charms along the curvaceous coastlines.

They walked here. There were no more plants now, nothing but the field of gaillardia, a kind of small yellow flower with red petals; and here and there, the consecrated graves rose, their outstretched arms outlined against the sky, giving the whole environment the aspect of a cemetery.

At one of the crossways, Wang's daughter, Chu-Su, saw a historic coral building that always scared her because she had heard a story that inside this structure, there were many spirits victimized by the war. She hesitated between two paths running among thorny slopes.

She could remember asking her father when she was a little girl, "Who are the spirits in this building?"

"It is a long story." Zhu Wang saw his daughter's face full of curiosity and said in a serious voice, "In the early seventeenth century, pirates, smugglers, the French, the Japanese, the Spanish, and the Dutch from the southeastern bank of China gathered in the Taiwan Strait to pursue trading advantages at sea. The flames of war continually broke out in waters around Formosa. Penghu, located in a strategic position of Eastern Asia, became a coveted prize for foreign powers. Hence, wars broke out every year and also left many dead bodies of soldiers, which were buried together in this building. So now, as you see, this building has historical value."

"Dad, is it true that dead persons become ghosts?" Chu-Su inquired; she didn't really understand her father's words, but she cared about the possibility of ghosts.

"When a human being dies, he or she becomes a ghost. The ghosts who receive offerings from people settle down and are not dangerous. Otherwise, they present unseemly behavior as they bother and bring misfortune to people. Anyway, they shouldn't bother us because we have no feud with them. My dear, there is nothing to fear," Zhu Wang replied.

Although Father usually said that, Chu-Su still fluttered with fear whenever she arrived at this place. Now she walked through the building again. She laid the offerings on the ground and put her hands together as she bowed to worship the spirits respectfully. In her hurry, she stirred up the sand under her feet, and some of the sand flew into her right eye, so she couldn't open her eyes and had to stop walking.

"Help, I can't see because I have sand in one eye," she yelled out to her brother.

"Sis, what's up?" Zhu Ling asked.

"My eye hurts. It is too painful to walk on."

"Stop moving and then open your eyes. Let me blow the sand away."

"It is still uncomfortable." Chu-Su unceasingly wiped away tears.

"Maybe I am not blowing hard enough!"

As time went by, Chu-Su and Zhu Ling fell far behind their parents because of Chu-Su's accident. When they arrived at the tomb of their grandparents, the cemetery ground had already been swept clean by Papa and Mama. The whole spot seemed faded and eaten into by the sea wind; the tombstone was covered by the grayish lichen splashed pale buff. They apologized for their delay, and then in front of the grave, Chu-Su carefully set the food on the table and put the flowers in the bottles on both sides. Everything was ready. Zhu Wang lit incense.

While they paid respect to their ancestors, they saw a group of people coming toward them. They were members of the Lu family. From the expressions on their faces, it was clear they were coming with ill feelings toward the Zhu family.

"You are also visiting a grave here?" the wife of Zhu Wang asked their neighbors.

"Hum! Hum!" replied the wife of Lu.

"What's up?" Zhu Wang asked.

"You are an evil person," the wife of Lu glowered angrily at Wang. "My son is seriously hurt by your dirty trick. Now he is still in too much pain to walk."

"Whatever does that mean?" Wang's wife inquired.

"How dare your husband do a bad thing like that?" she said, out of breath. "Evil intentions will be repaid by evil results. He not only harmed my son, but also harmed several other kids."

Now Chu-Su understood what Lu's wife was talking about—Papa had recently hammered nails on boards to avoid more thefts in the garden during the harvest season. Papa hid his secret traps on the ground throughout the garden.

"Oh, I did not know who stole my guavas," Wang said, "but it is your own fault. I never wished you any sort of harm, but you stole my guavas."

"Your bad life will come to a bad end," Lu's wife threatened Wang.

"You stole my things! What on earth can you say to that? You are acting like you are the victim when it is me who is the victim." Wang sputtered a lot and was vexed. "As a matter of fact, the proper way is that even when you are starving, you don't steal the things which do not belong to you."

Friends might turn into enemies when there was a shortage of food on this infertile island. But eventually, Wang's secret traps resulted in no one daring to steal the harvest of his hard work anymore. Now that he didn't have to worry about thieves, he could easily plant enough fruit to support his whole family.

After one year passed, however, just when he now had more time to enjoy living, Wang's wife suddenly died in an awful accident. Afterward, he not only gave up his diligent planting but he also didn't want his children to go on with the job of planting. The garden of guavas and even the leaves of most plants and trees in this village area gradually stopped growing. The color of growing grass faded as Wang became more and more depressed.

Things look phantasmal in the dimness of the dusk; and imperceptibly but inexorably, Chu-Su longed for a chance to, one day, see the light in her family again.

2-2

A Pumpkin Grievance

Autumn came to Waian dock the way water swamped the fishing boats, which hit in waves, moving more and more into the village until it was completely under its sway. Thus Exue could use the noise of this powerful seasonal wind to covertly pull up a big pumpkin in the garden of her newly adopted home. She wanted to give the pumpkin to her birth mother, who lived next door. Auntie Yao had just come to the back door when Exue picked up the pumpkin. She didn't know whether Auntie Yao actually saw her stealing the pumpkin. Auntie Yao was here to play the game Ten-Hu with Exue's adoptive mother.

"Auntie Yao might have missed seeing me steal the pumpkin," Exue thought hopefully. By the time Auntie Yao came inside the house, Exue knew she must immediately hide the pumpkin somewhere to avoid someone finding out about the theft, so she took the opportunity to take it next door to her birth mama, who lived alone in poverty. She was concerned about how her true mama was getting by since Exue had been adopted by the Pumpkin family.

Exue was a very shy, withdrawn skinny girl. She was especially nervous when she was with people. She had a way of ducking her chin as if she was embarrassed when she spoke, and she spoke very little in a low voice. These behaviors were more obvious after the Pumpkin couple adopted her when she was ten years old. Over the course of two years with her adoptive parents, she often secretly visited her needy birth mother even though she was warned not to do so.

The game of Ten-Hu in Penghu was like Chinese mah-jongg that needed four players in a team. In fact, it had a rule that one more player was still needed if there were only three. Thus Yao came at the right time. The three waiting women moved over to give more room for Yao. She settled down and properly dealt all the cards. While she was waiting for another woman to play a card, she recklessly asked Mrs. Pumpkin, "Are you bringing in a good pumpkin harvest this year?"

"Because of the lack of rain, my pumpkin harvest is bad," replied Mrs. Pumpkin, thoroughly helpless.

As the women called out gaming terms such as *a pair*, *match up*, *catch on*, their voices rose and fell inside the room. Then suddenly, there was a loud noise from the yard outside.

"Oh damn! Has Big Man come here?" someone yelled out.

The four women hastily hid all the gambling cards under the table. The Japanese regarded gambling as a criminal act. The hostess, Mrs. Pumpkin, went to inquire what had happened. Fortunately, it was not the so-called Big Man; it was Mr. Pumpkin.

Why oh why were people scared of the Japanese police? Because the authorities disapproved of the occupied people gambling, the emperor of Japan fundamentally insisted upon his authority over the colony being respected. Otherwise, they would be severely punished by Big Man. This was the result of all the changes brought in by the new government—no one dared to act against Japanese rules.

Even though there were severe penalties, such as flogging or imprisonment, the villagers still secretly played Ten-Hu because this gambling was their only entertainment. In order to enjoy their only pleasure, they used flattery and bribed the Japanese police to look the other way.

"Damnable conduct!" Mr. Pumpkin was muttering all at once about the pumpkin that had disappeared from the yard.

"I saw it still here last night. I think someone has stolen it," Mrs. Pumpkin replied. Her husband went outside, and then she suddenly thought of Yao's unusual behavior. Did Yao steal it? She sprang up and rushed from the house.

"What is happening outside?" everyone asked, except Yao, who seemed to be deeply thinking about something.

"I am right about Yao stealing the pumpkin," Mrs. Pumpkin decided. She went back into the house.

"I regret that someone stole my pumpkin," Mrs. Pumpkin announced angrily. "I have no desire to play anymore. Today's game is finished, you can all go."

After the hostess had asked her unwelcome guests to leave, she neglected to walk them outside so she could talk with her husband. The group of speechless and uneasy women rapidly went on their way home. Exue, pale and trembling, was still there, doing the housework. Her mouth was turned down at the corners by the time Auntie Yao looked at her with confused eyes on her way out.

"I'm almost sure. I'm almost sure the pumpkin was stolen by Yao," Mrs. Pumpkin said to her husband.

"Oh fuck! I wanted to send it to the Big Man who is the supervisor of our village."

"Do you have to send it to him?" Mrs. Pumpkin asked, muttering about the low harvest.

"Our town holds the festival of ancestor worship every year. Now it's our turn to host the event. In order to improve the relationship between the police and the local community, I want to make a gift of the pumpkin to the police so that I can get more concessions for our event." He gave his wife a meaningful look.

"Taoism, our religion, is totally different from Japan's religion. Thus the Japanese have made very strict laws with their colonies to promote their Japanization. The Japanese authority has a strong desire to assimilate Taiwanese culture into Japanese culture."

Exue peeped worriedly through the door hole to see what was going on outside where her stepparents were talking. She trembled with fear.

Two days later, one Sunday morning, a fishing leader stood near the temple and asked, "Who wants to join a group to catch fish this afternoon? We still need four more people."

"I want to join it," Mr. Pumpkin replied loudly.

Ten men formed one team, which was a typical fishing group in the Waian area. From fishing nets to stone weirs, from plant gardens to masked women, from silver anchovies to seaweed-harvesting season, the sea business was handed down from generation to generation as their sweat blossomed into seawater. Fishermen collected in boats liked groups of workhorses. In their desire for more harvest, their diligent hands constantly cast fishnets into the very deep ocean.

In the Waian zone, all plants were going bad, yet fishing was going well. Looking into the still water, they could see exactly what took place, how the silver anchovies, octopi, blowfish, and other sea life came together; and then they made a concerted effort to pull the net out. Every moment, with rapid action, the fishermen hauled in their nets, driving their boats toward the seashore, hand over hand, then throwing all the fish to the women who were waiting for their husbands or brothers to come back and share their own part.

But now night was falling, and the equipment had been folded up. Mrs. Pumpkin took a big fish package and followed her husband home.

"Is Exue at home?" Mr. Pumpkin suddenly stopped walking to talk his wife.

"Yes."

"I heard Yao's husband say that the pumpkin was stolen by Exue."

"Oh." Mrs. Pumpkin stood in shocked silence.

Damp and hot under a heavy black sky, at last they arrived home.

"Exue? Exue?" Mrs. Pumpkin desperately yelled out. "You bitch! Where are you? Get out here without delay."

Exue had just returned from her birth mother's home. She sensed something was amiss and felt like a wayward lamb. She shuffled her feet as she stood and twisted her hands tightly together in front of Mrs. Pumpkin.

"What in blazes were you doing? How dare you steal the pumpkin!"

"Not me." Exue replied nervously.

"You are a liar. Really a troublemaker." At that moment, the atmosphere was fierce. Mrs. Pumpkin wanted to punish this bitch. She bent forward to look for a bundle of firewood in the corner. Grasping the firewood in one hand, her blows beat down on Exue like hard-driving rain.

"Oh, no, please stop . . . Mama, if I stole it, I will die." Exue made this oath so that Mrs. Pumpkin would stop flogging her.

"You desire to die? Very well, I agree. Go, go."

Looking at the mad, accusing face of her adoptive mother, Exue felt a sudden urge to run away. But it happened that after walking and crying for a long time through rocks, thorns and wind, she at last came upon a path. And all paths lead to the sea. The tiny village was far behind her now, and as she advanced through this last promontory of Taiwan Strait, the gray sky around her became gloomier and the country, more mournful. A neighbor passed by her and yelled, "Girl! It is too late to stay here alone. Go, go back home!" Now in the area of the dark seashore, she had been warned of danger. She glanced behind her, and then she ran home.

It was late when she crept home. The light was on in the living room, which was a bad sign. Mother would be waiting up to scold her again.

"Didn't you say that you want to die? Why have you come home now?" Mrs. Pumpkin still jeered at her as Exue appeared in the doorway.

So now Exue decided that everything was over, forever and ever. She went forth on her way again, more disheartened, lamenting her fate and not stopping as she hastened toward the ocean.

A tremendous tumult arose all about as if all the ghosts of hell had gathered together. Voices could be heard above, shrieking, bellowing, and yelling, as from a great distance. It was only the wind, the great breath generating all this disorder; the voice of the invisible power from the ocean deeply attracted her. Yes, she wanted to join this part of ocean, and she would love to listen to the wind in the ocean, and it would be good to leave the burden of her life.

"Ah, Ocean! Here I am!" She jumped into the water from the top of a rock. Immediately, she disappeared, vanished into thin air.

However, she had left all her grievances tightly bound to this land of Waian.

2-3

Going Home to Marry

Every year, April brought a lovely spring. In 1925, the weather was so charming that had it not been for Exue's suicide, it would have been a season of great cheer. Relatives left their jobs in Taiwan to show off their achievements and earnings, and everywhere was the joy of family activities and group consciousness in the small town of Waian.

This day was the festival of ancestor worship, and the Pumpkin family was the host of the event. The village leader announced a message to villagers from the temple yard.

"Who wants to eat meat or other foods? All of you can go to the house of Mr. Pumpkin to take whatever you want."

For the people of the sea, worshipping ancestors and God carried the greatest significance. And floating over all of them was a deep religious sentiment, a feeling of bygone days, with respect for ancient veneration and the symbols that protected it. Hearing the announcement, neighbors gradually swept into the house of the Pumpkin family for the most important event of the year. The smoke of incense that had been lit to worship ancestors slowly flowed throughout the Pumpkin house where villagers' faces showed their longing for shelter and safety.

Men and women assembled in front of the house; inside the house, host and hostess welcomed their guests. They were all joyful, except Yao, who said nothing and remained grave and sad. She did not go in to drink with the crowd. She thought something was wrong at the corners.

"Hi, Yao, why you don't join them? Come on," demanded Mrs. Pumpkin.

"I am just wondering about the relationship between a series of unfortunate accidents in my family and the event of Exue's suicide."

"Oh! You are talking about Exue, my adopted daughter, who was really a stupid girl." Mrs. Pumpkin sighed out her helplessness. "At that time, I said I wanted her to die. That wasn't really what I meant. In fact, I just was driven mad by anger. Unfortunately, she took action."

"I can't understand why her soul constantly comes to me and wraps herself around me. Alas, recently, I often have nightmares about her, and she looks at me with sad, staring eyes." Yao sighed deeply at the thought.

"Have you considered that you saw through her thieving action when she plucked the pumpkin out? So she comes to complain to you, I guess," someone warned Yao.

"Oh, is that so? But it is so unfair to me," said Yao.

The result of Exue's suicide had been the topic of widespread gossip for several months; indeed, after Exue killed herself, strange things were happening in this small town. For example, not only was Yao's son-in-law—who was also Zhu Chu-Su's brother—unexpectedly killed in a sea accident, but Yao's daughter often wanted to kill herself. Furthermore, one could hear the sorrowful crying of a female soul arising from the shore over and over again around midnight.

Ever since the Japanese came to Penghu, they were seen as terrible ghosts by the residents of this land because the government of Japan left strict instructions to inflict torture as punishment on all their prisoners. So the villagers didn't dare to break the rules. Thus a Japanese policeman was called Big Man, and a child would stop wailing when he or she heard the words "The Big Man is coming." The result of Exue's suicide was that now there was yet another threat—"Exue is coming"—to scare disobedient children.

The purpose of giving comfort to the soul of Exue was added to the festival of ancestor worship. They prayed, offered foods, collected paper money to burn, and played a Taiwanese opera to show respect for their ancestors and soothe Exue's spirit so that they would be safe. Filled with joy and sorrow, people appeared peaceful with the scent of reverent incense all around them. At this time, the aroma of incense and delicious foods filled the whole village.

At this same hour, over on the other side of the earth, Lee Zi-Shan was on board the *Feng Shan Wan*, on the Strait of Taiwan. The ship was very heavy with many passengers on this special day; Zi-Shan, the longed-for son, had followed hundreds of other Penghu workers returning from their workplace in the southern Taiwan city of Kaohsiung.

It was getting close to afternoon, and the ship was still struggling through driving rain and high winds. Some people couldn't bear sitting in the rocking ship, and they began to vomit, which seemed the price they should pay before they came home. Yet some of the men could talk freely; they had been drinking wine, and the sheer enjoyment of life lit up their straightforward, truthful faces. Now they were loitering in their cabin, chatting in their Penghu accents about amusing news from Kaohsiung.

"Japanese kids were so dumb that we could easily cheat them out of their money when we played the glass balls. Hey, that was really cool." A young fellow roared with laughter.

"What you were doing was very bad."

"You don't need to pretend to be kindhearted. As my uncle said, they are living on our land, eating our food, and using our materials. Of course, we can take something from them. We can't cope with the adults, so the next best thing to do is to deal with their children." They broke into another peal of laughter.

The men were dressed alike in high-class clothing and Western-style trousers; on their feet, they wore leather shoes. Their style of dress was an expression of the success of their businesses in Taiwan. Because they had little chance of work except fishing in their hometown of Waian, a lot of young people went to Kaohsiung to make money. After working diligently for several years, they came home rich and covered in glory.

Sitting in a corner, Zi-Shan, who liked these men very much, had gone to Kaohsiung; and now he was coming back home to visit his mother, Shiang-Sao, and his fiancée, Zhu Chu-Su. While he listened to the conversation of his friends, a smile lifted the corners of his mouth because he had also had the experience of winning at gambling games with those Japanese children.

At twenty, Zi-Shan was a thin young man, but was as steady as an older man. His hair was nearly flat, but his beard was a little bit rough. Even though he was a silent person, when he talked, his clear, calm voice flowed like a brook over a shallow bed.

His grave brown eyes looked intently through the window into the broad expanse of rough waters as though he was expecting at any moment to find his missing father, but he never saw him. An unclear image of his father had often imprinted on his mind since he was five years old, and his mother had told him that his father had drowned in the sea.

Although his father abandoned them to move to Taiwan to live alone, their life needed to go on. When his mother had to choose one of her two sons to be adopted by a rich family, she made the difficult decision to choose his elder brother, Zi-Tian, who was so shrewd that he had enough courage to deal with changes in his life. His mother kept Zi-Shan beside her. Since then, mother and son relied upon each other for life.

Once he asked his mom why Father had never come back home. Then he was beaten by his dear mom who otherwise never beat him even when severe situations happened. Thereafter, he didn't dare talk about Father. But when he couldn't stand the feeling of starving or when he saw his playmates enjoying time with their fathers, he would hide himself in a blanket to sob uncontrollably.

Uncle Yi-Ren came to their family following Zi-Shan's rescue from drowning when he was a little child. Although he no longer starved, he still didn't like Uncle Yi-Ren, Mother's lover. But to please Mother, he would pretend to like his uncle because he really cared about Mother's feelings.

Lee Zi-Shan's elder brother, Lee Zi-Tian, who was adopted by another family in an earlier time, now traded in marine products and was a successful businessman in Taiwan. Zi-Tian was trying to recruit more workers from his hometown to develop his business.

By the time Zi-Shan was fourteen years old and had finished elementary school, he was recruited by his elder brother. It was exciting to go to Taiwan to make money. For this purpose, he not only might have a chance to find his father in Taiwan, but he and Mother wouldn't have to rely on the support of Uncle Yi-Ren anymore. However, almost everything that could go wrong did go wrong.

Unfortunately, Zi-Shan had to return home very quickly. The reason for leaving his job was that he couldn't bear the sight of his snobbish brother. At the same time, his stepfather Yi-Ren was killed in a sea accident. He was worried about his mother, so he was anxious to return home as soon as possible.

In spite of his lack of income, he had a good time with Mother in his hometown. Additionally, he met his love. The first day he had seen her—this Chu-Su, the most beautiful girl in the fishing village—was the year after his arrival at Waian. It was on the fifteenth night of the first lunar month, the day of the Lantern Festival. The loud gongs and drums of the ceremony pounded relentlessly, and believers bustled in front of the shrine in Noble Wun's temple. Blessed by God, they took home several kilograms of rice turtles. It seemed like they also took a ton of good luck.

Zi-Shan had a clear memory of all these things together. Now, excited and merry, a great joy seized him at the idea that Zhu Chu-Su would now become a member of his own family. Although he was recognized as an obedient child, he had fallen in love with Chu-Su, neglecting Mother's wish that he marry a girl she preferred, who didn't need any money to be paid at the betrothal. But his mother finally agreed that he could propose to Chu-Su. Indeed, his loving mother always touched his mind even though he lived on a tight budget. "It was a family where you always worked for things," Zi-Shan recalled. "Success was something you earned. I grew up watching my mama live that, and it stuck."

Falling in love with Chu-Su, he seemed to mature a lot overnight. Six months later, he decided that he would go to the Port of Kaohsiung again to find work, not only because of his desire to get married and start a career, but also since he had to make more money to pay for the betrothal. He had to pay a high price to Chu-Su's family.

The Port of Kaohsiung was located on the southwestern coast of Taiwan. Building up the city of Kaohsiung was a strong goal of the Japanese while they occupied the region; moreover, Kaohsiung was also a place where the people of Penghu hoped to get job opportunities.

When Zi-Shan went to Kaohsiung, it was 1925. The feeling was very different from three years ago when he was an immature teenager. Now the first important thing he needed to do was look for his father's place after he got off from a twelve-hour ship ride.

Unfortunately, even though he searched tirelessly, he couldn't find the location where his father was living.

"Man, do you want to find the Second Tiger Papa?" asked a passerby.

"What is the Tiger Papa?" Zi-Shan replied.

"I guess you are looking for the man, Lee Shiang, whose nickname is the Second Tiger Papa because he led a group of anti-Japanese when the first Japanese were coming."

"You knew that!" said Zi-Shan. He was shocked by how famous his father was here.

"Aha! I know that many heroic groups died in defense of liberty when Taiwan was ceded to Japan," this very kind and helpful passerby explained to Zi-Shan. "It was mostly believed that some members of the Tiger Papa group have escaped to China to settle down. The Second Tiger Papa, Lee Shiang, probably was one of them that escaped to China to find shelter from the Japanese because the Japanese government wanted to break up these groups."

"Lee Shiang is my father!" Zi-Shan was proud of his father. It slipped out of his lips.

"Wow, the son of the Second Tiger Papa."

"Now I don't know where to go."

"Do you have any relations here?"

"Yes, I have one brother here," he said disappointedly. "But I don't want to rely on him."

"Let me think . . . Do you want to be a porter in the Port of Kaohsiung?"

"Sure, may I?"

"You are from my village and look like an honest man. I feel duty-bound to help you."

"It gives me great pleasure to meet you."

It was said that the Port of Kaohsiung's development was begun in 1908 by Japan. Thus there was a lot of hard work to do. The situation required a lot of laborers to achieve so much construction.

In fact, there were job opportunities all over Taiwan. Zi-Shan chose to be a porter even though it was very hard work because the wage was better than other jobs were paid. Not only was he hardworking, but he was also very thrifty. In less than two years, he had saved a lot of money and decided to go back home to Waian.

By midday, the ship, *Feng Shan Wan*, was docked at the port of Magong, Penghu. Zi-Shan needed to transfer to another ferry to get to his homeland as Waian country was a small island located on the western side of Penghu. The boat rolled gently with the everlasting wail of the wind. Zi-Shan couldn't bear to wait in the slowly swinging boat. Even though the boat hadn't yet drawn alongside the shore, he jumped down from the boat and made haste to run to his sweet home.

"Nobody is in the house. Everyone has gone to the temple fair," an old woman told him.

Zi-Shan started off at a run again to the temple fair. It was too crowded to look for his mother in the spiraling smoke and the noisy gongs and drums of the ceremonial march. He didn't know what was happening in his homeland that would require such a big event.

"Mom, I am here!" At last Zi-Shan found his mother in the middle of the crowd.

"My dear, you finally came back home." Shiang-Sao wiped her tear-streaked cheek with the back of her hand.

"Mother, you must see how much I earned in Taiwan." Zi-Shan wanted to show off the money to his mother.

"Foolish child! Don't show it off here." Shiang-Sao pushed down Zi-Shan's hand.

After a while, he would have liked to know where Chu-Su was, but he did not dare ask about her.

"Ah! The incident of Exue gave rise to a lot of talk in this town." Shiang-Sao sighed deeply at the thought. "After Exue committed suicide, a series of bad events happened in the family of Chu-Su."

"How is Chu-Su?"

"It is a long story. First, her brother, Zhu Ling, suddenly passed away in a sea accident, and secondly, her father became an absolutely useless person who indulged in drinking every day and gave up planting the guava trees in his garden," Shiang-Sao said. "Her family is a mess, but fortunately, Chu-Su has gone to Neian to find a babysitting job to help her family's finances."

"Mom, I want to marry Chu-Su and bring you to Kaohsiung to live. I have already prepared a home for you and Chu-Su there."

"Yes?" said Shiang-Sao, who did not understand what her son was talking about.

"After I marry Chu-Su, I hope you and Chu-Su will move to Kaohsiung."

Zi-Shan's suggestion came as a shock to Shiang-Sao. Yet she saw a serious face in front of her, so she said, "I fear that I am not well suited to moving to a new place to live, but I also worry about your young brother being left here alone. Maybe you two should go there first."

"Of course, he can go with us if he likes."

"I will think about it," Shiang-Sao replied.

"Mom, please."

"If you really long to marry Chu-Su, you must take immediate action to avoid any trouble happening," Shiang-Sao soberly advised her son.

2-4

The Struggle Between Daughter and Daughter-in-Law

Penghu enjoyed a cornucopia of fish in its surrounding seas; the island of Waian was rich in rockfish in the winter. At the time of the fishermen's leave-taking, the preparations for the busy season occupied everyone. It is true in the month of February that when the rockfish came, any man could be a fisherman.

Before dawn the men went to sea to catch fish and the women went to the rocky coast to find wild laver, sea snails, and clams. After this, they did housework—the people of Waian were diligent in their work.

One spring day in 1926, Chu-Su was woken by a smell of heavy smoke spiraling from the kitchen. She guessed her mother-in-law had risen to do the housework. She shyly looked at the man, Zi-Shan, who slept beside her. For seven days they had been husband and wife. She threw off the blanket and ran to the kitchen to help her mother-in-law light a fire in a quiet dark corner.

"Mother, you woke up so early. You should go to sleep again," Chu-Su said carefully to Shiang-Sao. "Let me do it alone."

"Yah! That would be useful," Shiang-Sao snapped with heavy sarcasm. "But I am not fortunate enough to be able to sleep longer."

"Please excuse me," murmured the new bride, now completely abashed.

"Wow! It's chilly today." Zi-Shan rubbed his hands together and asked his two women, "Why should you two be up so bright and early in such cold weather?"

At this moment, a bright fire burst from the pile of firewood. Suddenly, the fire not only shone brightly in the dusky cookroom but also the chilly feeling began to disperse.

Afterward, Shiang-Sao sighed with relief and said to sleepy-eyed Zi-Shan, "Don't be lazy! Great pains quickly find ease." Then with one more sigh, Shiang-Sao, who had been kneeling in front of the fire, tried to stand up, but this action made her feel dizzy. Zi-Shan and Chu-Su quickly rushed up to hold her.

"Don't worry, this is my old ailment." She showed them that she was all right. Then she added, "But recently, I feel my eyes are having some trouble. I cannot easily see things anymore."

The new couple was shocked by the words of Shiang-Sao. After a silence, Zi-Shan spoke to his new bride, "We need to be more patient with Mother. In fact, she did not have good fortune in her life, but she is also upset to think of me leaving here next week."

Chu-Su gazed at her husband for a while.

"Mother seems to loathe me because I have no dowry," she said.

"Don't worry. Even though she has a bad temper, she is really a sympathetic woman. I will arrange for you and Mother to go to Taiwan as soon as possible."

"I've got plenty of things to deal with. There's no need to rush." Chu-Su breathed a sigh of anxiety and said to Zi-Shan, "I worry about my sick father. I cannot forget my own family even though I'm married to you."

"Now you are a member of my family, so you should care more about the Lee family than your own."

"Females are always undervalued. A married woman is treated like dirty water that is thrown on the ground to disappear into the earth."

"It isn't so serious." He looked at Chu-Su steadily and expressed his growing concern, "I worry that you are too busy with two families to care about me."

"Nothing worries me," she sputtered and seemed vexed. But all kinds of thoughts raced through her mind. She thought that even though Zi-Shan respected his mother very much, he stood up to the anger of his mother and showed great courage to marry her. What a lovely man, and he was now her husband. Her mood gradually improved. Finally, she shyly scanned Zi-Shan's face.

"If you go to Kaohsiung next week, I may be able to do a job for the Yang family," she said.

"What?" he inquired impatiently.

"I can go to Neian, the village next to Waian."

"Are you really in love with that fellow Yang-En? I heard a rumor."

"Humph! What are you talking about?" Chu-Su was now white with rage. "Don't you know this is the season rich in rockfish? Everyone is busy here, and I can make some money to help."

"You should do your duty as a daughter-in-law. It is better for you to be at home with Mother."

"I don't know what on earth you mean." Chu-Su came very near to crying.

At this moment, Zi-Shan's mother came in the door with firewood in her arms. She knew that it was a sign of bad luck for a new couple to argue in the morning.

"What has gone wrong with you two?" She wanted to smooth things over. So she gave orders to the couple. Zi-Shan went to the old well to draw water, and Chu-Su went to make rice cakes with her mother-in-law. Shiang-Sao's upset expression disappeared.

Zi-Shan was happy to relieve his mother's anxiety, but Chu-Su couldn't accept the sudden changes in Mother-in-law's attitude. Chu-Su secretly wiped her tear-streaked cheeks with the back of her hands and then followed Shiang-Sao to prepare the rice cakes.

After looking at his mother and wife working together, Zi-Shan ran to the backyard to fill two water buckets.

To avoid the cold wind outside, Shiang-Sao brought two cloth wrappers for them to wrap around their heads. Outside they found themselves in the cold bitter wind of the dusky morning.

"Auntie Dou is a really, really kind woman. She set up a rice mill to support our neighborhood. We can make as many cakes as we want to in the future. But we should be as early as possible. Otherwise, we need to line up for a long time on this festival day," said Shiang-Sao.

Lowering her head, Chu-Su carried two buckets of rice loaded on her shoulders as she followed her mother-in-law step-by-step. They used the light of the moon to find their way to the rice mill. At first they were not able to work together in a harmonious way, but after a half hour, they found a way to help each other effectively. Finally, when they finished their work at daybreak, Shiang-Sao dealt out another task to her daughter-in-law. She said, "You should collect some firewood since later we will need to use a lot to cook the rice cake."

"Yes, Mama," replied Chu-Su. Actually, she was at the end of her tether after three hours of hard work.

While they were on their way home, Zi-Shan yelled out to Shiang-Sao, "Mom! Uncle Tian has just told me that he wants you to go to his home to sing Nankuan music."

The special voice of Shiang-Sao was discovered by Tian, who was the leader of the Nankuan Music Club. The twelve members of this society came from Neian and Waian when the club began, and since then the Nankuan Music Club provided great entertainment to the people of Waian. Even though Shiang-Sao was unable to read or write, she could sing the words perfectly. This pastime comforted Shiang-Sao through many days of wind and storm.

When Shiang-Sao went to Tian's home to sing Nankuan music, Chu-Su handed over responsibility for some of the unfinished housework to Zi-Shan because she wanted to go to the backyard to collect firewood.

To speak truly, Chu-Su was really on her way home to see her father. She had only visited her parental home once, two days after she was married. As her father always said, "A grown daughter cannot be kept unmarried for long." But Chu-Su thought that on the other side of the fence, being a male had much more value than being a female because she had to leave her own family to suit another family.

She had but a confused memory of her wedding. Her friends looked with envy as she married a man who was not only the most handsome man in this area but also had a job in Taiwan. Excited and joyful, yet with her heart aching, she felt anguish seize her at the idea of leaving her own family because she was worried over her father's health. Moreover, the Exue incident also involved her family in a series of troubles, such as her brother's death and her sister-in-law's illness. Yet when Zi-Shan came back home from Kaohsiung, she didn't hesitate when he suddenly proposed to her.

She had been walking for a half hour, inhaling the fishy breeze whistling up the hill as many people passed by her. While she was still climbing up the hill, she saw a familiar face, Yang-En, who was carrying two buckets of fish on his shoulders. She backed up a few steps to look for another way to go. But then she stopped, hesitant and afraid.

"Chu-Su, I—I wish to speak to you, please."

"Ah! What are you doing here, Yang-En?" she queried, lowering her voice and snatching off her cloth wrapper.

"The Japanese cop here likes the rockfish, so I'm taking a gift of these fish to him."

"I see. I have to go."

"Wait," pleaded Yang-En. "Chu-Su . . . I would like you to be our helper again if your husband wants to go to Kaohsiung. Recently, our fish factory is going well, but we need more help."

She said nothing. She looked around quickly, worrying that someone was commenting on them in whispers. She started to leave Yang-En in a hurry.

"Please don't rush off. I haven't finished." Yang-En said earnestly.

No, she needed to rush to her father's home. That was the most important thing for her to do now.

Then the pathway rose again, and she found herself commanding a view of immense horizons and the smell of a cattle shed—she breathed in the bracing air of sea heights and the irritating odor of cow dung. From the cattle pen on the cliff, the gray waters of the Pacific Ocean where her brother had disappeared in a shipwreck could be seen in the far distance. What surprised her now was that she was charmed by the smell of the sea wind and cow dung mixed together. Walking here, she must try to remain calm as she approached her parents' home. Yet here she always gave her thoughts free rein.

It was said that this cape was close to the opposite shores of Tang-Shan (mainland China). Now her mind dwelled on the relationship between Tang-Shan and Lee Shiang, who was Zi-Shan's father. When he failed to join the action against Japan,

Lee Shiang went into hiding in Tang-Shan to avoid being arrested by the Japanese authorities.

In the past, even though she had been unfamiliar with the name of Tang-Shan, she had longed to face the sea wind and see the faraway opposite shore and imagine her future. For example, she knew that she would have a considerate husband and very clever children who were different from this area's rural children.

Indeed, she already had a husband who was able to go to the urban district of Taiwan to make money, and this made her the object of envy of all her girlfriends. Now her dream had come true. Yet she was sorely troubled by her happiness for it seemed something too impossible, as unstable as a joyful dream. Besides, would Zi-Shan want to leave again? Would she always be too deeply concerned about her own family?

As she neared her father's house in this lost region, all things seemed rougher and more desolate because their big guava garden had been neglected for a long time. Sea breezes that made people stronger made shorter and stubbier plants, such as gaillardia and cactus.

When she walked into the house, she saw her father's hand holding a bottle of wine.

"Dad, how are you doing? I've come home to visit you."

"You are alone? Where is Zi-Shan?"

"He didn't know I was coming here. I miss you so much, Dad." She choked down her tears.

"My dear, now that you are a daughter-in-law, you need to know the three obediences and four virtues of woman." Although Zhu Wang was a little drunk, he still clearly reminded his daughter, "Chu-Su, you must focus on your husband's family and keep our family's fine reputation." He breathed a sigh of regret and said to his daughter again, "Remember! Don't care too much about your original family after you are married."

"Dad, you don't want to know how I am doing in the family of Zi-Shan?" Chu-Su was almost crying. Poor Father! Even though he had suffered a misfortune, he still cared about his reputation. No wonder people prefer a male in childbirth. Once again, Chu-Su had a queer sense of sorrow as she thought to herself, "It is an unworthy existence being a female."

Then her father cried, "Alas! We are a decent family, and we have always behaved ourselves, but we aren't blessed by God. You see, a series of miserable events happened in our family. To begin with, your mother passed away, then your elder brother died in a sea accident, and your sister-in-law . . ." He frequently lifted the bottle of wine to his lips, and his tears fell down like rain.

It was then that her little brother appeared and gave Chu-Su some relief. She was anxious to return home because she had already spent too much time away from her duties outside. Now she realized some strange ideas about herself. It was true; when living with her married family, she worried about her parent's family. On the other hand, when visiting her parent's home, she cared about her married family. In fact, she needed to return home before sunset. She hadn't yet finished the work of collecting firewood.

The sun, already quite low, descended even more; thus night had obviously come. As the great ball of flame fell into the leaden-colored zone that surrounded the sea in the wintertime, it grew yellow, and its outer rim became more clear and real. Now it could be looked at straight on as if it were the moon. Growing up in this ocean land, Chu-Su longed for whatever the sea brought to her village; only the ocean energy could be a comfort to the hardworking people of Waian.

She walked hastily along the irregular path to descend to her destination. Passing right by the police station, she heard the voice of the Big Man shouting at someone. She didn't know who had violated a rule again in the village. In fact, everyone was in terror when the Japanese police were angry. Hastening her steps, she went toward the place that was both strange and familiar at the same time; although she was consigned to Zi-Shan in this life, she didn't feel comfortable yet in his home. Once she dreamed that they were very dear to each other, yet she woke up and found that they were strangers. Was marriage both a blessing and a burden?

Now it was too late to collect much firewood. She didn't know how she would face her displeased mother-in-law.

入船高雄

PART THREE

Coming to Kaohsiung
(1929-1939)

3-1

Lee Zi-Tian

On the western side of the Port of Kaohsiung one fine Sunday morning in July 1929, a fleet of boats followed a big boat toward the shore. The big boat was about to be burned as the main event of the Wangchuan boat-burning ceremony. Under the sunshiny sky, a huge crowd rejoiced wildly at this local custom. There was a great clamor in Kaohsiung as tremendous flames from the burning Wangchuan boat filled the air, and uproarious gongs and drums beat the time of the ceremonial march. Once every year, the God of Nobility took the burning boat of Wangchuan on patrol to protect people. Smoke slowly fluttered to the shore where everyone prayed for a better life.

Believers crowded on the seashore. Pushing through the huge crowd, Lee Zi-Tian earnestly touched the Wangchuan boat to receive protection from the God of Nobility and attain his desire for good luck in the future. Meanwhile, a cargo boat was gradually sailing toward shore. Zi-Tian quickly ran to welcome the boat.

"Young fellow, here are huge amounts of stuff. We need more workers," the captain said to Zi-Tian who was now on deck.

"I can do it all. Yes, even if you have only me it is okay," replied Zi-Tian.

"Where are all those people going?"

"They are all going to see the boat-burning ceremony." The cargo boat hadn't fully docked yet, but Zi-Tian wanted to start doing the job.

"Penghu guy, don't rush, take it easy. You'll have a lot of work this time."

The boat rolled gently with the wind's ceaseless howl, as repetitious as a Waian song moaned by a sleeper. Zi-Tian rolled up his trousers and sat in the sand, impatiently waiting for the boat to dock.

Closing his eyes, at first he could not distinguish what he was seeing behind his eyes. First it looked like a drop in the ocean. Then it grew into a shimmering mirror that had no objects to reflect, and in the distance, it became a wild cloud; beyond that were many memories in front of his mind.

In fact, Waian wasn't just his birthplace. It was also the place of his suffering. In the early days, his father left his family high and dry. This resulted in Zi-Tian stealing food to avoid starvation. But once, he was caught by the store owner and was severely punished by the Japanese police. Finally, his mother wiped away her bitter tears and decided that he should be adopted by the Lu family who lived in their neighborhood without a son. Even though he had a nicer existence, he was uncomfortable with the Lu family because he wanted to live, not just exist.

After he had been married to the Lu's daughter for half a year, he went to downtown Penghu, which was called Magong, to do a Japanese-cooking job, but he was unsuited for this work. In the meantime, he met a good man who introduced him to Taiwan. The opposite shore of Taiwan had many good opportunities to look for a job, especially during the period of building the harbor and other parts of Kaohsiung under Japanese rule, which led to the modernization of the city. Indeed, it became a source of hope for the Penghu people. Zi-Tian resigned almost immediately from his cooking job to start his future in Kaohsiung.

But the beginning of his new life was a struggle between letting go of the long-established customs of Waian and adjusting to the new ways of Kaohsiung. Learning how to survive in a new place was a big job for him. First of all, he was always annoying other workers because he bent over backward to do his work.

"Pig of Penghu, come on." Crowds of angry workers protested against him and tried to stir up trouble for him.

Zi-Tian fought back. "You are not my boss. Why do I need to obey you?" Now he was stronger than before. He would no longer be meek and timid. He unloaded heavy bags from his shoulders and stood up straight to accept the challenge.

"Kaohsiung is our place. Of course, we are your boss!" The mob had a magnificent air of authority.

"You're talking nonsense!" He jumped on one of workers and tried to strangle him.

This became an irreconcilable conflict between rival factions within the workplace. Finally, they were arrested by the Japanese police.

The police neglected to notice that Zi-Tian's head was cut and bleeding and only blamed him for the trouble. "Huh? Penghu guy again, you really are a troublemaker! Tell me what is wrong?"

"They beat me first!" He felt frustrated at this accident, yet he stuck his neck out to defend himself. He went away very troubled. Indeed, he got very hot under the collar when he realized he was considered an inferior person because he came from Penghu. He looked up to the sky and said to himself, "Fuck it! Why do I, a Penghu guy, need to lower myself to suit a gang of Kaohsiung?" He breathed a sigh of regret. "No, absolutely not! I will not only win honor for Penghu, but I will be a roaring success."

After that, during his two-year struggle to achieve good karma, he became used to dealing well with the people where he lived. Nowadays, he was an office boy cleaning for a Japanese company.

But even though he already had a regular job, he still had a good chance to win another job when the cargo vessel entered the Kaohsiung harbor.

Zi-Tian returned from his dreamland of remembrances to see clearly again; the cheerful sun shone on the remains of the ritual as the cargo tanker came in. Thank God nobody looked down upon him now. This was his time, and he entered the boat to move things.

"Young guy, do you want to make more money? I have a good idea," said the captain who aroused Zi-Tian's interest.

"Oh . . . more moncy for what?" asked Zi-Tian, puzzled.

"We will have a shipment of Fukien wood coming from the mainland to Kaohsiung next month," the captain said to Zi-Tian. "A good opportunity is coming to you."

"What opportunity?"

"You know—after the ship unloads the wood, it needs to carry some goods back to Fukien because an empty ship is easily capsized."

"You mean you need some goods from us."

"That is strictly correct," said the captain. "But what kind of the goods should we fill it with?"

There was a moment of complete silence. Then Zi-Tian said seriously, "I can help. I can try to persuade the head of the Japanese sugar company to provide the goods—sugar. Yes, I can try to discuss this with him; he's my good friend."

"I know you are a smart guy. Okay, the cargo will be sugar, and the matter of the ship I can handle," said the captain. "Let's cooperate to get the work done smoothly. Ha-ha!"

Zi-Tian and the captain became more and more excited as they discussed their great future together. At the same time, a crowd gathered on the seashore to pray for good luck. Under the summer sun, the sky was so blue that Zi-Tian felt like a bird flying high, as if an even better tomorrow lay ahead of him.

In fact, in 1913, Japanese authorities had arranged to combine two species of sugarcane to make new stronger sugarcane that would avoid disease. Several years later, their experiment was successful. The accounts showed Taiwan was only inferior to Cuba and India in the world of sugar industry; hence, Taiwan was called *Eastern Sweet Island.*

And so the more Taiwan developed its sugar industry, the more good luck Zi-Tian had. Sugar was the favorite product of mainland Fukien (China) so that Zi-Tian was able to get more and more contracts for his marine transportation business—in other words, he was a bit of an opportunist who made a fortune through his undertakings out at sea. The situation transformed him from a lowly office boy to an important exporter of sugar and wood.

The more profits he made, the more actively Zi-Tian invested. To begin with, he needed more workers to develop his business, and most of the workers were recruited from his hometown, Penghu, Waian; this time, his younger brother, Zi-Shan, was one of these Penghu migrant workers.

To speak truly, even though the brothers hadn't been together for a long time, Zi-Tian had not been very welcoming to his younger brother who had come with a group of Penghu migrant workers to Kaohsiung to work for him. After barely glancing at Zi-Shan, he turned his eyes away as if he were vexed with this meeting and in a hurry to go. Zi-Shan was disappointed in Zi-Tian—he really thought his elder brother would be excited to meet him in this strange land. What a difference there was between Zi-Shan's passion and Zi-Tian's coolness! "How nonsensical and empty is Kaohsiung!" Zi-Shan thought.

"Hey, man, you must be polite to the Japanese. Remember! Don't turn the Japanese off because we are making a lot of money from them," Zi-Tian warned Zi-Shan.

"Make money? You must take the way of honor to do it." Zi-Shan disagreed with his brother's way of doing business.

"Your mother raised scum!" Zi-Tian barked at Zi-Shan.

"I don't know what on earth you mean. If my mother isn't your mother, who is?" Zi-Shan spoke with confidence because his elder brother knew that he was in the right.

"How dare you talk to me in such a way!" Zi-Tian gave Zi-Shan a box on the ear.

"Even if I starve to death, I don't want to rely on his help anymore," Zi-Shan said to himself, as he fought back the tears and decided to escape from the power of Zi-Tian.

Dispirited, Zi-Shan walked by a train loaded with sugar to think about his future. Suddenly, he was attracted to a pile of wood on the ground near the tracks, and he went over to examine it, but he soon got arrested for his behavior.

"Don't you know it's a crime to steal wood?" asked the Japanese policeman.

"I wasn't—," Zi-Shan had never disobeyed the law. He was very much embarrassed.

"Unless you have a guarantor, I will have to detain you for questioning."

"Lee Zi-Tian is my elder brother."

"You are Zi-Tian's brother!" Fondling his beard, the policeman looked at Zi-Shan's honest face and then waved his hand to signal that he could go away. It was true; he, Zi-Shan, had to rely entirely on the name of Zi-Tian for release. This fact contradicted how he wanted his life to be. Everything was going wrong. He really couldn't comprehend what the facts were now. Lee Zi-Tian was not his cherished brother anymore.

"What a difficult city Kaohsiung is!" he thought. "It is altogether snobbish and altogether harsh and forbidding."

Consequently, after not even half a year of working for his brother, Zi-Shan wanted to go home to his sweet hometown, Waian, and enjoy the love of his mother even if he didn't like Uncle Yi-Ren, his mother's lover. In fact, feeling uncomfortable with his Uncle Yi-Ren was his excuse for leaving in the first place, so he could ignore Mother's tears as he followed the other migrant workers into Kaohsiung to work for his elder brother. But things hadn't turned out according to his wishes.

That year, at the age of seventeen, Zi-Shan experienced failure in Kaohsiung. His elder brother, on the other hand, continued his successful adventure.

One morning in Kaohsiung, the sun was shining on several ships under the name of Lee Zi-Tian passing through the Taiwan Strait to Penghu. Developing a ship trade was not only good for the Penghu people but it also increased Zi-Tian's business.

At that quiet moment, that same sun could be seen in Waian where it was about to rise. It was, indeed, the same daystar beheld at the same precise moment of its never-ending round, but here it did not shine so brightly. Higher up in the blue sky, it kept shedding a soft white light on Lu Shan as she stood outside on her front balcony, baking fish and every moment waiting for her husband, Lee Zi-Tian, to come back; but . . .

3-2

A Craving for Togetherness

In Waian, near the end of October in 1932, the wind bellowed out in its deep voice with a rumble of rage and again repeated its warnings. The sea waves were ever increasing, and masses of water were thrown with such violence that they tore apart everything in their way. Most of the plants on the island had faded by the time the northeasterly monsoons of winter brought strong winds laden with salt.

This weather didn't suit going out to sea. A gloomy mood pervaded the whole fishing village. However, in front of the temple of the Noble Wun, which was full of flags, lightning flashed as if to announce the upcoming festival. In other words, even though the weather was very dull, the whole village still seemed to be in a festive mood.

Indeed, devoted prayers for safety and security were going on. The surroundings of the temple represented spiritual dependency and a place of ceremony.

After one month as husband and wife, Zi-Shan went to Kaohsiung to make money, and Chu-Su stayed in Waian for more than one year. At this time of religious devotion, prayers for safety and security occupied everyone. Chu-Su and her mother-in-law were busily preparing offerings before daybreak. Chu-Su's brother-in-law, Li Zi-Song, was also on the job heaping up salt for pickling squid and fish.

While all the adults busied themselves with their work, the children engaged in their own games. For example, two-year-old Lee Lian-Ren, son of Chu-Su, struggled to climb a chair and pull a paper off the wall. Finally, he got it and put it into his mouth to scratch his new itchy teeth. In the meantime, his action was seen by eight-year-old Lian-Yuan, who was his cousin. Actually, Lian-Yuan was sent here by his mother, Lu Shan, to ask Auntie Chu-Su when she wanted to go to the temple to attend worship because his mother was ready to go. But he had seen many pieces of paper fall here and there.

He knew this paper that had been on the wall was very important to his auntie, so he yelled out quickly and anxiously, "Auntie Chu-Su! A paper was torn into many pieces in the living room by Lian-Ren."

The paper was calligraphy of a masterpiece work that was written by Zhu Fo-Sh, Chu-Su's grandfather, who was a wise man of Penghu Island. He enjoyed writing in verse from the Diamond Sutra taught by Buddha to give advice to his students who learned moral culture from him. Chu-Su had preserved her grandpa's masterworks.

All the world's phenomena and ideas
Are unreal, like a dream,
Like magic, and like an image.

These treasured calligraphic works were not only Chu-Su's proudest possessions but also the source of her spiritual strength. Her husband, Zi-Shan, used to tease about her behavior, saying, "Your grandpa's work is the best dowry he gave you."

But now her best dowry was torn into small pieces by her son, which upset Chu-Su very much. She lifted her hand to strike her son's delicate face. The little boy was wailing miserably, which provoked his grandma's fury at Chu-Su.

"The works are of no use at all. You don't need to educate your son like that!" Shiang-Sao shouted at her daughter-in-law, and then turning round, she tenderly embraced her grandson. "Don't cry, my dear, Grandma will take you to the temple to pray for you."

Chu-Su suffered through this painful episode, and then she didn't know how she ended up following Lian-Yuan, who was actually the eldest grandson of Shiang-Sao, to his house to accompany his mother to worship at the temple.

As they walked along together, Lian-Yuan neglected to notice Chu-Su's dark mood, so he felt free to ask her naively, "Auntie! I have never seen my daddy. I miss him very much. Can you tell me what he's like?"

"His name is Lee Zi-Tian, and he is also my husband's brother," Chu-Su forgot her own worries as she replied patiently. "When he was ten, he was adopted by your Lu family and matched up to your mother when he was eighteen."

"I said I miss Daddy, but Mummy was always sad . . . crying."

"For her, alas, her husband leaving home for a long time and never coming back to care for you was very bad." She breathed a sigh of regret and seemed to say to herself, "Even though your dad and Lian-Ren's dad are blood siblings, their characters are totally different. A story is going around that not only does your dad, Lee Zi-Tian, have a very successful business in Taiwan but he also has a wife there, so . . ."

"Auntie, what are you saying?" Lian-Yuan didn't understand what Chu-Su was talking about.

"Yes, of course, you are too little to understand the world of adults." She patted her little nephew on his head pityingly as she continued her conversation with him. "Your mom is a very obedient daughter-in-law. Although Zi-Tian abandoned his family here, your mom still cares for Zi-Tian's mother."

Harder and harder the wind blew, forcing them to walk slowly. At last, they arrived at the house.

"Mom, I bring Auntie to our home." Lian-Yuan shook off the hand of Chu-Su to run toward Lu Shan.

"Oh, I waited a long time. I've always waited for a long time," Lu Shan said. Her look was very serious, like someone lost in a faraway land.

"Sis Shan, are you okay?" Chu-Su said courteously as she saw Lu Shan's pale complexion.

"Chu-Su, you are here," she gave Chu-Su a sad smile. At that moment, Chu-Su could see that she was reviving little by little.

"Let's go. We can go to temple together."

"Chu-Su, you know, when there are men without women beside them, trouble will happen like a love affair. My dear, listen to me. You must go to Taiwan as soon as possible to be with Zi-Shan," she advised Chu-Su.

"I think Zi-Shan isn't one of those men. Even though he goes to Taiwan, he comes back to Waian frequently," Chu-Su replied confidently. Chu-Su and Zi-Shan were like no other couple; they were more serious in their love than the common run. Chu-Su still carried herself very straight even when she was absorbed by a particular idea. She had an open mind, but she also had great dignity, which she inherited from the brave Netherland sailors—her ancestors. The expression in her eyes was both constant and tender.

"Do you know a common saying here—*Men keep mistresses in Taiwan; women keep empty beds in Waian*?" Lu Shan still considered all men the same. She tried to warn Chu-Su.

In fact, Zi-Shan had always wanted Chu-Su to go to Taiwan, but she didn't like to leave the place of her own birth and childhood. Moreover, her mother-in-law didn't want to live in a strange neighborhood. They were both fearful of unfamiliar

Taiwan. What was Chu-Su's overall impression of Taiwan? It was the place where her uncle, Zhu Dian, passed away when he joined the fight against Japan's authority, but it was also where her auntie's hometown had vanished off the face of the earth when the Japanese first landed. Nevertheless, Taiwan was the location of their hope for a better life because of their love for Zi-Shan, who still lived in Taiwan.

After several descending and ascending paths, they arrived at the Temple of Noble Wun. Floating everywhere were strong religious emotions and feelings of optimism that good luck would be received because of the great respect for and adoration of the ancient symbols that protect everyone and the great god Noble Wun. Every wall was covered by glittering lights heightening the splendor of the House of Noble Wun. Its steps were strewn with flowers and flags; the fragrance of incense and the votive offerings of villagers were all around the sacred tables.

A religious ritual was being performed on the stage. Rewarding troops and seeing off the Wangchuan boat, many mediums, interpreters, and exorcists constructed bridges between mortals and immortals. Belief was a process. The ceremony was humbling yet filled with joy and sorrow. In spite of the strong wind outside, the people of Waian appeared peaceful in the midst of the reverent scents of incense.

Chu-Su earnestly watched the ceremony. She was a very slim woman wearing a pink overcoat, which was the fashion of the day, and a long dark-green shawl. Shui-Zi, who was Chu-Su's sister-in-law, paid devout attention to the ceremony, but she also kept turning toward a man as they conversed with their eyes. Suddenly, Chu-Su came to a new understanding about Shui-Zi. She was seeing convincing evidence of the rumor that something was going on between her sister-in-law and that man.

Chu-Su calculated that her sister-in-law had remained in widowhood for around two years. It was true; Chu-Su's brother had died two years ago when he was killed in a sea accident. In fact, Shui-Zi was usually an obedient woman, but she was unfortunately fond of fooling around once in a while. Chu-Su worried about how her elderly father would feel if he knew his daughter-in-law, Shui-Zi, was going to marry again.

Chu-Su put her palms together in devoted worship. She said her prayers at length for all the dead members of her family—mother, brother, and uncle; then she prayed again with renewed strength and confidence for her father. As for her husband's family, praying for her mother-in-law was enough.

About one month later, in November, the weather around Waian Island was of that rare kind that the villagers call the period of ebb tide; in other words, in the air, nothing moved, as if all the breezes were exhausted and their task of signaling when to collect the best seafood was done. With this in mind, Chu-Su wanted to go to the seashore to collect some seafood to make a good meal for her mother-in-law. She knew a special area of beach where there was a wide variety of fish. Even though Zi-Shan often warned her to avoid this dangerous area, which was also the place where her brother drowned, she still wanted to go there and find some seafood to please her mother-in-law. Between Chu-Su and her mother-in-law, their relationship had gradually improved because they had the same focus on their beloved Lee Zi-Shan.

The heat and the sun were not reduced by the winter season as Chu-Su continued to walk alone across the hills of Waian in the direction of the beach. First, she passed an abandoned garden. The long fence had fallen in long ago, after her mother passed away, and enormous guava trees had grown on the spot where her family's business had once thrived.

As she neared her destination in this lost country, everything looked more rugged and desolate. Sea breezes made plants shorter and stubbier. Seaweeds and fish of all kinds were scattered over the paths as well as leaves of sea purslane, gaillardias, and cacti; their briny smell mixed with the fragrance of heather.

She had been walking for the last hour with a light step despite oppressive memories of her family's loss as she inhaled the healthy open breeze whistling up the hills. Unexpectedly, she heard voices from behind a leafy space. Chu-Su, pale and trembling, stood there by the side on the cliff, unable to move, with her soul captured by the strange voices. She heard a woman's groan and a man's heavy breath as they made love to each other. At the sudden realization of what she had come across, she felt small. Her first instinct was to run, but she knew the noise would make her presence known to the lovers. Actually, the two people lying together on the earth seemed too absorbed with each other to notice anything else happening. Quietly and carefully, Chu-Su took a peek at them. When she was able to see that the woman was her sister-in-law, Shui-Zi, she was shocked. She knelt down on the ground and started to cry softly and murmured, "My dear brother, you don't need to care about them. You've already left this world. You must have peace of mind to get into the cycle of reincarnation."

After finishing her prayer, Chu-Su rushed on to her beach destination. Two mating dragonflies flew right in front of her face. The smell of fish and seaweed everywhere seemed to reinforce that the desire for food and sex was part of human nature. The wind from the sea came in from all sides, blowing her clothes about and caressing her breasts and itchy nipples. Suddenly, she felt intense heat throughout her body, which meant that her menstruation would soon begin. She raised her hands to massage her nipples and thought that she wanted to breast-feed her baby, but then she knew that would not relieve her real desire. A craving for togetherness with Zi-Shan suddenly entered her mind.

Chu-Su's unstable mood continued as she walked to her destination. She stopped again, started again, hesitant and frightened every step of the way. Finally, she had an idea that after she finished her work, she should go to the temple to ask the great god Noble Wun if this was an appropriate time to go to Kaohsiung to be with her husband, Lee Zi-Shan.

3-3

Lee Zi-Shan

The ocean city Kaohsiung was where Lee Zi-Shan's workplace was located on the southwest coast of Taiwan, which was situated alongside the Taiwan Strait and Bashi Channel.

During the nineteenth century, Kaohsiung had already made its mark on the international stage, becoming the most important trading district within Taiwan. During the twentieth century, Kaohsiung became the sixth biggest container port in the world, and because of its convenient location in the center of the Asian Pacific region, it owned the most prosperous deep-sea fishing industry in the world.

The port of Kaohsiung was important because it served as the sugar-exporting port of Taiwan as the cane sugar industry became more and more vital to the Taiwanese economy during Japanese rule. Thus, it spurred the development of Kaohsiung with the construction of the port and railways. Building up the city of Kaohsiung was a strong goal of the Japanese while they occupied the region. For this purpose, Japanese authorities required a lot of the Taiwanese workforce to join the building project.

The harbor-improvement work began in 1908, but after twenty years, Kaohsiung still continued to expand and the laborers' work became even more arduous.

In 1934, one September evening after a day of hard labor, Zi-Shan ran across the shore wall to the quay to check the schedule of a ship from Penghu. He had received information that Chu-Su would come here soon. There was only one ship a month from Penghu to Taiwan, but he was really hoping to pick up his wife and son this time because he had already failed twice in this attempt.

He couldn't stop coughing when he ran to the pier because he was so excited about the family reunion he anticipated would happen soon. Counting on his fingers, it was almost four years since he left his hometown of Penghu to come here. He supposed that his son, Lian-Ren, who would be four years old now, would probably have grown by leaps and bounds. Thinking about his sweet family, he was full of the joys of spring. But Zi-Shan didn't recognize his own limited strength due to all the hard work he had done on behalf of his family over the past four years. As a result of the damage to his lungs, lately he couldn't stop coughing after he finished working.

"Hey, young man, what's up? Another fit of coughing again?" Dr. Lin, who was both Lee Zi-Shan's landlord and physician, had asked him recently.

"Yah," Zi-Shan sighed deeply. "Especially after I did the extra work of carrying twenty more bags on top of the one hundred I'd already carried." Then he continued to cough for a long time.

"It may be necessary to struggle in life at a young age, but it doesn't mean it is necessary for you to have to go all out," advised Dr. Lin as he placed bowls on Zi-Shan's chest to apply pressure and ease his congestion.

Lee Zi-Shan replied earnestly, "The work can be extremely difficult, but it has its rewards."

"Don't rush. You'll be around for a long time," Dr. Lin said.

"I want my family to have a good life here, and I must be ready for a rainy day for them."

"I know your brother has a great business here and has proved popular with the Japanese authorities. You can rely on him to help you."

"I don't need to rely on others. I want to rely on myself. Additionally, the burden of asking favors of someone is heavier than the work of labor."

"You guys must all try and help each other, especially in a foreign land."

"One cannot generalize about our relationship. But thanks for your advice." Zi-Shan put on his clothes, and then he went to pay, but he was stopped by Dr. Lin's wife who said, "My dear, you don't need to pay. We are all family." Then she added kindly, "You are a very devoted and considerate son. You must be your parents' pride."

"Thank you very much. Whenever I am in difficulty, you always kindly come to my assistance. You are like my parents. Yes, that's very kind of you, but you know if there is no payment, there is no healing."

"Don't say that. You know, you seem like my son Lin Huo. We have not seen our son for a long time. My poor son . . ." As she spoke about her beloved son, Mrs. Lin's eyes filled with tears.

Lin Huo, the Lin family's only son, had the rare honor of being a Taiwanese student at the Japanese public school. Lee Zi-Shan recalled meeting him several times when he rented a small room in the Lins' house three years ago. It was Zi-Shan's impression that Lin Huo was an enthusiastic young person, but he couldn't bear seeing anything that seemed unfair. He remembered one night Lin Huo hit a soldier, a Japanese officer, in defiance of the law because the soldier had been flirting with his sister. He added insult to injury when he called that officer a rat after he had already beaten him up. Because of this incident, Lin Huo desperately fled for his life to mainland China.

A year after Lin Huo fled, a rumor started that he had joined an anti-imperialism group that was composed of young patriots from Taiwan who now lived in Shanghai. Their actions supported the anti-Japanese group in Taiwan. This kind of activity was so dangerous that his parents were anxious about his safety.

In fact, this kind of difficult situation really hit home with Zi-Shan. His father had had the experience of the fighting against the Japanese authorities, and then he had also fled to China to avoid arrest when he was found out by Japanese authorities. So Zi-Shan totally understood the Lin family's feelings. Actually, he had complete confidence in Dr. Lin, and whenever the Lin couple worried about their beloved son, Zi-Shan always tried to comfort them.

"Don't worry too much. Heaven helps good people, and every cloud has a silver lining!"

In fact, even though the world always filled the human soul with pain, it expected happy songs in return. In the same way, Zi-Shan would always look at himself with a sense of shame, but view everyone else in his life with a sense of gratitude. This kind of personality stemmed from his childhood with his mother when they had to rely upon each other. He had always been hungry, especially when his family lived in abject poverty. Once he felt guilty about his mother falling ill because she hadn't eaten anything so that he and his brother could eat what little food there was. Since then he always wanted to see his mother eating first whenever they had a meal together.

During his difficult childhood, he was not only hungry for food but he was also hungry for knowledge. One day, his mother said to him, "I have good news. You are so desirous of studying that the teacher wants to teach you, and your studies with him will be free of charge."

"Wow, you mean I can go to the inner room with the others to attend his class?"

"Yes, my dear," Shiang-Sao said to her son knowingly. "But you must remember one thing—to be grateful and repay kindness when you benefit from someone."

This event had a great influence on him. Indeed, Zi-Shan had a motto to assure his good conduct. It was something like the sayings of Tseng Shen, a disciple of Confucius:

"I examine myself three times a day,
Have I been unfaithful when planning for others?
Have I been unreliable in dealing with friends?
Have I learned but not practiced?"

Therefore, Zi-Shan always kept his thoughts sincere. His brother, Zi-Tian, on the other hand, only cared about profitability and had become a snob; furthermore, his wife was not very friendly toward her brother-in-law, Zi-Shan. That was to say their relationship was very bad. Even though life was hard in Taiwan, Zi-Shan had to struggle for himself and didn't ask for help from his rich brother.

In the early days, young people from Penghu usually came to Taiwan to learn a small trade or skill in order to make a living away from their hometown. But it would often take them a long time to reach this goal. However, there was another kind of person from Penghu who had more endurance to do hard labor, as in Zi-Shan's case. He had come back to Kaohsiung several times. But now he knew he'd prefer to do hard work rather than ask for his wealthy brother's help.

As the time for his family reunion drew nearer, Zi-Shan was so excited that he rushed to the wharf even though his cough grew worse as he pushed through the crowd, hoping to see that his wife and son had arrived at last. Finally, he stood back by the gate with joy beaming from his eyes.

Oh yes, there they were. He saw Chu-Su carrying her belongings wrapped in a cloth in her right hand and leading their son, Lian-Ren, with her left hand. She stopped and looked through the crowd, but couldn't see Zi-Shan.

"Hey, Chu-Su, I am here!" he cried and went striding along to meet her after he caught sight of her.

"Zi-Shan!" she cried. "Zi-Shan! Oh! Is it you? It is such a long time since we have seen each other."

"Yes, a long time. Is Mother okay?" Zi-Shan couldn't bear to wait to ask about his mother.

"Sure, she is okay." Chu-Su was surprised to hear Zi-Shan ask about his mother first and not his son. "Now then, Zi-Shan, isn't your son really the very last person in the world you would have expected to see?"

"Ah! My dear, you are as welcome as you are unexpected." Zi-Shan was in a hurry to bend forward to embrace and kiss Lian-Ren. "Hey, let me see how tall you've grown!"

Chu-Su said nothing. She was tired from the long trip, and she was a little worried about landing in this foreign city where she would face new challenges. Gazing at her husband, she felt that they were strangers and dear to each other at the same time.

Indeed, day after day, month after month, year after year, the port absorbed many hopeful but fearful Penghu people coming to Kaohsiung to make a better living.

Zi-Shan bought a soda pop from a shop. He popped the bottle open, and its contents overflowed. He said, "Have a drink, it tastes nice and will energize you."

Fearing that all the pop would overflow from the bottle, Chu-Su quickly drank it down in one gulp. It's sweet, cold, smoky taste refreshed her. She looked up and felt guilty about the empty bottle in her hand. And then she smiled, exposing a set of amazingly white teeth to Zi-Shan. He gazed at her; there she stood before him, the same slight, graceful figure to whom he had said farewell years ago in the town where they had a date in front of the temple of Waian.

When the family got to Zi-Shan's place at midnight, Dr. Lin and his wife were in the living room, anxiously awaiting them. They looked very pale and drawn.

"Zi-Shan, at last you are home! I hope you can accompany me to go Taichung tomorrow."

"What's happened?" asked Zi-Shan.

"It is said that my son, Lin Huo, was sent to Taiwan from China. Now he's now under arrest in the Taichung jail."

"Alas! How could this be possible?"

"Their secret group was discovered by a Japanese spy in Shanghai."

"This is awful!" Zi-Shan blurted out without thinking because he knew how terribly Lin Huo would be tortured by the Japanese police. He looked like a whipped dog as he stood there, feeling unable to help his friends. Mrs. Lin was on her knees quietly weeping in a corner.

Through the sadness, everything looked ghostly in the dimness of this dark night. Tears of joy, tears of grief—Chu-Su's bittersweet first day in a foreign community. She had a pressing desire to go to bed because today's events were more than she could cope with and understand. She wanted to sleep until morning and wake up to see this ocean city where her family had new hope for their future.

3-4

A Diligent Couple

Morning—the true morning light—at last came; as in the days of when the world began, it had divided the light from the darkness. And now in 1939, Chu-Su had finally discovered a good way to live on the Kaohsiung River after she had been settled in the ocean city for several months.

Kaohsiung River, its clear water sometimes lined by long green grass, reflected the water-friendly image of Kaohsiung. There was a diversity of fish where freshwater mixed with the seawater in the river. Through the entire river flowed well-nourished water; the water was filled by well-nourished fish, and then all the fish were eaten by well-nourished humans. Thinking about how they would have the benefit of a good, natural source of food because they lived near this river, Chu-Su was filled with joy. She pointed her finger outside and said to her husband, "Zi-Shan, I have a great idea. We should catch fish from this river!"

But he did not reply. He shook his head gently without taking his eyes from his work—he was making a closet.

"The situation just requires that we have a cast net and a bamboo raft—that's all." She completely ignored his indifferent attitude. She wanted to try out her idea.

"Ah! Ah! You want to be a fisherwoman? Do you know, it's easier to know the why than to do a thing?"

"I can do it! It is easy to knit a cast net in three days. As for a raft, that will also be easy to get."

"Come on! It is a big job. Even though we came from Fisherman's Island, we are not really fisher people," Zi-Shan replied.

"There are many kinds of fish in this river. They are a gift from our loving and kind Buddha," she said. "And if we do well, we can sell some of the fish to make money."

"What shall we do if we fail?"

"We can still reach our destination one day." After some thought, she added, "My grandpa always said to us '*More gain for more pay.*' You'll see—we can try it," she said firmly. Although it was a big job, she thought, she would show what a woman can do and what a woman can endure.

Zi-Shan burned the candle at both ends day and night to make more money for the family to live well; thus, there was no room in his mind to care about a river crowded with many kinds of fish just in front of their home. His wife, on the other hand, wracked her brain about how to use the river to improve the family economy. She was in a hurry to achieve her main purpose, which was to welcome other family members to Kaohsiung. Bringing them to a better life here was her greatest hope.

Ha-Ma-Shan was the fishing harbor of south Kaohsiung where they first arrived from Penghu, and it was also the location of many Japanese residents. Their landlord, Dr. Lin, not only had his license to practice medicine because he had set the broken bone of a Japanese officer's son, but he had also managed to save his son, Lin Huo, who was in Taichung prison. After that, Dr. Lin moved to Yan-Cheng to open a clinic, and then the Zi-Shan family moved near the river.

Working in the Port of Kaohsiung allowed Zi-Shan to earn a good income, but it forced him to work too hard in order to keep his job. Although he showed great perseverance in the face of any difficulty, he couldn't bear being treated so badly by the foreman. It was too difficult to work in the port of Kaohsiung. He thought if he could find any other way to make money, of course, he would do it immediately.

At this time, he watched Chu-Su enthusiastically making her preparations to catch fish two days after she suggested the idea. Zi-Shan took great pleasure in changing from cold to hot about Chu Su's fishing project in just one week. Zi-Shan decided it was time to quit his work in the port and join the business of catching fish. The couple worked as a team; the bamboo raft was handled by Chu-Su, and the fishing net was cast by Zi-Shan. They wanted to get the ball rolling on their new project.

The fishing went slowly, but there were few hands for the work, and they knew that practice would make them perfect. They continued to fish for over one year so successfully that they felt like the fish in the river swimming smoothly together. Chu-Su not only caught fish with Zi-Shan, but she also peddled their fish from door to door. The fishing went on very well, and with so much to do, there was no time for weariness.

Chu-Su went downtown to sell the fish once or twice a week. She totally dedicated her life to her fishing work. And the family had certainly improved their income. Their endeavor was not for nothing.

But one day on a sunny afternoon, while she was dealing with Madam Gao-Mu—who was the wife of a Japanese officer—Chu-Su suddenly felt dizzy and fainted, falling to the ground. She was having a miscarriage. In fact, she had been feeling under the weather for a while, but she had ignored her pain because she was so intent on her work. Her miscarriage resulted in Zi-Shan washing his hands of fishing. Money was not more important than health, he thought. He wanted to earn money by himself from now on.

Chu-Su felt better after her miscarriage but still needed to rest for several days although she did not admit to any suffering at all.

Chu-Su owed some change to Madam Gao-Mu, so she was going there to return it to her and to ask her for more work.

When she arrived there, Madame Gao-Mu asked, "Chu-Su, are you much better?"

"Oh! Madam Gao-Mu. I just came to your home to return your money."

"How is your fishing business?"

"My husband doesn't want me to do this work anymore," she said helplessly. "Madam, could you do me a favor?"

"What is happening?"

"I mean, do you have any job for me, something like washing, cooking, or babysitting?" she asked humbly.

"Hmm . . ." Madam Gao-Mu breathed a sigh as she thought for a while, and then she suddenly asked Chu-Su, "What kind of vocation does your husband have?"

"I guess he can do any kind of job," Chu-Su replied.

"I heard news from my husband that the aluminum company will need a couple of new workers next month," Madam Gao-Mu said. "If your husband wishes to do it, my husband can help him."

"Wonderful!" Chu-Su was moved and excited.

"He will stand a good chance of getting the job, don't worry. I know you are an enterprising woman, and I will do my best to help you and your family."

"Thanks a lot." Chu-Su respectfully saluted this kind Japanese woman.

In order to consolidate the colony, the Japanese authorities undertook many developments. They wanted to make Kaohsiung an important center of industry and commerce in Taiwan by producing high-quality aluminum and iron there. They were taking the necessary first steps toward industrializing southern Taiwan. Kaohsiung was the first base of the Japanese invasion of the South Pacific.

Thus, the aluminum company was established in 1935, and of course, it also brought a great opportunity for Zi-Shan to get a good job.

In the beginning, he was dispatched to the aluminum oxide section of the factory, which was very hard work. Before refining the aluminum, it was ground into powder, and then it became red pulp by blending it with saltwater. Unfortunately, the saltwater often hurt his eyes. The grinding machine operated all day long, so he needed to work twelve hours a day.

New job challenges confronted him every day. Even though he struggled in this work, he liked the good relationship between the foreman and the workers. His work was very highly regarded because he put a lot of effort into the job and did it well. It was true, no one could easily endure the extreme heat generated by the factory machinery but Zi-Shan, who accepted danger as being part of his work, never complained about it. His hard work was of great value to the whole family, including relatives still living in Penghu, he thought.

At last, he could bring his mother to live with them. But he was both happy and concerned when he welcomed his mother, Shiang-Sao, to Kaohsiung. Unfortunately, she couldn't live in Kaohsiung by herself. She was almost totally blind, and everything was more comfortable for her in her home country. Now she couldn't bear living in the strange city of Kaohsiung even though her son was here.

One day she waited for Zi-Shan to come home from work and pleaded with him, "My life is in the clouds here. Please let me go back to Waian."

"Hi, Mom! You see I've brought a friend who is good at playing a two-stringed instrument, and he wants to accompany you singing Nanyue." Zi-Shan went on his knees to kneel in front of his mother. In order to make her feel better, he had arranged for her to be able to sing Nanyue.

"You are welcome, very welcome." She heard someone ahead of her and greeted the guest with politeness.

"Auntie Shiang-Sao, I heard your voice is special and you sing very well."

At this time, Chu-Su came home after finishing her washing job in a Japanese home. She said hello to the guest and then headed to the kitchen to prepare food.

"Hi, Chu-Su. There are three portions of medicines for Mother's eyes. You should heat them carefully after each meal," Zi-Shan said to his wife.

"Don't worry. I will do it well," Chu-Su replied obediently. Then she added, "I have news. The concrete company in Banping Mountain is short of employees now. I want my brother to come here to apply for a job with them." She said that at the same time as she poured a package of leftovers from the Japanese home into the pot.

"Ayo! Something smells odd." Zi-Shan frowned at the leftovers.

"It is okay. I'll just cook it for a while, and then we'll have one more dish for dinner today. Japanese people really are wasteful of their food," Chu-Su said.

But after some thought, she asked him, "What is your opinion of me inviting my younger brother Zhu Kam here?"

"It is up to you."

Six months after he arrived in Kaohsiung, Chu-Su's brother was in a dreadful accident in the concrete company fire. Several workers died in this mishap. When his body was pulled out from the concrete, it was changed beyond recognition, and because of her brother's death, there would be no more sons born to carry on the Zhu family name.

After her brother died, Chu-Su felt even more responsible for her family. She kept gazing toward her faraway home country—Waian, Penghu. The gloomy sky reflected her sadness, and her heart wandered, wailing with the restless wind.

"Console yourself with the thought that you did your best," Zi-Shan put a comforting arm around her. "What is the use of worrying?"

She said nothing. It was midnight, sleeping time, so she didn't want to make any noise that would wake up the other members of their family sleeping in this small room together. Yielding to her husband's desire for her in this night of weariness, she gave herself up to lying with him without a struggle, placing her trust in her sweetheart. She knew that all her sadness would be relieved at the moment of their sexual climax.

When the night of dark tenderness was over, the sun came up and another busy day began.

"A brother is a blood relative, and since blood is thicker than water, the relationship is long; but a spouse is a partner through a marriage contract, so the relationship can change and be short." That was a motto of Shiang-Sao, and she had often reminded Zi-Shan. Surely, he understood the meaning of his mother's words: brotherly love.

Finally, as if Zi-Shan at last heard his mother's words, he decided to visit his rich but cold brother. One fine day, after his mother had lived with them for one year, he came to his brother's luxurious house where a board with "Lee Zi-Tian" written on it was nailed on the right side of the door, and another board with the words "The model family of the Japanese language" was nailed on the left side of the door. A servant asked him the purpose of his visit and then guided him to a grand living room. In fact, he'd come here several times to ask his brother to visit their mother, who was missing him very much; but Zi-Tian had never come to Zi-Shan's home.

"How can you be so indifferent to the sufferings of a mother who cherishes you and misses you day and night?" Zi-Shan queried.

"I want to visit her," Zi-Tian, who was wearing a kimono, replied in Japanese. Even though he was Taiwanese, he seemed more like a Japanese man. He was a little hesitant when he spoke. "But I have not much time. I have to make shipping arrangements, and I have a great many other things to deal with."

"What do you take me for?" Zi-Shan talked in Taiwanese. He ignored his brother's attempt to explain himself. "The purpose of my visit is just to ask you to see a poor blind mother. I don't want to hear about your busy business." He said this in a demanding, furious voice.

But later, as Zi-Shan approached his home, where four more children had been born since Chu-Su and his oldest son arrived here, he turned thoughtful and began to breathe more heavily because he had no idea how to explain his brother's heartlessness to his mother.

"Yesterday, I had a vivid dream about Zi-Tian—he wanted me to live with him. It is a good omen," Shiang-Sao said to Chu-Su. Then she heard steps outside and stretched out her hands, "Zi-Shan, are you home?"

"Yes, Mom, I am here."

"Hip, hip, hooray! Papa is home. It's time for dinner!" The children's shouts of joy shook the house.

"Why so late coming home today? Fortunately, Mom has had a nice dream, and she has a strong feeling that Zi-Tian will visit here." Chu-Su felt relieved when Zi-Shan came into the room, and then she went to the kitchen to prepare dinner.

They were totally different: the small house that was his sweet home and the gorgeous house that was his brother's home.

We all live in this world that we both love and detest. Zi-Shan prayed to Buddha to give him the strength to bear his joys and sorrows lightly, to give him the strength to make his love fruitful in service. In the kitchen, Chu-Su asked Buddha to help her face her problems with her mother-in-law.

顛倒歲月

PART FOUR
Upside-Down Days
(1940-1946)

4-1

Delicate Grasses

In 1942, to Zi-Tian—who recalled how hungry and miserable his family in Waian, Penghu, had been throughout his childhood—the chance to make money was the means of creating a life of human dignity after he grew up and arrived in Taiwan to start a new life. Indeed, conditions of extreme poverty seemed only to increase his creative powers, and the pressure of difficult existence made him push harder to get a good position during the years of Japanese occupation. In order to succeed, he had needed to become an integral part of Japanese society; the statue in front of his house came to symbolize for him all that he had proudly achieved in Japanese circles.

"People must have food if they are to think and act," he told himself. Here was a need more important than all others. Thus, aside from the shipping business, he was inclined to sell many kinds of food to Japan and China, such as dried codfish, squid, seaweed, salt fish, silver carp, and so on. These foods were imported from abroad, and he had made a significant breakthrough in this area. In fact, a man was bound to be successful if only he would do his best.

"The poor struggle to be rich, the rich to be richer." This was a portrait of the life of Lee Zi-Tian. In the absence of titled

Taiwanese nobility in the age of Japanese colonization, financial success was accepted as the highest success, and Zi-Tian was a shining example of this.

Even though he neglected his first wife and one son in Penghu, he obtained and supported a young concubine in Taiwan, and she gave birth to five children. Actually, he forgot about his son in Penghu, but he always showed off his five sons in Taiwan and paid for them to have the best education.

Rarely had a family from Penghu become so successful in Taiwan. In fact, Zi-Tian paid over twenty thousand yuan each year in taxes. Thus Lee Zi-Tian was very highly regarded by Japan's officers. Since 1937, the Japanese authorities recruited more soldiers from Taiwan's young people to fight in China and the Malaysia Islands to increase Japanese power. They were called volunteers, but actually, they had no choice. The decision as to who were chosen to join the battle depended on the officer's likes and dislikes. In the Zi-Tian family, fortunately, the five sons weren't chosen, so they didn't need to join the fight in the far South. Did their rich father have influence on this decision? Who knew? On the other hand, when they had to participate in the wave of patriotism that honored Japan, they contributed all their gold to the Japan government.

Furthermore, the Japanese authorities set up the economic police in 1938 to control the people of the colony. The result of all these rules being put into practice was that not only did adults look like frightened birds when they saw the police approaching them, but also crying children, who were told that the Big Man (Japanese policeman) was attracted to the sound of their crying, suddenly stopped crying and ran off to hide.

In the Kaohsiung district of San-Kuai-Cuo, there was a small simple house that sat beside a river. The kitchen faced a narrow brook where the family threw out fish bones and other food wastes. Many mosquitoes and flies hovered over the brook. But a few wild grasses grew up in scattered silt gaps and sprouted tender leaves, thriving in every strong wind and heavy rain. The life of these grasses reflected the life of the Lee Zi-Shan family.

One fine Monday in July 1938, two policemen arrived. They looked awe-inspiring in their uniforms; each of them wore shiny boots, an embroidered cap, and a sword tied around his waist. They were holding a volunteer soldier application and looking to see if they had the right address. At last they saw it. When they knocked at the door, wood flaked off everywhere.

"Is somebody in here?"

"Yes . . . who is . . . ?" Shiang-Sao answered the voice outside and hurried to open the door.

"We are police with information for you."

"What's going on?" When Shiang-Sao knew the guests were Japanese policemen, she faced toward them in awe even though her eyes couldn't see them. Her granddaughter suddenly stopped her crying and started to shake.

"Is this the home of Lee Lian-Ren?"

"Yes, yes, Lian-Ren is my grandson," said Shiang-Sao.

"Is nobody here except for you?"

"Oh, my son is working at the aluminum company, and my daughter-in-law is working at a Japanese place, washing clothing . . . probably they will come back soon," she replied carefully.

"Your grandson is officially registered as a volunteer soldier. Today we bring the application form to him, and then he needs to have a health examination."

"There won't be trouble will there?" she asked anxiously.

"No, not at all if he just follows the rules."

"Oh, thanks a lot." She seized two papers from the police. "Of course," she said to them in her peculiar Penghu manner.

There was very little space in the living room for the police to make themselves comfortable. But before they left, they had recognized that she might have the honor of identifying herself as the mother of a rich man.

"Ma'am, are you the mother of the rich man, Lee Zi-Tian?"

"Sure! Sure! He is my eldest son." She was so excited.

"I have seen you there. Who lives here?"

"This is my second son's place. I moved here from my first son's a couple months ago." She began to prattle about her own affairs. "I couldn't bear staying there because that daughter-in-law was awfully mean to me. For example, she actually blamed me for the loss of their confiscated gold. Oh heck, she treated me like dirt." It was as if she had met a close friend to whom she could pour out her heart.

In the natural course of events, the two brothers' situations being totally different came as a shock to the two policemen.

Later, Chu-Su and the policemen encountered each other on the opposite side of the road. She didn't know what had happened in her home, but recently, she was particularly anxious about her elder son, Lian-Ren, because he often complained bitterly that he had been unfairly treated in the workplace. She hurried home.

As Chu-Su returned, the baby girl, Lian-Zi, promptly stretched out her little hands for her mama's embrace and started crying again.

"At last you are home." Shiang-Sao took a deep breath. "No wonder people prefer the weight of a ton of bricks to taking care of a little baby."

"I have one more place to wash clothing, and then we will have four more yuan each month." Even though she was exhausted after work, she was excited to increase the family's income. Lian-Zi was smiling through tears while her mother pressed her to her bosom.

"Don't hang on to your mom too much. Mom needs to make more money for you," Chu-Su said, feeling both love and frustration as she patted the girl's little hip.

As Shiang-Sao handed Lian-Ren's soldier application to Chu-Su, there was a rattling noise from outside. Chu-Su jumped to her feet, completely thunderstruck. She blinked her eyes hard. She looked carefully all around the river. And she saw a familiar figure. Lian-Yi? Oh yes, it was her second son being chased by a crowd. Good gracious! She rushed out in time to catch her bleeding son in her arms; her face was white as snow.

"What does this mean?" she demanded to the crowd.

"This thief needed to learn a lesson. You must repay our kindness because we didn't take him to a police station." They left Chu-Su and her son with those cruel words.

Then Chu-Su said sadly, "My dear, if a thing doesn't belong to you, you don't want to casually take it."

"On the way home, I picked sugarcane on the roadside to drink it's juice because I was dying of thirst while I shouldered the heavy firewood." Lian-Yi looked helplessly at his mother.

"From now on, I want to do this work instead of you," Chu-Su said firmly.

The weather was very humid, and the river, anticipating the approach of a typhoon, was restless and heaving. Chu-Su thought about the many inexorable desires of children that gave her agony.

"Mom, I want to join the Japanese army," Lian-Ren had announced two weeks ago.

"What makes you want to do this?"

"My boss is always finding fault with me, and there are too many things to be done, but also my wage is so much less than Japanese workers." He was resentful at being treated unfairly in his workplace.

"You need to treasure your job in the Japanese company," Chu-Su tried to smooth his feelings.

"So what?"

"Life is so difficult that we should be more patient."

"Do you know if I join the Japanese army, we could get more advantages for our family? Such as more food, more honor."

Chu-Su thought her son was just saying these things because he was not happy at work. But he joined the army, and then she was worried about where his childish desire would take him.

About three months later, a flag of honor fluttered in front of the Lee family's door after Lian-Ren passed the health examination, and then he started his army training.

As their eldest brother wore his military uniform and showed off his spectacular appearance, his three brothers waved excitedly.

"When I am an adult, I also want to be a soldier like that," said Lian-Li. Among the brothers, he was the third eldest and smarter than the others. Whenever he entered a contest, he would win the prizes. He had won the national Japanese language contests, the Japanese writing contests, and more. Certainly, he was an excellent student at the so-called Public School.

During this period of Japanese occupation, Penghu's and Taiwan's educational system was transformed into a discriminatory one. A well-equipped school, named the Primary School, was run for Japanese children only; and a poorly-equipped school, named the Public School, was created for Penghu or Taiwanese children.

Lian-Yi wasn't a good student in the Public School because he often carelessly spoke Taiwanese instead of Japanese, and then he was punished for his speaking. He used to get teased about his stingy activities in the class, such as always picking up pencils that others gave up so he could use them again for a time. He couldn't deal with the taunts of classmates. However, he was highly skilled at insulting Lee Chun-Li, who was an adopted daughter of the Lee family and was being prepared to become his bride. When Chun-Li was insulted by him, she would complain tearfully to their parents.

"My parents are not your papa and mama. Shame on you." Lian-Yi had been so proud of his words.

"You're talking nonsense!" Chu-Su exclaimed angrily. "You are really a useless man who bullies the weak and fears the strong."

Lian-Yi was so badly scolded by his mother that he sought protection in the arms of his grandmother.

"Who hasn't been bullied by another in this dark time?" asked Shiang-Sao. There seemed to be hidden meaning between the lines.

Chu-Su couldn't say any more after her mother-in-law gave her such displeased looks. She picked her little daughter up in her arms and walked away on the horns of her difficult dilemma, and her third and fourth son followed her outside as well. It was summertime for all that—hot, humid, and troubling, with its buzzing flies and young perfumed grasses.

The more children, the less space in this small rental house, and with the additional expense of medications for Shiang-Sao's eye disease, they could barely survive. For so long, Chu-Su had mused on the possibility of their rich brother Zi-Tian's help. She had thought that Shiang-Sao, being both Tian's and Shan's mother, might make it reasonable to ask for help.

"What are you talking about?" Zi-Shan was strongly opposed to her idea. "Even if I, Lee Zi-Shan, starve to death, I will not ask somebody else to support my mother!"

"Actually, it is a piece of cake for a millionaire," Chu-Su murmured to herself and felt helpless.

"Rich as he is, I don't need to ask for anything from him."

Shiang-Sao decided to avoid supper in protest at this kind of argument because she thought that her daughter-in-law considered her an unwelcome person.

Goodness knows, from the bottom of her heart, Chu-Su had never been unwelcoming to her mother-in-law when she came to Taiwan from Penghu. She knew it was Zi-Shan's goal to bring his mother to Taiwan to live with them. In fact, Chu-Su was thinking about asking her brother-in-law, Zi-Tian, to help them financially. This would make it possible to bring Shiang-Sao to live with them. Zi-Shan was in a very bad situation, whereas his brother was doing very well.

Now was no time to think of unfairness, Chu-Su thought. Now was the time to think of only one thing. That she needed to do her best for this family. Come what may, she mustn't lose her courage. Such was life!

Summer advanced, and at the end of August, many diverse kinds of fish and a lot of freshwater fish arrived together in the San-Kuai-Cuo River and nearby ditches. On summer evenings, the family did not sit up late, in order to save their lights; when the weather was nice, the children would go to the ditch to catch fish. One early evening, Chu-Su and her three children were walking to a ditch.

Suddenly, Lian-Li yelled out to his young brother when he saw a group of fish swimming in the ditch. "Lian-Shi, we should go catch some fish for dinner here."

As Chu-Su warned her children to be careful, she saw three people bringing cloth wrappers to her house. When she recognized them, she ran forward to welcome them—Lian-Yuan, his wife, and his mother, Lee Lu Shan—the Penghu wife of Lee Zi-Tian, who was their rich brother. This millionaire brother had two wives. One of them was in Taiwan, and the other one was in Penghu. Finally, six months ago, Zi-Tian agreed that his Penghu wife, Lee Lu Shan; their son, Lian-Yuan; and his wife could come to Taiwan to live with him and his Taiwan family. Chu-Su had heard that the two wives weren't getting along very well. And this time, she knew it was worse between them when she saw this family of three people coming here to ask for help.

Lee Lu Shan suddenly became very tearful when she met Chu-Su. Lee Lian-Yuan, who was Lee Lu Shan's son, picked up on his mother's inability to say anything, so he said, "Auntie Chu-Su, my mom couldn't bear living with Aunt Gao-Zhao. They often fought bitterly with each other."

"I have no patience with that bitch," Lee Lu Shan said angrily as she wiped away her tears.

Although they came to escape from a bad home environment, it was so wonderful to meet relatives from her hometown—Penghu.

Chu-Su liked bringing a treasure to show off to her almost-blind mother-in-law. She went down on her knees and said to Shiang-Sao, "Mother! What a surprise! Can you guess who is here?"

"Mother!" Lee Lu Shan also went down on her knees in front of Shiang-Sao.

"Grandma!" the Lian-Yuan couple bowed to Shiang-Sao as well.

"My dear, my baby!" Shiang-Sao hugged them tightly.

Chu-Su felt great relief when she saw her mother-in-law was now as happy as a clam. She needed to prepare a room for their guests and then prepare dinner for everyone.

Zi-Shan came home after he finished work. He was very happy to see Mother's excitement, and he extended a warm welcome to the Lee Lu Shan family. While he immersed himself in the sweet mood of his home, he heard the words of his wife from the kitchen, "Children, get a few fish from the river today so that you will have food to add to your box lunch tomorrow."

Around the decaying small house with its gloomy walls grew jasmine flowers, and many kinds of grass. Even the mossy roof was filled with wildflowers. Although the grasses and flowers hadn't enough space to grow up, they were still spirited and indomitable as they faced the strong wind and heavy rain. As long as there were roots, there was life.

4-2

Surviving Japanese Colonization

After the Japanese invasion, there was increasing pressure for the Taiwanese to adopt Japanese ways in order to improve their position in society. Thus they had to accept the movement of Japanese authorities to promote Japanization through newspapers, radio stations, and schools.

Generation after generation, Taiwanese were born and raised in Taiwan, yet they were regarded as inferior people even though they were born in their own land. Everything about life in Taiwan was turned upside down. They were living in their own country; they were living in a foreign country.

One June afternoon in 1944, after a boring Japanese language class, eight-year-old Lian-Shi rushed out of the classroom in his bare feet to go home. Even though his feet were really hurting him on the rugged road, he still ran steadily while he was thinking about bunches of beautiful bananas. He finally arrived home and put his schoolbag on the table, and then he wanted to go outside right away. He didn't like to be cooped up at home.

His young sister, Lian-Zi, said, "Brother, where are you going? I want to go with you."

In the meantime, his grandma, Shiang-Sao, heard the noise and came out. When she realized somebody had come in, she asked, "Is Lian-Shi here? Your mama wants you to pick up some firewood that's near the ditch. Don't go running around."

"Ao, eu, ou, ya, oa," Lian-Shi said some Japanese letters in order to confuse his illiterate grandma so he could run away outside.

"Oh damn! What are you talking about?"

While Shiang-Sao complained, Lian-Shi turned on his heel and fled. His young sister followed him outside.

"Why do you follow me? You are really a troublemaker."

"Fourth Brother, I can give you my favorite pencil," Lian-Zi said.

Brother and sister had already argued with each other over this pencil because it was a high-quality pencil. Finally, their father decided to give it to Lian-Zi so her brother was very upset.

"Are you trying to bribe me?" Lian-Shi stopped walking. He didn't believe that his sister's pencil would belong to him. He took a long look at Lian-Zi, and suddenly, he added, "Maybe you will be useful to me."

"Really?" said Lian-Zi expectantly.

Lian-Shi pulled his sister's hand so that they were like two dragonflies flying through the streets and alleys, and then they slowed down in front of a warehouse. Lian-Zi imitated her brother's stealthy walking and gazing around. Her requests to be with Lian-Shi were often rejected because she was very much in the way. Now she was permitted to come with him for the first time, so even though she was panting like an ox, she had a strong curiosity to find out what would happen next.

However, her brother didn't want to hand over any responsibility to her. He just wanted her to wait at the back door. If she were to see the Japanese police coming, she was to notify him immediately. How could she notify him? She had no idea. But she realized that something suspicious was happening when she saw his sneaky behavior.

She wanted to cry, but she didn't dare. She said, "Brother! I . . . I need to pee."

"You needn't be afraid! Later you will have bananas to eat, and we can also sell them. Look at them!" Her eyes followed his finger's direction; she saw a couple of shadows bending over to take the bananas and then hastily fleeing from the warehouse.

"Are we going to be banana thieves? No . . . no . . . Mother will punish us for such a bad thing."

"You are a big mouth," he said and then in a completely adult tone said, "The bananas were planted by our farmers, we are just asking for some back from the Japanese. You are too young to understand it. Don't say what should not be said."

As Lian-Zi waited at the door for her brother, time seemed to slow down, and she really did not like the dangerous atmosphere of the alley. No wonder Mother had said that they needed to stay home. She wondered if her mother had finished washing the clothes yet. Why was Brother staying inside for such a long time? To pass the time, she entered an old cramped porch, worn away and daubed over with whitewash. Suddenly, she saw a Japanese policeman walking across the street. She yelled out loudly, "Brother! Be careful! A Japanese policeman is coming!"

Unfortunately, she not only warned her brother but she also alerted the Japanese policeman.

"Oops!" She knew she had made a mistake and tears rolled down her face.

"Ba gai ya lou! The truth is out! You are a thief raised by a pack of dogs." The policeman shook his head when he saw Lian-Shi holding a bunch of bananas. The cruel policeman punched and kicked Lian-Shi as if he were a ball he was playing with. Lian-Zi wept over her brother being carried away by force. She was so upset she wet her pants. That incident was so unexpected she caught her breath in shock. "Mama! What am I going to do?" She was trembling with deep sorrow and fear.

She didn't know how she managed to walk on her two shaky legs to the workplace to ask Mrs. Gao, her mother's Japanese employer for help.

"What's happened, my dear?" Mrs. Gao came to the door when she heard Lian-Zi's sorrowful crying. "I will do what I can to help. Don't cry."

Finally, Mrs. Gao understood what had happened after the little girl gestured wildly about the event.

The policeman's cruelty and Mrs. Gao's kindness—what totally different impressions of these two Japanese people went through Lian-Zi's mind!

Although Lian-Zi settled down after Mrs. Gao heard about why she was so miserable and upset, she was still very worried about her brother. Walking home, she felt like an injured lamb uneasily limping its way home. Her legs were so weak she could hardly stand. She was drooping and fainting as she staggered toward her anxious mother's arms in front of a narrow alley—her mother had been looking for them.

When Lian-Zi woke up, a crowd of their friends and neighbors had gathered outside to discuss what had happened to her brother. She was really tired and couldn't stand up easily. She sat on the ground and held onto her mother's leg. Her eyes saw a lot of feet; and then she started to observe them one by one, all of which—except for Senior Auntie who wore tiny embroidered shoes—were bare, chapped feet exposed to the cold, muddy ground. She was uncomfortable with these dirty feet, but she also didn't like Senior Auntie's unsteady feet even though she wore shoes. She wanted a pair of Da Mei (Japanese-style shoes) like Mrs. Gao's daughter, who had a pair of beautiful pink Da Mei. She and the daughter of Mother's employer were the same age.

Recently, Lian-Zi's mother had picked up a pair of old Da Mei that had been cast away by her employer. Unfortunately, Lian-Zi's feet were bigger than Mrs. Gao's daughter's. Even though she couldn't put her feet into the smaller Da Mei, she still tried and tried until she got a cramp in her feet. Finally, the next best thing was to touch them every day. Father said that he would buy a pair for her next New Year.

Suddenly, those feet were moving chaotically. She raised her head. Wow! Brother had been brought home by Mr. and Mrs. Gao. Everyone enthusiastically said "Thank you so much" to this compassionate couple.

"Don't do that. You need to wash your son's scratches now." Mrs. Gao held Chu-Su's hands up when Chu-Su wanted to kowtow to them.

Lian-Zi stood up quickly when she saw that her brother was home. Her tears were now tears of joyfulness, totally different from a few hours ago.

Afterward, Chu-Su decided to bring both Lian-Shi and Lian-Zi with her to her washing job to avoid the brother and sister going around outside and doing foolish things again. First, Chu-Su must apologize to her employer, and then her children needed to stay beside her obediently. Lian-Zi watched Mother's hardworking hands scrub a pile of dirty clothes. Her mother's hands created a lot of white froth, and her chapped fingers were bleeding. Even though the weather was chilly, her mother still perspired profusely.

And Lian-Zi said to herself with perhaps a hint of sadness, "Mama! When I grow up, I will make a lot of money, and you won't need to wash clothes to make money anymore."

On the other hand, Lian-Shi, her fourth brother—who usually couldn't sit still for a more than a little while as he longed to be outside, jumping up and down—didn't dare go far away and out of Mother's sight. If he could go outside, he would pick up some firewood near the employer's house for his mother's pleasure, but she wanted him by her side.

After being beaten by the Japanese policeman, Lian-Shi settled down a little bit; but he still argued with Lian-Zi about things such as pencils, papers, and erasers. Lian-Zi thought how Lian-Shi was different from her third brother, Lian-Li, who was kinder to her and was considered the most intelligent child by their parents.

Chu-Su was such a hardworking and responsible woman that many families desired to hire her to help them with their housework. In fact, she needed to do all these jobs so that she could earn enough money to give her family a better future.

Once when Lian-Zi followed her mother into a gorgeous house that her mother was to take care of for three days, she tasted a delicious meal of white rice with pig oil and soy sauce. After that, she could always remember the taste of the food, and she would describe the wonderful smell to her playmates. They looked with envy at her experience and asked if they could eat it as well.

So one day she asked her mother, who was working on her knees to wash the floor, "Mom, my friends want to eat a meal like the one we ate before."

At this moment, Mother's employer came to the door, displeasure on her face. Lian-Zi knew she had gotten herself into trouble. She ran away from her mother and went to her girlfriend to express the distress that she felt about creating her mother's dilemma. She hated herself very much.

God finds himself by creating; children find themselves by continually making mistakes, and adults find themselves by working ceaselessly.

Lu Shan, along with her son and her daughter-in-law, had taken refuge with Zi-Shan's family for over half a year as the situation worsened at her husband's home. Now the abundant breast milk of her daughter-in-law, Mei-Zhi, after she gave birth two months ago, gave Chu-Su a good idea. When Chu-Su saw Mei-Zhi's breast milk being thrown away every few hours, she

said to Mei-Zhi, "You shouldn't waste your breast milk. As far as I
know, some rich men long for breast milk as a lovely tonic."

"Auntie's meaning is that I could sell my breast milk to some
rich men?"

"That's right!"

"Where can we find these men?"

"Let me think about it."

"You and Uncle are very kind and helpful people. I deeply
appreciate you."

"We are people who not only come from Penghu but we are
also close relatives that certainly need to help each other."

"We always make trouble, and you always help us."

"Don't talk like that. You know better," said Chu-Su. The
expression in her eyes was both steady and tender as she said,
"There are expanses in our life that are difficult, yet there are the
open spaces where our busy days have their light and air."

Chu-Su's hands pulled her long hair as if she had a lot of
worries. She lifted her head and drew her long hair back on the
side, pulling her thick tresses above her ears and then winding her
hair into a bun at the back of her head. This is a hairstyle that has
survived from remote times and gives quite an old-fashioned look
to the women of Penghu.

Chu-Su did her best to sell Mei-Zhi's breast milk. As a result,
she found a rich customer on San-Kuai-Cuo Street. Now Mei-Zhi
must eat many green apples with fish so that she would have
enough breast milk to make more money.

Who had the time to take milk to sell to this rich family once
a day? At a family meeting, it was decided that Lian-Zi was the
only available person to do this job.

After a half-hour walk, Lian-Zi passed through a few fields
and walked along several streets into a bright yard with two big
banyan trees in front of a rich man's house. On the topmost
branches of these ancient banyan trees was interwoven a

transparent canopy of leaves. Here everything was light and green; here and there were sunbeams that burst through the leafy branches and lots of shady space to play hide-and-seek or chat. Then there was the gorgeous house. A sweet fragrance greeted Lian-Zi; it reminded her of the home of her uncle Lee Zi-Tian. After she had delivered the milk and waited for the rich man to pay the money to her, she longed to sit under the trees and watch the children playing hide-and-seek. She desired to join them, but her Taiwanese accent was always unwelcome, and children teased her about it. She was also subject to their jokes about her bare feet.

After she returned home, Lian-Zi asked her father, "Papa, why are we not Japanese?" Then she said again, "I would like to be Japanese."

"We can be like the humble grass that can live well with the help of a little dew," Zi-Shan answered seriously even though he was busy repairing a broken door. "They are living their Japanese lives. Of course, we are living our Penghu lives."

"Papa, would you please take me to Uncle Zi-Tian's home?" Lian-Zi considered that her uncle's success was not only a mark of honor to the Japanese but also a mark of honor to her.

In the meantime, Shiang-Sao also pushed herself ahead to say to Zi-Shan, "Brotherhood is blood. Blood is thicker than water. You two absolutely need to see each other."

In fact, Shiang-Sao had always encouraged Zi-Shan in this way. However, Zi-Shan didn't want to give someone like his rich brother additional splendor, but he did give timely assistance to those who needed it. For example, he often helped his Penghu brother, Zi-Song, who had the same mother but a different father. On the other hand, he was cold as ice with his millionaire brother in Taiwan. Even though Shiang-Sao deeply knew the traits of Zi-Shan's character, she still did as she saw fit. This son was always obedient to her wishes except on this point.

"Daddy, what is a slave of Manchu? Why do the Japanese always call me that?" Lian-Zi leaned lightly against her father's shoulder even as he carried on his work. Around her neck, she was wearing a gold-colored amulet that swayed back and forth as if echoing her curiosity. She never let go of a question once she had asked it.

Her father stared at her, thunderstruck after she asked this question. But Zi-Shan still answered her seriously, "It is very arrogant of the Japanese to assume that the Taiwanese are the slaves of the Ch'ing dynasty [1644-1911]. This is the Japanese way of shaming the Taiwanese."

Lian-Zi didn't understand what her father was saying.

"At your time of life, my dear girl, it is more than you can understand."

Zi-Shan bent over to resume his work. But after some thought, he raised his knife and said to himself, "If the sword handle is not powerful, does it matter if the sword blade is sharp?" And then he began to sweat over his repair job.

However, Zi-Shan ignored his sweat dropping on the broken window as he thought, "The sword blade cannot be polished without friction, nor can man be perfected without trials."

4-3

Escaping the Air Raids

Toward the end of May, in 1944, a southern warmth-dispersing languor spread toward the north, occasionally transmitting the sound of an air-raid alarm as the rays from a distant sun rose over the Waian seas. Often the air was calm but depressed because the surroundings were filled with horror.

In the fishing village of Waian, the weather was calm and fine; despite that, a vague uneasiness seemed to hover about. A confused dread emanated from the air as well as the sea, which so many beings usually trusted. There was now an everlasting threat that they could only pray would end. They recited deeply felt prayers at the Buddhist altar in the Kind Navigation Temple located in the middle hills, three miles north of the Waian Sea, and they also piously recited the *sutra of four sentences of repent and reform* to relieve their stress:

> *For all bad karma created in the past,*
> *Based upon beginningless greed, anger and stupidity,*
> *Born of body, mouth and mind,*
> *I now repent and reform.*

Was there sin in humans from birth? Did they need to confess their sins to Buddha so that he would forgive them? It seemed to be the only place their souls could find comfort, especially in these endless, miserable days.

The old man's name was Zhu Wang. Afternoon was falling as the old man, carrying a basket, walked with great difficulty beside the temple in a region of gently rolling hills as he headed toward an abandoned garden. A long time ago, the guava he grew in this garden once supported his family. Nowadays, the guava garden was completely overgrown with weeds. He looked for some wild vegetables to fill his belly; his hands were trembling with hunger, but even though he took a long time to look for the wild vegetables, his basket remained empty.

"I cannot fail myself and die because I can't find a meal, old man," he said to himself as he continued on his journey, being careful to avoid the bombs falling from the air. "Now that I need more time to find some food to eat, Buddha helps me with the six-word *Na-Mo-E-Mi-Two-Bha* chant, and I recite *repent and reform* many times. But I cannot say them now. Consider them said," he thought. "I'll say them later."

Staring at his neighbors' backs as they knelt at the altar, he seemed to feel the shadow of anxiety huddling under the constant threat of air raids.

He was really old, both physically and spiritually. He lived his life alone because his wife and two sons had passed away, one after the other. His deceased sons had died in Taiwan. And his daughter, Chu-Su, was still living in Taiwan after she married Lee Zi-Shan. Taiwan was both a woeful and hopeful place for him. Chu-Su had asked him to come to Taiwan to live with them. Ah, but there was no reason to live with his married daughter, he thought.

In fact, he had lived alone in Waian for a long time. However, not only did this so-called Waian, Penghu—his motherland—belong to the foreign country of Japan, but now he also needed to dodge American bombs that could drop from the sky at any time. What on earth was happening to this world? Did hardworking dogs need to pay the debt run up by greedy pigs? And did we deserve what has been to done to us?

The region of Taiwan and Penghu seemed to be very important to both Japan and America since the attack on Pearl Harbor. The Japanese attack on Pearl Harbor resulted in an explosion of anger from the United States. But both these countries' actions led the people of Taiwan and Penghu into a life of poverty.

When Japan waged war with the USA, the Japanese Office of the Taiwan Provincial governor-general was, of course, dedicated wholeheartedly to the war; and thus it consumed a large amount of their energy. Consequently, the Taiwanese people suffered a miserable life through lack of food, medicine, and general materials. The ruler didn't have enough food and neither did the common people who were colonized in Taiwan and Penghu.

To the hungry villagers, food was so all-important that they ignored the danger of air attack. A team of four or five people sailed for three days on a schooner to Taiwan to pick up food that was considered garbage by the Taiwanese. Even so, Taiwan's unwanted food was regarded as a treasure by the people of Waian. But their plan met with little success. They were hit by bombs halfway through their voyage, and Zhu Wang's son-in-law was killed. They couldn't tell why his heart stopped. It was never asked or known or remembered.

Moreover, if winter was coming, it would be a good time for bedbugs to grow as clothes, blankets, and mattresses became comfortable places for these insects. Then villagers would not only face the economic problems confronting their country, they must also contend with these insects that could bleed them dry.

On the other hand, if a cold current of wind and rain were coming, it could be a blessing because the fish would freeze to death under the sea and on the land; this would be good news for the people, who could easily get enough food to fill their empty stomachs.

One morning, before five o'clock, while all were dreaming quietly under the winding sheet of fog, they heard a clamor of voices. Zhu Wang's voice seemed both excited and alarmed to his neighbors, "Friends! Hurry and wake up!" His finger pointed at the big waves at sea level and added, "Look! I'm sure there are several big fish floating up on the water again. Wow, we might have a big harvest today."

Men got up and rushed for bamboo poles, boat hooks—anything they could lay their hands on to use. They were almost close enough to catch the fish, leaning over the water, staring at them with eyes distended by the surprise of awakening and waiting. Nearer objects were seen more clearly under the colorless light. They took care not to inhale the air too deeply to avoid the wet cold from penetrating their lungs. A huge unforeseen gray form rose very high and drifted right beside them. Then suddenly, someone yelled out, "My goodness! It-it . . . is a corpse. There isn't any big fish."

Much changed within a short time. Cowardly men immediately ran away from the water, but a few men of courage pulled the body of someone who had been killed by an air raid from water to seashore, and then they buried the body to comfort its spirit in order to stop it from becoming a hungry ghost in the future.

Where was the enemy that dropped so many bombs in a ceaseless outbreak of hatred on this small village? The freedom of these poor residents seemed to belong to other countries. The hostility between Japan and the USA resulted in a pitiful life for the people of Penghu.

Upon this particular day, there was no air-raid alarm going off near the Kind Navigation Temple. The villagers made a pilgrimage to the temple and then, one by one, found their way home. Zhu Wang looked at the result of his search in his basket. Even though there was not too much, it would let him eat for two or three days if he rationed them carefully.

"Uncle Wang! Are you worshipping Buddha at this time?" a neighbor passed right by him and asked him.

"Prayer is useless to me."

"Did your daughter send money to you recently?"

"There has been no news about Chu-Su from Taiwan since the American air attacks started."

"So you need to pray for her even more."

"As a married daughter, of course, she belongs to others," Zhu Wang said helplessly. "If she were a boy, alas, I might be happier because she would be beside me for more time."

The wind from the sea came in from all sides, blowing and swaying Zhu Wang's thin weak shape. Listening to the wind, the ever-present sad memory of his family came to him. Suddenly, he realized what he was listening to! A bomb hurtled through the air. He stopped short to listen again.

Hiss! Again the whine breaking the silence of the air—a shrill, continuous voice, a kind of prolonged sound until one had a strong impression that the bombs suddenly hit their targets and caused fatalities. *Boom! Boom! Boom!* Again and yet again! The bombs fell in regular showers now. Two or three bombs were still flying about; they could be seen bouncing like deadly balls in the green. But many people, including the old man, Zhu Wang, were killed in this American air raid. By now Buddha couldn't say anything except a series of words, "Sin, sin, sin."

That wretched day of October 23, 1944, the United States Air Force moved threateningly toward Waian space instead of Penghu's military headquarters. They dropped three big bombs of five hundred kilograms and many small bombs of three hundred kilograms on Waian. What was the meaning of this strong action by the United States? By the summer of 1943, America had employed its strategy to finish fighting in Taiwan. But was this attack aimed at the Japanese fleet admiral Yamamoto who had already been killed in the Solomon Islands when his aircraft was shot down during an ambush by American fighter planes?

Does the history of human beings need to wait patiently for the day of freedom for the oppressed person? Or do humans have to endure their suffering over and over again?

Zhu Wang was killed by the bombs on the grassy fields of Waian. And at this same hour, on the other side of the Taiwan Sea in Kaohsiung, which was also very heavily attacked by air raids that afternoon, Chu-Su, the daughter that Zhu Wang had greatly missed, angrily spanked her own daughter Lian-Zi.

"If you don't stop crying, I will kick you out, let you be killed by the bombs."

"I want Papa to go with us," Lian-Zi held her father tightly.

"Don't cry, honey," Zi-Shan wiped away his weepy daughter's tears and held her in his arms. "Papa must make money here. You guys must evacuate to Jiu-Qu-Tan because it is a safe area, and then I will go there as soon as possible. Okay?"

Now Chu-Su put down the stick with which she had just spanked her daughter and collapsed her tired body into a corner.

"I don't know why my eye keeps twitching. Is my dad having some kind of trouble over there?" Chu-Su asked her husband, her heart loaded with worry.

"Don't worry so much. Dad will be fine." Zi-Shan went on, "You have to hurry to get on the oxcart, so you can arrive at Jiu-Qu-Tang before dark."

By now his mother, Shiang-Sao, was ready to go; but it was difficult for her to get in the oxcart because of her very poor sight, and she was unsteady on her small feet even though she was holding a staff.

"Mother, be careful. Your seat is here." Zi-Shan saw his mother come out, and he made haste to hold his nearly blind mother. "Hey, where is Lian-Li, Lian-Shi? Why does nobody help Grandma?"

"Zi-Shan, take good care of yourself. From now on you'll be alone here," Shiang-Sao said, reluctant to leave her son.

"Don't worry about me, Mother. I can look after myself. Actually, one person can easily run from an air raid. I will assess my situation and be as quick as possible to look for any chance to get back to you." Although Zi-Shan looked relaxed, his voice expressed his worry. As the family left, Zi-Shan gravely watched Lian-Yuan, who was the only strong man among the family members. Lian-Yuan realized what Zi-Shan's look meant and said, "Uncle Zi-Shan, don't be anxious for us. I will do my best to take care of everyone."

As Zi-Shan's figure became smaller and smaller, Lian-Zi wept louder and louder. But even though there was melancholy in the wind and sorrow in the grass, the family had to encourage one another to keep their lives going. After the world had kissed them and infused their souls with its pain, was it asking for songs in return?

Hiding and peeping through the trees that lined the path on the way to Jiu-Qu-Tang, the moon was in full view when they arrived at their destination. Looking up at the moon and feeling the silence of the countryside, Lian-Zi felt a deep heartache, full of mystery that chilled her very soul; she knew now that her dad couldn't be seen. She was filled with sorrow as she faced yet another hard time.

The day of evacuation, Zi-Shan's mother, Shiang-Sao, and his wife, Chu-Su, longed to return to their hometown. The lifestyle of Waian—such as drawing water from ancient wells, catching fish from the brook, and seeking the herbs from wild areas—would greatly reduce their fear of the air raids.

But Lian-Zi was happy that her mother no longer worked for the Japanese so that she could see Mother whenever or wherever she wanted to, and her brothers didn't go to school so she had them to play with her. However, they often felt hungry because of Chu-Su's reduced income, and now they couldn't get leftovers from Chu-Su's Japanese master.

While they are growing up, children often get hungry, so Chu-Su wanted them to go to sleep early in order to escape their feeling of starvation for a while, but they often woke up with empty stomachs at midnight. Lian-Shi couldn't bear feeling hungry and usually beat a cat to vent his anger.

"Dammit! What are you doing?!" Chu-Su sounded a sharp warning to end her son's violent action against the poor cat, but she couldn't stop him. Angrily, she grasped a stick to hit him as she scolded, "If you want to be full of food all the time, you might as well not be born into this world where there is always hunger."

Shiang-Sao heard the fury of her daughter-in-law from outside. She took hasty but shaky steps as she stretched out her hands in the air to help her touch anything in her path, and then she said shiveringly, "You beat your son for wanting food, yet you willingly feed me, a worthless old woman who is just a waste of food!"

"Grandma, please sit down, don't be angry," said Lian-Li, third child of the Lee family who was always polite and considerate toward his family.

Chu-Su took a quick look at her mother-in-law and laid down the broom. Her expression was very serious, like someone lost in deep thought. Recently, she had often had a nightmare in which her father's bleeding face fixed his gaze on her and wanted to say something to her.

Even though life was a burden these days, there was still a blessing. The most important and cheerful event occurred when Zi-Shan rode home on his bicycle. He was spotted first by his joyful daughter each time he returned, and then she ran to welcome her dad back home as quickly as she could.

"My sweetheart, how do you know your papa is home?" Zi-Shan bent down and kissed her.

"Dada, I have to tell you that Brother isn't a good child. He's being beaten by Mama." She couldn't wait to tell her father about what was happening in their family.

"What is that, Dada?" She wanted to open a large package that was bound to the bike.

"This is a piece of canvas. We can trade it with a neighbor, and then we will have enough for a goose. Do you like it?"

"What is the use of canvas? What do they want it for?"

"They want this strong cloth to make many things such as bags, tents, or shoes."

The family would have goose to eat, but more importantly, they would be reunited with their beloved father. During these hard times, their only blessing was that they could see their father come home from his workplace in Kaohsiung. However, this kind of blessing was very rare because Zi-Shan didn't easily give up the opportunity to work for the aluminum company.

There were several ways to live in an evacuation situation in order to protect themselves and still have a good time. One way was creating smoke to avoid being seen by the United States Air Force. Thus the family needed to build a pile of dried leaves and branches on the ground and light them to make smoke that filled the sky in order to confuse the bombers. It required great skill to do this work well. There couldn't be too much fire, but if the flames didn't go higher and higher, they must add fresh branches or leaves. Collecting these branches and leaves was the job of the smaller ones in the family, so Lian-Zi and Emei, Uncle Lian-Yuan's daughter, were the best candidates. Even though doing this work covered their faces and bodies with dirt and soot, Lian-Zi was very happy to do so because she desired to compete with Emei as to who was quicker than the other.

Nevertheless, this good time for Lian-Zi came to an upsetting end when Emei fell ill, and then Lian-Shi, her fourth brother, also got sick. They had both contracted malaria, which was a serious virus. The trouble was that there were no doctors in their rural area, and the urban doctor didn't dare to make a house call during these days of constant air raids.

Zi-Shan heard of his family's bad news, but he couldn't come home immediately. The situation was getting more dangerous. Blind Shiang-Sao wailed day and night.

Lian-Yuan, who was the only strong man in the family, heard there was a clinic in Bingdong that specialized in treating malaria. But how could they make the journey that was more than an hour long? They had no oxcart or bicycle to ride to Bingdong. The two children became more and more ill. Now the family was more worried about this unforeseen problem of children sick with malaria than their constant hunger.

Finally, Lian-Yuan decided to first carry Lian-Shi on his back to Bingdong. Then he would return to carry his own daughter, Emei, to see the doctor.

"We each carry one and go there together," Chu-Su suggested firmly.

"You can't do that. It will be too dangerous to get there."

"Time is limited. The quicker we get there, the better."

"Aunt Chu-Su, you must stay home to take care of many things, and your strength is limited. Let me go there alone. I will come back as soon as possible."

It was hard work for Lian-Yuan to carry his cousin, Lian-Shi, on his back for the two hours it took to reach Bingdong clinic. Lian-Shi was lucky enough to be placed in the hands of a doctor. But when Lian-Yuan headed back home to pick up his own daughter, he was hit by a bomb. Fortunately, he was discovered by a kind stranger who escorted him home. Sadly, the delay caused by the bomb could have been avoided, but Lian-Yuan was in such a hurry to get home that he didn't hear the air-raid alarm go off.

If anything could go wrong, it did. When Lian-Yuan arrived home, Emei was barely breathing. Zi-Shan received the message and hastened home, but it was too late; Emei passed away.

Many people in the Jiu-Qu-Tang region died of malaria. Although they avoided the attack of US airplanes, the whole village was still covered by the darkness of death.

Zi-Shan had never dreaded facing any challenge, and he seldom was brought to tears by difficult situations when he became an adult. However, that sorrowful day, he curled up in a corner to weep. He seemed to cry out against all the misfortune of these times.

After dealing with the family disaster, Zi-Shan went to the Bingdong clinic to bring his son back home. The only soothing thing was that Lian-Shi was out of danger this time. Although the family was hungry and poor, they were warm and happy. But the event of Emei's death brought great distress to Zi-Shan and Chu-Su; they were filled with guilt at having failed the Lu Shan family. Their children grew up quickly after the tragedy of Emei's death; Lian-Zi no longer expected to be spoiled by her parents.

Despite the disaster of the air raids, there was a subtle feeling of understanding that the aim of the United States was to defeat Japan, not Taiwan. If the war could bring Taiwan liberation, the United States' actions might be forgiven.

At the end of the Sino-Japanese War in 1895, China had relinquished Taiwan (then Formosa) to Japan, according to the Treaty of Shimonoseki between China and Japan that was signed on April 17, 1895. In 1945, after its defeat in World War II, Japan surrendered sovereignty over Taiwan to the Allied force. Taiwan's fifty years as a Japanese colony finally came to an end.

On August 15, 1945, the Japanese emperor announced, "Japan renounces all right, title, claim to Formosa and the Pescadores." Suddenly, the skies of Taiwan and Penghu Island put a new complexion on the people's situation: under the Japanese, dark clouds had gathered, but now that the people of Taiwan and Penghu were free, the skies offered them a gorgeous view. Thus when things look dark in the dimness of seemingly endless dusk, we know that people living on earth should wait for the morning and wake up to see their world in the light.

It is said that the emperor of Japan sent an imperial order explaining that Japan wouldn't surrender to China, so they surrendered themselves to United States, Britain, and the Soviet Union.

No matter who surrendered to whom, human history still waits patiently for the triumph of the oppressed people.

浮亂港都

PART FIVE

Chaotic Kaohsiung
(1947-1954)

5-1

Foreign Moon

The heavy clouds now seemed to shine in through the windowpanes and brighten everything. Even though the Chinese city of Tianjin was buried under a big snowfall for the first time in twenty years, Lee Shiang still felt very warm in his heart because he had received good news from the Taiwan Association that there was a sailing from Tianjin to Taiwan on March 20. Now, finally in 1948, he had a slim hope of returning home to Taiwan, so he didn't mind the cold air that chilled his bones.

Lee Shiang wore a fashion long since out of date—a gray coat; his dark eyes, in which the whole of his long-lost youth seemed to be reflected and which contrasted strangely with his snow-white hair, gazed calmly at the sights around him as he peered out the window. There was a crowd of poverty-stricken people in the big courtyard shared by many low-income families who all suffered lives of great hardship. He had been living here for two years, and it had felt like a never-ending nightmare.

In the early morning, the vegetable peddler yelled a warning to an old man who bought on credit but never repaid his debts; two neighboring women were fighting in the front yard for just two coals; the landlord was driving out a young couple who couldn't pay the rent.

Complaining voices were rising and falling in the ruined courtyard.

"The Japanese devils already surrendered and went away. We will have a good day in the future. So what are you guys fighting about now?"

"If you are a person of great ability, you may receive things from the Japanese as you like. But don't be like an outcast person who is a complete nuisance all day long over a tiny matter."

"You don't have a right to take over this property just because the Japanese have left."

"What the fuck does he think he's doing? Why is it that we couldn't take over the things that the Japanese left behind, but we let others take them over instead?"

In fact, originally, everyone was equal, with the land belonging to everyone. However, the Sino-Japanese War created different groups of people who disagreed about who owned what. For example, now China was divided into regions known as the frontline, the rear-line, the enemy-occupied area, the war zones, and the recovered area. At the end of the Sino-Japanese War, some people were sure that if they hadn't used their wisdom to defeat the Japanese, the enemy-occupied areas wouldn't have achieved victory against the Japanese. Thus the rear-line people believed that they were superior to the recovered-area people. So it seemed that even though the Chinese people defeated the Japanese, the war continued among themselves.

The Sino-Japanese War victory meant the end of the foreign war, yet it was the beginning of a civil war in China. Is it human nature to always want to fight? Or did the Chinese continue to fight because they were so used to struggling that they were afraid if they stopped fighting, they would lose their spirit?

One month ago, Lee Shiang felt very depressed about his application to return to Taiwan. He hadn't had any news yet. After he had placed his overcoat in a corner, he raised his freezing and trembling hands to light the kerosene lamp, but the oil was used up. He sat down in the chair dispiritedly and, folding his hands, seemed to be resting after he had spent all day dealing with his application to return to Taiwan. While he sat thus, it gradually grew darker; before long, a moonbeam came streaming through the windowpanes and into the mirror on the wall as if his life of transition was being reflected in the mirror.

When he had first come to China, he had not only had to avoid the Japanese authorities who would have arrested him for his rebellion against Japan, but he also had great ambitions in this dreamland called China. However, his dream proved difficult to achieve when he was given abusive treatment by local people. Surely, if there wasn't enough space for Chinese people in their own country, why should they welcome him? It seemed to Lee Shiang that the Chinese people were so arrogant that they considered themselves better than other people from Taiwan or Korea.

And at this difficult time, Lee Shiang, who was regarded as a longed-for, heartless lover by his family in Penghu, socialized with local villains and struggled with dark and murky chaos in his heart.

At this time, the Taiwanese people regarded China as their motherland. But although Lee Shiang was at first praised for his behavior against Japan by motherland China, he was a hot-tempered man, and now he suffered from lots of scolding from motherland China. When stepmother Japan had mistreated him, he could defect with confidence because he knew that he was in the right; but when he was abused by motherland China, Lee Shiang only felt confused. Outwardly hopeful and merry, inwardly his heart ached as he felt an anguish that destroyed his vision of this country being his dreamland. Finally, he chose to captain a ship that was leaving China and wander all over the world.

As he managed to save some money, his hot temper calmed down a lot as he measured his travels by the hourglass and followed the shipping lanes that crisscrossed the map of the seas. He loaded in one port and unloaded in another, resting against each pier. As he heard the ship's whistle, he felt homesick, but when he finally decided to settle down, he was already fifty-five years old.

Even though he felt homesick for Penghu, Waian, he didn't want to go back to the place that was still a Japanese colony. It seemed impossible for him to go back home because there was a big ocean between China and Taiwan.

One day, Lee Shiang and his Korean friend, Piao-Taiqi, who also worked on the ship, came ashore at Tianjin and went to a restaurant to have a drink. Later they greatly enjoyed walking along the street after being at sea for such a long time even though it was very cold. Although their bleary eyes were dim, they could still distinguish where they were going. Suddenly, Piao-Taiqi patted Lee Shiang's shoulder to suggest, "Brother Lee, how about we emigrate to Yu-Lin?"

"Do you mean the Yu-Lin harbor of Hainan Island in China?" asked Lee Shiang.

"Yes!" Piao-Taiqi nodded his head seriously.

Piao-Taiqi, who was a Korean, was his best friend; it was true because Lee Shiang had fled for his life from Taiwan to China where only Koreans could become good friends with him.

"Ya. They seem to abound with fish around that island."

Lee Shiang thought for a while and then asked, "What are you driving at?"

"We can get into the fishing business. First, we should make a plan to follow, and then we need to raise money."

Unfortunately, before they finished their discussion, a beggar rushed out from the darkness to beg them for help. Lee Shiang put his hand into his pocket to look for some change for the beggar, but he couldn't find any, so he turned away from the beggar to continue his walk with his friend. The beggar began to cry and pleaded with them to help him.

"Fuck you! What is going on?" Lee Shiang felt furious.

"Here you go." Finally, Piao-Taiqi had found some change that he gave to the beggar as he sent him away.

Lee Shiang's slight drunkenness disappeared quickly after this event. A halo surrounded the dreary moon that emitted mournful moonlight on Tianjin.

Looking back, China was a Japanese world for a long period. Even though Shanghai's and Nanjing's battles had ended several years ago, here and there remained the shadowy aftereffects of war, such as large groups of beggars, high unemployment, and economic depression.

In 1931, the Japanese army headquarters secretly formulated the principles, steps, and measures for invading Northeast China. After careful preparation for the invasion, the Japanese imperialists blatantly launched the September 18 Incident, an important battle that was a prelude to large-scale invasions to China, then Asia and the Pacific region.

Because it was far away from the areas of conflict, Hainan Island would be a nice place to live. Thus, Lee Shiang said decisively, "We don't need to work on a ship again. We can move to Hainan Island to catch fish instead."

Three months later, Lee Shiang and Piao-Taiqi began their new life; they resigned from shipping work to leave for Hainan Island and make their dream come true. As their plans went well, the two sang the individual songs of their respective countries. Lee Shiang sang in Taiwanese, and Piao-Taiqi sang in Korean. Even though their languages were different, they could harmonize very well with each other. Their joyful singing expressed how pleased they were.

Unfortunately, halfway along their journey, they met a group of robbers. They were robbed of everything, down to their last coin. They nearly died of fright in the strange area and struggled for ten days in a small town. Finally, they canceled their plans and returned to Tianjin.

And now, they had not only lost their jobs but their dream had also been destroyed. They didn't know how they would get by in their old age. They wanted to ask for help, but all their friends knew more poverty and frustration than them.

During this difficult time, somewhat to Lee Shiang's surprise, based on his resident certificate from the Chinese government, he was hired as a translator for a Japanese company because he could speak both Japanese and Taiwanese. A source of livelihood was the most important thing in life; indeed, for a person who recalled how hungry and miserable he had been for so long, the chance to make money was not only a means of living a better life but of reattaining human dignity. He even regretted his behavior that year he had been fighting against the Japanese force. In fact, his energy had already been low after he fled to China and experienced a series of difficult situations, such as the hostility of the Chinese people and his struggle to find work.

What then was the relationship between Japan and China? The September 18 incident in 1931, a great battle between the Chinese people and Japanese army, aroused people's angry resistance against Japan all over China. Moreover, after the Marco Polo Bridge incident in 1937, another battle between Chinese and Japanese armies, the amalgamated army recruited many Chinese people to further launch a protracted, comprehensive, and armed anti-Japanese struggle. They then effectively coordinated the nationwide war of resistance against Japan, led by the Communist Party of China and, finally, gained victory over Japan in 1945.

The storm of last night had crowned this morning with golden peace and fallen angels; likewise, the light of victory cheered the Chinese people, but there was still great poverty and many other troubles to resolve. Even though the snow and wind had ceased, the sky was still filled with dark clouds.

A neighbor jeered at Lee Shiang, "The Japanese eventually surrendered themselves, which is good for our China, but it is bad for you Taiwanese."

"What are you talking about?"

"Taiwanese people are a servile people who must be controlled by another country." The neighbor looked like he wanted to pick a fight. This kind of social stigma made Lee Shiang furious; he just glared at the neighbor and went directly to his room, which resulted in the neighbor opening his mouth but finding nothing to say in response to Lee Shiang's abrupt departure.

After Lee Shiang had placed his hat and the bank information on the table, he was very tired, so he sat down in the armchair and, folding his hands, tried to rest as he recalled his meeting with the bank clerk:

"What on earth is this? Why do I have so little?" Lee Shiang checked and checked, but he still found that a lot of his money was missing.

"The purchasing power of Chinese currency has been cut. Now $200 is only worth $1," the clerk explained the money rules of the transfer.

"But I should have the same as him," Lee Shiang complained, pointing to the man behind him. While he and this man had waited in line, they had discussed their finances and figured out how much money they should have, which had turned out to be the same amount. But Lee Shiang now found out that he had much less than the other man.

"Man, what is wrong with you? The other guy has his own Guan Jin currency [the Guan Jin currency refers to that which was issued by the Central Bank of China between 1930 and 1948. This currency was initially used for customs payments]. Do you have Guan Jin currency?" the clerk asked.

"Guan Jin currency?" Lee Shiang murmured to himself.

"Next!" the clerk yelled, clearly indicating that Lee Shiang should go away. Seeing a long line behind him, Lee Shiang stepped away, but he did so very unwillingly.

As he went back home, deeply disappointed, he was jeered at by his neighbor. Lee Shiang was getting desperate and low spirited. He almost suffered a severe asthma attack. Now he continued to sit in the armchair and rubbed his hands anxiously.

Suddenly, he leaped out of his chair and quickly went to his desk where he opened the top drawer. There was a newspaper dated January 14. He read again and again about the rules of possession that applied to the Taiwanese and Koreans after Japan surrendered. Thanks to his ability to read Chinese, he got the main idea. He wondered why the Chinese government treated Taiwanese people—who were also Chinese—like dirt, as if they were from another country like Korea. He was filled with suspicion. He needed to look for somebody that he could discuss this issue with.

The sky was covered with gray, which darkened toward its lower edge near the horizon and gradually reflected on the gate of a big country yard, making it look even gloomier. Everlasting night or everlasting day—no one could say what it was. There were twenty families gathered together in this area. The door of their courtyard had twenty names on it. On one side, the name of Lee Shiang hung on the door; on the other side of the door was the name of Piao Taiqi. They had dwelt here for one year after their Hainan Island plan failed. Lee Shiang went to visit his best friend, Piao Taiqi,

"Man, do you want to move somewhere?" Lee Shiang asked. He saw Piao Taiqi packing some things into a big bag.

"Yes, it is said that our Korea will become independent soon, so I want to enjoy free air." Piao Taiqi stopped packing to talk to Lee Shiang. "There is a sailing to Korea next month. I hope I can get on it."

Lee Shiang lowered his head to think about his own and his friend's fortunes after Japan had been defeated. It seemed good for Koreans like Piao Taiqi, yet it was bad for Taiwanese like him, who stayed in China. He pulled out the newspaper from his pocket to show the article to Piao Paiqi. Each time he had read this article about the Chinese authorities setting up the rule of law, Lee Shiang always plunged into a deep depression. Now Piao Taiqi read it.

"It means all Taiwanese and Korean belongings are controlled by the Chinese government," Piao Taiqi said.

"It is really unfair to us."

"It is okay because neither of us have any property anyway."

Lee Shiang sighed deeply at the thought and said nothing.

"Man, do you have something troubling you?" Piao Taiqi asked.

"My Japanese boss, Yamomato, who was very kind to me, gave me one of his houses at Lao Nong Tou when he was sent back to Japan," Lee Shiang explained.

"I can't complain about how the Chinese government treats the Koreans, but treating you Taiwanese the same as us is totally unreasonable. After all, you are the same family." Piao Taiqi was filled with sympathy for Lee Shiang.

A chilly north wind drifted through the window. The broken door resulted in a great sad sound filling all the air. In the thickly veiled sky, gaps broke out here and there like skylights in a dome trying to reveal ghosts, one by one, in every corner.

"Brother Lee! I have advised you to go back to Taiwan. It is the best way. Now the Eighth Route Army has obtained Soviet Russia's help in the province of Man Zhou, and the Chinese government also will want to get rid of those who disagree with authority. So the Chinese Civil War will start soon. It seems more chaotic than when Japan was here." Piao Taiqi was trying to get across his opinion that their friendship was cemented in adversity.

Before Piao Taiqi's suggestion, Lee Shiang had already decided to go back to Taiwan. Because of Japan's surrender, he had lost his job as translator; he couldn't sustain a living here anymore. If he didn't go back to Taiwan, where else could he go? He had to return to Taiwan in order to achieve a better life.

The Chinese government was busy with the civil war and thus didn't care where Taiwanese or Koreans went. Eager to return home, Lee Shiang began to aggressively ask how he could return to Taiwan. He was determined to get back to Taiwan no matter how difficult it was. At last, he got the information he needed from Mr. Cal Dui, a member of the Townsmen Association. With his help, Lee Shiang managed to squeeze onto a crowded ship that was sailing to north Taiwan on March 23.

The grass seeks her people in the earth; the wanderer seeks the solitude of his original homeplace.

5-2

Forgetting Father's Name

Taking his cigarette butt from his lips, Zi-Tian threw it to the sky. Some ashes scattered on the ground while other ashes hit the wooden wall. Zi-Tian looked into the endless smog and thought about his father, Lee Shiang, who had abandoned their family when Zi-Tian was just a baby. He had just gotten the news that their so-called father was coming home soon, yet he felt neither excited nor surprised when he found out.

It was 1948, and Zi-Tian was now a member of the Penghu Association from which all Penghu people in Taiwan could get help if they had any problems. This day they had a meeting to discuss how to renovate the association's office that was damaged by American bombs. Before the meeting, Zi-Tian saw his coworker, Mr. Xu, bringing a letter, which he read word for word to Zi-Tian,

"'Lee Shiang, from Penghu, age seventy-four, who has two sons, Lee Zi-Tian and Lee Zi-Shan, who live in Kaohsiung, Taiwan.'"

The name of Lee Shiang was so strange to Zi-Tian that he did not even raise his head as Mr. Xu read the letter,

"Finally, your father returns to Taiwan. Congratulations!"

"Father? Where does this father come from?" he lifted his head to ask confusedly as he continued on with his work.

"He is coming from China! Look! He will take the Tianjin ship on March 20 and arrive in Ji-Long a week later."

"Who will pick him up?"

"Of course, it is *your* duty. You are his son."

The problem was how dangerous it was to travel to north Taiwan at this difficult time. Last year several arrogant Chinese officers shot a Taiwanese woman who wouldn't let them have cigarettes without paying for them. When other Taiwanese people heard about this incident, they were very angry and fought with the Chinese army from north to south Taiwan. Even though the violence had slowed down a little, there was still widespread anger, so it was highly dangerous to travel. One time, when the director of the Penghu Association went to the north government office to negotiate with an officer about business, he almost got shot. Moreover, Lee Zi-Tian's concubine, Gao-Zhao, who often strongly advised against him travelling, was far away from home at this time.

The aim of the Penghu Association was to improve on the friendship and advantages among townspeople and make Kaohsiung a good place to live. For example, the association helped thirty Penghu villagers, who were in a very difficult situation, move from Hainan Island in China to Taiwan last month. At that time, Zi-Tian had also helped out these people. Could he neglect his own father? No, but it was just so shocking to deal with his father's return.

Meanwhile, in his home, as the sun's flames grew higher and higher, Zi-Tian's sons, arguing with one another in the living room, found the sun's rays reflected on the granite walls irritating to their eyes.

"Don't let your father, who is in poor health, know that you guys are always arguing with each other about money," said

Gao-Zhao, who was their mother. "You all must consider what the meaning of being a parent is."

She sputtered her words and was very vexed. In her so-called rich family, her sons' greed for even more money was all they could think about and was the major reason for all their squabbles.

Looking at them, Gao-Zhao felt a deep, helpless anguish that froze her very soul, especially for her fourth son, Lian-Si. Silent for a while and with perhaps a hint of sadness, she scolded him.

"I gave you a lot of money to do the business of building, but you did nothing. This is your business. You don't need to argue about who didn't give you a hand."

"I don't want to haggle over something, but you, my mother, are so unfair to me among all my brothers," said Lian-Si, and then he forced his cough a little more so that she should suffer remorse.

"You dare to say that to me, your mother." Gao-Zhao was now white with rage. Furthermore, she heard her second and fourth daughter-in-laws quarreling with each other again in the corner. Her face turned from white to red as she continued, "We diligently raised you one by one and gave you everything to give you the best education. Now you are married and have started nice careers, yet you do not care about each other, and you argue with each other about money all the time without ever considering your parents' hard work. Your father and I are objects of ridicule in this family. What kind of earth is this! One never knows!"

She could not say anything more. Her words were choked by her sobbing. She felt helpless that she couldn't make herself understood by her children.

The sun was becoming brighter and brighter, causing a glare on the glass that covered a drawing; and then as it rose higher, the glass reflected back into her eyes so that it hurt sharply, and she closed her eyes to avoid looking at it.

The picture that Gao-Zhao couldn't bear to look at was *The Image of Five Sons* drawn by the famous artist, Mr. Liu, who was the only person of Penghu who had graduated from the Japanese art college. Finishing this masterpiece, Mr. Liu said to Lee Zi-Tian, "My friend, your achievements have made the people of Penghu very proud of you. Not only do you have a successful business in Taiwan but you also have five excellent sons. I think very highly of you, so I drew a picture to say happy birthday to you!"

When Lee Zi-Tian accepted this big canvas from his good friend, he joyfully gazed at the drawing for a long time. Behind the five sons there was the kitchen; gold and dust, among other things, covered the floor. But he really had no idea what the meaning of the picture was. He focused his confused eyes at Mr. Liu to find out the answer.

And Mr. Liu threw out an explanation. He said slowly, like a poet chanting his poetry, "Siblings come nearest to unite when they are great in humility. Thus the dust could become gold. On the other hand, siblings grow far apart when they argue about anything. Thus the gold could become excrement."

"This is a kind of motto. Live and let live among brothers." Zi-Tian laughed his approval.

At that time, Zi-Tian's eldest son was studying in Japan, but the other four sons were living together in their father's big and luxurious house in the middle of Kaohsiung. Everything was okay except that they could not accept Lian-Yuan, who was actually Zi-Tian's eldest son, born by his first wife in Penghu. However, these brothers were continually getting married, and then their relationships became worse. Even though money may make the world go around, sometimes it is useless.

This rich and powerful family had gradually faded, especially when Cai-Lian married the fourth son and came into the Lee family. This fourth daughter-in-law was called a bad-luck woman by Gao-Zhao.

"She is naturally indelicate," Gao-Zhao complained to her fourth son. "I don't know why you chose this bad woman to come to our home."

"What are you talking about?" Mother's words made Lian-Si angry. He went on expressing his rage, "Cai-Lian's diligence and obedience are beyond compare to anyone in this family. She did a lot of housework when the housekeeper quit last year. She just cannot please you, and you always scold her. You are an unfair mother-in-law. You have different rules for each of your daughter-in-laws."

Furthermore, honest Lian-Si was always arguing with his mother. He had a sense of justice; he especially didn't like their family neglecting Lian-Yuan, who was their brother from a different mother, and this point was a source of great rage on the part of his mother so that she totally disappointed her fourth son.

"It is a ridiculous thing," Lian-Si always said of this issue. "Our rich family has a poor son."

"Hold your tongue about what is not your business. You certainly have a genius for getting into trouble." Gao-Zhao was very angry, and with perhaps a hint of sadness, she added, "If I put money into the toilet there would at least be a loud sound in response. But it is useless to give you so much money to do your building trade because your business always fails."

Lian-Si stared at his mother. There was a moment of complete silence. Then he flashed back at her with a kind of resentfulness, "We are all your children, but you have treated me most unfairly. Is it possible that I'm not Zi-Tian's son?"

At this time, Zi-Tian could hear the sound of something going wrong in another room, and he rushed toward that sound. When he saw a group of his beloved family members arguing with each other, his commanding eyes looked around at everyone. He lit his cigarette butt slowly, and then he raised his head to ask, as cool as a cucumber, "What on earth does this mean? Let me know who is not Zi-Tian's son!"

Suddenly, everybody was silent; they all stood staring at each other as no one dared to speak or even move or breathe, except Gao-Zhao, whose angry eyes continued to stare at Lian-Si. Although Lian-Si felt deeply wronged, he swallowed his words even though it greatly frustrated him to say nothing.

The brothers showed their respect for their father, so Zi-Tian's temper calmed down a little bit. In the meantime, Cai-Lian reverently took a chair to her father-in-law and gently said, "Dad! Please take a seat." But Zi-Tian didn't sit down at once. He looked around and around this big living room. When his eyes touched on the wall of his favorite masterpiece *The Image of Five Sons*, he exclaimed suddenly, "I, Lee Zi-Tian, got where I am by working hard to be in a situation that allowed me to support you all and give you a high quality education, and yet . . ." He stopped here and prepared to sit down to talk with his sons.

At the same time, the gardener hurried into the room to stand in front of Zi-Tian and say courteously, "Master! Chu-Su, Zi-Shan's wife, is here to see you."

"Very nice. Let her come in," Zi-Tian answered joyfully. But the gardener couldn't believed his boss's warm response, so he stood there, hesitating to move.

"What are you waiting for? She's visiting at a good time. I just want to discuss something with Zi-Shan"

"Oh! Yes, I will ask her come in." The gardener scurried out of the house to where Chu-Su was waiting.

"Is my brother-in-law at home?" Chu-Su asked the gardener carefully. After walking one hour, her fair complexion had turned a little red. Her eight-year-old daughter, Lian-Zi, was holding her mother's hand tightly and looking up into the grown-ups' faces excitedly.

"Yes, my master is in a good mood today. You are coming at the right time."

When they came in to the big luxurious house, the scented flowers attracted Lian-Zi. She gasped in admiration and yelled in surprise, "Uncle's home is so beautiful!"

"Don't be too loud," Chu-Su said.

"Follow me please. I'll show you the way." The gardener turned his head to them.

A beautiful stone fountain was set in the middle of the garden. The powerful water suddenly created such a strong cascade that Lian-Zi was startled. But she kept silent and snuggled up to her mother.

They walked through the porch and passed by a glass building where they could see some indistinct figures in the room. Chu-Su took a deep breath before she came in. She hoped her plan would be acceptable to her brother-in-law, Zi-Tian.

When Chu-Su and Lian-Zi entered the living room, many people were there. Lian-Zi followed her mother's example and also said hello to them.

"Uncle! Auntie! Brothers! Sister-in-law!" Lian-Zi said in a timid voice.

"Hi, little Lian-Zi. How are you?" Lian-Si warmly took her hand, and he wiped the sweat from her face so that Lian-Zi relaxed a lot. And then she began to explain her new name.

"My daddy said that the Japanese have gone, so my last name doesn't need to add the word *Zi* anymore. So now my name is just two words: *Lee Lian*," she said seriously, but no one was listening except Lian-Si.

In fact, the adults were thinking about their individual problems. All of them went to another room except Uncle and Auntie.

"I have heard news about our father. He is still alive and will come home soon," Zi-Tian said without asking about how his brother and his family were doing.

"That's great. Where is he?" Chu-Su asked excitedly.

"The question is who has the free time to pick him up!" Zi-Tian said, and he continued to worry. "The north of Taiwan is so far away . . ."

Gao-Zhao interrupted her husband to express her opinion. "Recently, going outside is very dangerous, especially after the events of February 28. Part of the north is still chaotic." There was a moment of complete silence. Chu-Su wondered why it was such a difficult thing to go to meet their father when there were so many members of the Lee family.

At this moment, Zi-Tian asked Chu-Su, "Does Zi-Shan have time to go to Taipei to pick up Father?"

"Even though he has no time, he can still do it," Chu-Su answered confidently.

"It is perfect!" Zi-Tian seemed to have unloaded his heavy burden. His pale face showed his need for a few moments of repose. He closed his eyes to take a rest, and he almost forgot that his guests, Chu-Su and Lian-Zi, were still here.

"Brother . . ." Chu-Su wished to speak but did not say anything else.

Zi-Tian opened the eyes and prepared to listen.

"I mean, recently, Zi-Shan and I took a fancy to a house on Wen-Hua Road because we don't want to rent anymore. We want to have our own house."

"Do you need money?"

"No! No! We just need to take advantage of your name to buy it. Because you are a member of a savings and loan association, we can get a huge discount on the price."

"So that's how it is!" Zi-Tian responded with the first thing that came into his head.

This was absolutely true. At the beginning of Taiwan's recovery after the Japanese went back to their own country, Taiwan experienced two kinds of robbery. One of them was the Chinese people taking Taiwanese treasures with them to mainland China;

another kind was Taiwanese chief officers taking over Japanese companies for them. These two kinds of robbery were high-level problems.

On the other side of the fence, houses in which the Japanese had resided came under the authority of savings and loan associations to deal with them. When the Japanese left Taiwan to return Japan, the Taiwanese people applied for these empty houses, but they needed a member of a savings and loan association to help them buy it. Otherwise, not only did they pay higher prices but it was also difficult to register their ownership of the house. There was vastly different treatment between the members of the associations and these who were not members.

Zi-Tian thought, no wonder Chu-Su asked him to solve their problem. It was a good time to invest. Why hadn't he thought about that? Chu-Su peered at her brother-in-law as he maintained his silence. She was a little worried. She carefully asked, "Actually, the house that we live in now is too small. Additionally, if Father comes back here, there will be more space to let him live with us."

"Okay! You can use my name to buy the house," Zi-Tian said because he had heard the most important news from Chu-Su: his father could live with his brother, Zi-Shan.

5-3

The Suffering of Kaohsiung

The Japanese-style house in Kaohsiung contained many rooms of varying sizes, each including a paper door and a lattice window, but the rooms were seriously damaged. Zi-Shan opened the door and saw a huge pile of broken furniture. It was a scene of chaos that showed there had been nobody living here for a long time.

Even though this house was in such bad shape, it was a treasure for Zi-Shan's family. They had emigrated from Penghu to Kaohsiung twenty years ago. Now in 1948, they finally had their own house. It was great news for them, but they had had to wait until the Japanese went away before they could move into the broken-down house.

Now at last, they could sit together around a table that was six feet wide, ten feet long, and a half feet high. Lian-Zi and her brothers joyfully climbed up and jumped up and down on the tabletop. This secondhand table was a gift from Chu-Su's Japanese employer, Mr. Gao, which the family received four months ago; but it had been too big to set in their original small living room. Instead they had placed it in an upright position in the corner of the kitchen. Now that they had a bigger space, they set it up the right way.

After finishing the housework, Chu-Su sat down and slowly touched the smooth tabletop. She sighed deeply as she said, "A human is like a flower because it can't stay resplendent forever."

Chu-Su recalled that her employer, Mr. Gao, a Japanese officer, was very hospitable to her when she washed their clothes. She thought that if it hadn't been for Mr. Gao's help, her fourth son, Lian-Shi, wouldn't have been rescued from the Japanese soldier during a terrible event three years ago. The Gaos were good Japanese people, but unfortunately, the fate was the same for the kind Japanese people as the unkind Japanese people after the Japanese surrender. She remembered one afternoon, the Gao family came to her home to ask for protection from a group of Taiwanese people who were holding sticks as they ran to catch up to them. While Chu-Su was helping and comforting them, she heard Mr. Gao's daughter, who was filled with anger at the way they had been treated, ask, "What on earth is happening? Does the slave want to enslave us?"

It was a good question; why couldn't all human beings live together in peace?

"Mother! I am starving." Her children's yelling woke up Chu-Su from her memories. After only a short break, she could see that the sun was already setting. She needed to rush back to the kitchen. While she was busy with her cooking, her daughter, Lian-Zi, said to her, "Grandma's feet are aching again."

"You should go outside to check that our geese are safe!" Chu-Su ignored Lian-Zi's words because she wanted to get the cooking done. Meanwhile, Shiang-Sao was crying her head off and murmuring about her suffering. "Wu! Wu! I really have an evil life. I, like a beggar, only beg a mouthful of wine to stop my suffering, but nobody cares about me. I should die to avoid bothering anybody." She resented the way her daughter-in-law treated her.

Chu-Su stopped cooking when she suddenly heard her mother-in-law's increasingly loud sobs from the bedroom; she felt something like an insect crawling up her whole body. She must hurry to find the rice wine for her mother-in-law. Luckily, she found a little bit of red wine that was left from what Zi-Shan drank with his good friends several days ago. They sometimes met up to relax and have a few drinks. In a flurry, as she came running up to Shiang-Sao, she said carefully, "Mother! The wine is here."

Lee family members were often exhorted by their father, Zi-Shan, who pointed out, "Grandma can't see anymore, and now her legs are broken as well. This situation is very bad, so you must show deep consideration for Grandma's feelings!" It was true; after breaking her legs, Shiang-Sao couldn't lie down properly to sleep, and her arms hugged her legs as she cried all day long. Only the rice wine could relax her and relieve her suffering.

However, now, even after Shiang-Sao had already drunk the wine, her crying and suffering seemed worse than before. Chu-Su and the children didn't know how to deal with this situation. They all hoped their father would come home soon.

Zi-Shan finally arrived. He had heard his mother's suffering cries before he parked his bicycle in the yard at the front of house. He rushed to his mother and asked anxiously, "Mom! Are your legs hurting more? Let me ask the doctor to come."

"How am I to blame? She gave me rotten wine. What the devil is she doing?" Shiang-Sao made a serious complaint against her daughter-in-law to her son.

Zi-Shan angrily asked his children, "Where's your mom?"

"Mom is cooking in the kitchen," Lian-Zi answered in a timid voice.

Zi-Shan sprang up and rushed to the kitchen. He loudly scolded Chu-Su and slapped her face while she was busy with cooking. Chu-Su threw down the spatula to caress her aching left cheek and wept bitter tears of helplessness as she ran outside.

When Lian-Zi saw what happened to her mother, she started to sob uncontrollably and wanted to follow her mother. But she couldn't find her mother as she peered out into the blackness of the night.

"Mother! Mother! Where are you?" Lian-Zi's brothers also came out one by one. The siblings hugged one another, crying.

Even though they had moved into a bigger house, they were still surrounded by frustration. Zi-Shan was paralyzed on the floor by his mother, but his eyes saw the wine beside her. He stood up to taste the wine that his mother said was rotten. Then he was confused as he said carefully, "Mom, this bowl of wine is good. It isn't rotten as you said."

"What's the big idea?" Shiang-Sao disagreed.

"I mean, you can try it again."

"The taste isn't right obviously. I am an expert on rice wine now because I have been drinking it for several decades. Nobody can try to cheat me."

Zi-Shan suddenly understood something. He said, "Mom, this is red wine, not rice wine. Red wine and rice wine have a totally different taste. No wonder."

Night's darkness is a necessity of life as it bursts with the gold of the dawn as well. Likewise, it represents the alternation of the bitter and the sweet in life. After she had suffered many hardships for nearly sixty years, the most important person of Shiang-Sao's life, Lee Shiang, came back to her. One day Zi-Shan brought him home and said excitedly, "Mom, can you guess who is here?"

"Is . . . your . . . father?" Shiang-Sao opened her sightless eyes and reached out her trembling hands as if to catch something.

"Yes! Yes! It's me! It's me." Lee Shiang raised his fingers to test her vision as he swayed in front of her, but Shiang-Sao made no response. Lee Shiang was filled with complicated emotions as he realized his wife was really blind.

"How are you, Brother Shiang?" Shiang-Sao's voice was surprisingly calm.

"I'm fine." Lee Shiang was so embarrassed about himself that he had nothing to say in reply; he had abandoned his family for such a long time.

"Mom, I am Zi-Tian. Your eldest son is here." Zi-Tian had found a way out of this stalemate.

"Zi-Tian, my dear son! Finally, you come here to see me. I am so happy!" Shiang-Sao wanted to reach and fervently hug Zi-Tian. At last, all the family was reunited.

Zi-Shan said to Zi-Tian, "Brother, we are fortunate for your help in bringing Father home. Father can live here with us."

"Sure!" Zi-Tian was holding a tobacco pipe, and his feet didn't stop shuttling through each room to take a better look at this house.

Zi-Shan said to his brother, "There is some money I borrowed from you. I will return it immediately."

"Our parents are getting old. You need to spend a lot of money in the future, so you don't need to return it to me."

"Brother is brother, business is business. They should be clearly separated," Zi-Shan said seriously.

"Wait a minute—I think you could live in this house until you pass away. You shouldn't transfer it from my name to yours, just keep it in my name."

The words of his brother came as a shock to Zi-Shan. It meant when he died, his children wouldn't have a house to live in. It was nothing less than fraud. He wouldn't take it for anything. At this, he said angrily to Zi-Tian, "I think you're a terrible person!"

Zi-Shan was determined to look for another place to live in at once. He couldn't bear to live in this so-called Zi-Tian house anymore. In actual fact, he had asked for it. If he hadn't agreed with his wife to ask for his brother's help, he might not have accepted it.

Zi-Shan and Chu-Su rushed around every day, trying to find another house. At last, three months later, they found a remote house that was completely destroyed by a bomb. Although it was said that nobody dared to buy this house due to it being an unlucky place, they decided to buy it because they didn't have enough money to buy a better one.

Facing the ruined house, Chu-Su said to her husband, "As long as there is land and a foundation, it is okay. We both have hands to rebuild it."

"Yes, on the other hand, I need to become a member of a savings and loan association so that we can pay less," Zi-Shan said.

There were different reactions from family members when they wanted to move to another place. Lee Shiang kept silent as he watched the changing attitudes. After he'd returned from China to Taiwan to this home half a year ago, he was gradually getting to know the characters of his two sons, Zi-Tian and Zi-Shan. They had opposite views on everything; one of them tended to be snobbish while the other was more compassionate. Neither of these radically different temperaments of the brothers was a good way to associate with people. He would strongly advise against them, but no one wanted to hear him, just like the duck who listens to the thunder and can't hear anything else; indeed, he had left them for such a long time that there was nothing to talk about between the sons and the father. Moreover, recently, he'd had a severe asthma attack. He couldn't handle everything. Even his wife, Shiang-Sao, didn't feel happy after he returned home. Had he done so many wrongful acts when he was younger that he was down on his luck in his old age?

Lee Shiang felt a bit sad as he remembered his past experience when he was a Taiwanese hero brave enough to fight against the Japanese army and ride out a series of storms in his past life, but now he had nothing, not even one word that could help smooth out the problems of this family. Sometimes it's better to leave things as they were, he thought. Only Lian-Zi, who was the sole granddaughter of the Lee family, could sooth his loneliness. She always snuggled close to him to ask for hugs from her grandfather.

This day, a vendor peddled tofu pudding in the streets, making Lian-Zi itch to try some. When she desired to do something, she would look around at the situation, and then she would decide on her next step. She looked over at Third Brother, who was concentrating his attention on his homework, and she couldn't see Fourth Brother. Her mother was preparing to wash her hair. Lian-Zi knew her mother hadn't the time to keep an eye on her right now. Therefore, she moved softly and quietly to her grandfather, and said, "Grandpa! Tofu pudding is coming!"

"My dear, do you want to have some?"

She hurried to put her hand to her grandpa's mouth to stop his talking because she feared that somebody would hear what they were up to.

"You are a greedy girl!" Lee Shiang absolutely understood his granddaughter's meaning. As he stood up to get the money and go outside, he said softly to Lian-Zi, "My sweetheart, you hide here, and I'll go buy a tofu pudding for you. Okay?"

"Yes! Grandpa! I'll sit here waiting for you."

After five minutes, Lee Shiang held up a bowl of steaming hot tofu pudding.

"Grandpa! You eat first, we'll share."

"No, my dear, you can eat it all and remember to return the bowl to Uncle Tofu Pudding," he said at the same time as he put on his hat.

"Grandpa! Do you want to go outside?" Lian-Zi started to sob uncontrollably; she thought she couldn't enjoy the food without Grandpa.

"Yes, I will stroll along the street. If I come back late, you should tell them Grandpa might be at Uncle's place, okay? Don't rush. You'll enjoy your food more if you eat it slowly. My dear, take care!"

However, without Grandpa, Lian-zi lost her taste for the tofu pudding. She waited for a while, thinking she could share with Mother or Brother. When no one showed up, she poured out the pudding on the floor.

And she lay down on the floor and cried out in fear as though she had lost both her favorite food and her dear grandpapa.

The sun was setting, the moon was rising, and the night had fallen, but Grandfather had disappeared. After he went outside, he never reappeared.

"It is very late. Why hasn't father come back yet?"

"Lian-Zi said that her grandpa could possibly be visiting her uncle."

"Let Lian-Yi go to his uncle's place to take a look tomorrow."

"If everything is okay, we can move to our new house."

"We should thank Father for helping us buy the house."

"Father seems unhappy these days since he came back home from China."

"He almost has no friends except Mr. Cai Dui, who came from China three months ago."

"It is said that Mr. Cai Dui was caught by the government because he is a member of the Communist Party, which is the big enemy of the government." Talking about this sensitive political subject, Chu-Su lowered her voice.

Zi-Shan heaved a sigh, "I thought when the Japanese went back to their country and the national government came here from China that we would have a nicer living. But the way the situation is now, it is useless."

In bed, Lian-Zi listened carefully to her parents' conversation even though it was already midnight. She couldn't tell why her heart languished in the dark night's silence. She missed her dear grandpa and gradually fell into her nightmare—she saw her tall gray-haired grandfather walking slowly toward her. She wanted to welcome him, but while she was putting out her small hands to embrace him, he disappeared. She began to sob and follow her grandpa, and then she found out she had walked into a cemetery in the middle of a great wilderness. She didn't know how much time had passed. She seemed to hear an uproar—it cut through the quiet nighttime sky; then a tumult of shouting and screaming came from within the house.

"Oh damn! Our father has been arrested in the lockup near that hospital building." Chu-Su cried out in alarm as if the world would come to end.

The unfamiliar fate was black all round the Lee family, and among them was the sound of confusion as to why the authorities wanted to arrest a senior over seventy years old.

Moreover, it turned out that there was no time to rescue their father; sad news arrived from the jail that Lee Shiang had already passed away because he had suffered a severe asthma attack, and the relatives of Lee Shiang were called to receive his body from jail.

Things look phantasmal in the dimness of the dusk as people's hopes are lost in the dark and in the treetops like blots of ink. Can they wait for the morning and wake up to see their lives in the light during this sorrowful and joyful time?

5-4

Kaohsiung's Dying Flowers

Outside of Kaohsiung city, past many ruined fences, there was a yard overgrown with weeds and a shabby old house in the middle of it. On the right side of the house, there was a fire hydrant filled with bugs and rainwater. Clearly, no one had lived here for a long time.

In 1950, when the new owner wanted to move into this nearly destroyed dwelling, he had to take out the spider network under each door and window. But getting rid of all the spiderwebs was to the new residents like throwing off many worrisome ties to the past so that they were now free to go down the road to their future.

It was a really bleak place with a cemetery behind it, yet Chu-Su planned to use the field of grass and open area near the house to plant a vegetable garden and develop a pig-farming industry. In order to pay for the house, Lee family members were on the job every day. Lian-Zi used to enjoy lying on her mother's bosom, but now she threw herself into the work of raising poultry such as geese and chickens.

Even though Lian-Zi didn't fear her brothers' bullying because her parents had a saying that brothers must protect their only sister in the family, she was very scared of ghosts, especially at midnight. She heard that after people died, they became ghosts, but after her grandpa died, she never saw Grandfather come back even though her parents said they knew when Grandpa's soul had returned home. They were overcome with grief, just as Lian-Zi still had a sorrowful heart about Emei's death.

Death! It was a big problem for humans! Now Lian-Zi tried to avoid this unavoidable issue of human life. If someone broke her taboo to say something about her parents' death, she would be unhappy and impolite to them.

It was okay in the daytime, but it was an unendurable time for her at midnight, especially when her father worked night shifts. She would wake up at 2:00 AM and pray anxiously for her father because, at that time, her father had to pass by a terrible dark area of the cemetery. She had a vision of her father shaking with fright, and she murmured under her breath, "Bodhisattva Kuan-Yin! Please help my poor daddy! Let him pass by in safety." Then she waited to hear her father ride his bicycle into the yard so that she could finally relax enough to go to sleep.

By 1953, thirteen-year-old Lian-Zi couldn't endure any pain, even just a little ache, so she was called a chicken by her brothers. However, she was able to keep her painful worry about her parents a secret from everybody for a long time. If life was filled with struggle for Lian-Zi, it was also filled with worrying about her parents' lives. She was so scared that one day her lovely papa and mama would suddenly disappear. Of course, it wouldn't happen due to her constant prayers for them.

One fall afternoon, when Lian-Zi was taking care of the geese, she saw her mother hurt her leg and limp toward her daughter with a cry of pain. Lian-Zi barely had time to lay down her wooden stick when she saw that her mother was likely to fall down on the ground. She made a dash for her mother and caught her in her arms. Her mother had a deep gash on her leg down to the bone, and blood was pouring from her wound.

"Mom, what can I do?" Lian-Zi cried out in fear and hugged her mother tightly.

"My dear, don't cry, calm down!" Chu-Su said weakly. "First, you need to call upon Auntie Bie for help, okay?"

To get to Auntie Bie's place, Lian-Zi had to pass several farms and tombs. As she ran to her destination, she mumbled to herself, "Bodhisattva Kuan-Yin! Please don't let my mother die."

But when she arrived at Auntie's home, her prayer changed; her trembling lips cried to Auntie Bie, "Help me! Help me! My mother died."

"What are you talking about?" Auntie Bie asked confusedly.

"No! No! Not died, my mother is just hurt!" Lian-Zi sobbed as she corrected herself.

She dreaded others breaking her taboo to talk about her parents' dying, yet she had broken the taboo herself. Hating herself for her mistake, she headed home in tears, thinking she should be severely punished for her crime, so she pushed her fingernails into her hands until they were bleeding. Lian-Zi thought that the more pain she felt, the more reduced her crime would be.

After three days, Chu-Su couldn't rest anymore; she needed to get up to deal with the vegetable garden that she had just planted. She was hoping for a good harvest in springtime in order to make money for her family.

Each member of the Lee family did their work well. This busy time helped to ease the sorrow everyone felt after the death of Lee Shiang, but after that, Shiang-Sao very quietly sat in her sickbed all day long because she couldn't lie down on the bed. Zi-Shan was very sad to see his mother's suffering.

The family was in such bad condition that no one felt happy except Chun-Li, who was a girl adopted by the Lee family. She was originally meant to be matched with the second son of the Lee family, but she refused this marital arrangement and ran away to marry a Chinese officer. Now that she had come back home, she brought many gifts to assure a good reputation for her husband.

This day, as Chu-Su received a treasured military wool blanket from Chun-Li, she was concerned and asked, "Is it okay for you to bring these things here so often?"

"My husband is very kind. He always wants me to say hello to all of you."

"If he has time, I hope he can come here."

"Yes, he is very busy. It is said that he will have good news because he works hard and will soon be promoted to an admiral." Chun-Li was really proud of her husband.

"He will be an admiral?" Chu-Su didn't understand this naval term, but she was excited. "He has his own personal driver from the government. I think he is already an important officer."

"He is a graduate of the Japanese empire university. He is excellent." Chun-Li's eyes shone with happiness.

"As long as you are happy, we are happy as well."

Lian-Yi, who was originally meant to marry Chun-Li, listened disapprovingly to Chun-Li's words and said, "You are such a boaster!"

"What are you talking about?" Chun-Li retorted angrily. Now she wouldn't allow Lian-Yi to treat her like a weak girl.

Chu-Su looked at angry Chun-Li and was aware that a quarrel was beginning between the two of them, so she scolded Lian-Yi. "You didn't make any effort to succeed, but you blame others. You are useless!" And then Lian-Yi was so upset, his mother turned softly to comfort him. "Don't worry, I will find another girl for you."

There was a variety of seasons in southern Taiwan. After last month's fifteen floods, it was still occasionally raining heavily in February. Finally, on a rare clear day, Lian-Zi followed in Mother's footsteps to pick the flowers of the vegetables in the garden.

"We will have one more dish to eat. The basket is almost full of flowers," Chu-Su said to her daughter.

"Mama! I want to pick more because I long for a lot of this delicious food." Lian-Zi said.

"My dear, it is enough. We need to prepare the dinner early."

As they walked to the door, Chu-Su saw Chun-Li's maid hurriedly ride a bicycle to their place, and then she told them breathlessly, "Madam! It is awful. My boss has died."

"What? What? Please talk more clearly. I don't understand what you are saying."

"My boss's wife was notified by a staff member of the military department. It is said that my boss was executed by shooting." The maid choked with sobs.

"Don't tell me jokes. There is a measure in all things." Chu-Su was loathe to accept this bad news and waved her hands in protest.

"Madam, it is true. Please come with me quickly to Tsoying." The maid wanted Chu-Su to deal with this sudden calamity.

The Japanese government brought a policy that forced Japanization on the Taiwanese when Taiwan was her colony. After fifty years, the Japanese surrendered and went back to their country. After that, the Chinese national government came to Taiwan from China when the Communists took over; they also brought a series of policies that they forced on the Taiwanese, especially in order to punish Communists, such as an order of martial law that punished the Taiwanese for being related to or friendly with someone who had committed an offense. The fact was that Taiwan was again another country's colony. Taiwan is also called Formosa. Formosa means "beautiful." Unfortunately, living on this beautiful island, the people didn't have a beautiful life.

A colleague of Admiral Dig secretly told Chun-Li that Admiral Dig was suddenly detained and arrested on suspicion of being a Communist spy by the Naval Military Intelligence Bureau. They didn't wait to transfer him to a court to stand trial, and they also didn't have any appeal opportunities for prisoners. Thus, Admiral Dig and his eleven colleagues were killed in February 1953. They were shot on a sunny day at noon and laid down on the ground of Tsoying, mixing red with the sunshine and bringing unexpected woe.

The blood on the land looked like the piles of red mud that were discarded as useless materials by the aluminum company. Likewise, who knows how many innocent people, like Admiral Dig, died in the red mud, like dying flowers discarded as useless material by the national government.

Human beings are still waiting patiently for the triumph of the martyred people.

童夢的故地

PART SIX
An Old Haunt of Childhood
(1955-1986)

6-1

Collapsed in the Dust

The goose head was bent in a spiral at the edge of the basket, its legs thrust into its belly and its eyes closed to be more dignified to present to the Heavenly Emperor. The temple was filled with a great clamor and the scent of incense. Lian-Zi's thin hand tightly held her mother Chu-Su's arm. Her eyes were full of fear, but her mouth stayed silent as she peeped at the goose that had been alive for the past six months, but yesterday, Mama had killed it. Mama said, "The best is selected to offer as a sacrifice. This shows the greatest gratitude as we thank all heavenly bodies for having protected and taken good care of us."

If there was no sacrifice, how could there be a gift? Lian-Zi felt deep sadness as she gazed at her lovely goose friend laid at the altar of the temple.

Chu-Su knelt down in front of the Heavenly Emperor and raised joss sticks beside a feast of turtles and fruit offered to the God. She also made a vow that she would take two rice turtles from the temple and return four turtles to the god next year. After she finished praying, she took home ten kilograms of good luck. Lian-Zi joyfully held onto her mother's dress on the way home as she thought about eating the delicious rice turtles.

When Chu-Su arrived home, she respectfully lit a lamp and carefully put the turtles on the prayer table. Lian-Zi's brothers also looked joyfully at the colorful turtles and impatiently asked the grown-ups when they could eat them. Lian-Zi's grandma, Shiang-Sao, wanted every member of the family to pray for the Lantern Festival first, which was observed on the first full moon in a lunar year. It was an important festival in Taiwan and the Penghu area.

Even though Shiang-Sao was blind, she could read her grandchildren's minds. She spoke seriously to them, "We need to pray for three days and nights, and then we can eat them." In the kitchen, Chu-Su prepared other items for the prayer table. After filling the table with food, only then would the flustered Chu-Su smile sweetly.

Their big house was rented out to an American, and the rent was thirty American dollars. Then they rented another small house for one hundred Taiwanese dollars. Even though the living space of the home that they now lived in was much smaller, they were still happy to live in this limited space because they earned so much money each month; furthermore, they had more money to help their relatives and friends in Penghu, especially Lee Zi-Shan's little brother, who was with their mother. His own father had already passed away a long time ago.

"We should send some money to Mr. Dong, who looked after us the most when we had a difficult time in Waian," Zi-Shan said seriously.

"We already sent money to Mr. Dong last month. I think we should send some to Yang-En this month." Chu-Su just received the rent from the American; the American dollars were in her hand. She looked into her husband's eyes as she slowly said, "I sometimes ask him to go to my home to pray to my ancestors, so I need to pay him. Is it okay?"

"What? Yang-En? That Neian guy! You are still keeping in touch?"

"I am only asking him to go to my parents' home to burn incense to pray with respect to my ancestors. Our Zhu family must go on without any male children in this living world." Whenever Chu-Su mentioned her family, she would cry.

Talking about this issue gave Zi-Shan a heavy feeling as well.

"I should go to Penghu to deal with a most important matter about my relatives' grave. I want to put my parents and brothers together. Let them live in a nice place." Chu-Su longed for her husband's agreement on this matter.

"I always told you that moving a grave is taboo. You cannot ignore this taboo. Now you are a member of the Lee family. It is best that you not deal with the Zhu family matters," Zi-Shan strongly advised his wife.

Chu-Su's brow furrowed as she thought about how to reply to Zi-Shan, but she was interrupted by a sound from outside. It was her fourth son singing a marching song he had just learned at school,

"Attack! Attack! Attack the mainland! Mainland is our land. Mainland is our area."

"You sound like a dog begging for food when you sing this song," Chu-Su angrily scolded.

Unfortunately, Chu-Su's loud angry voice brought a pitiful groan from her mother-in-law, Shiang-Sao, crying, "It's a complete mess!"

Zi-Shan glanced accusingly at Chu-Su, and then he ran to his mother anxiously asking, "Mother! Are your feet painful again? I will rub your feet so you will feel more relaxed."

Zi-Shan seemed like two different people as he treated his mother so gently while giving his wife angry looks.

"Recently, my eye always jumps so I think my heart is becoming unstable," Shiang-Sao said worriedly. "Lian-Si hasn't come here for a long time. I don't know what is going on about his father Zi-Tian's liver condition. Liver disease is a difficult matter.

Actually, he can't afford to get sick because of all the sibling rivalry he has to deal with. Oh! My poor child!"

"It is a matter for young people, Mom. You don't need to worry so much," Zi-Shan advised his mother.

As mother and son talked about Zi-Tian's family troubles, Lian-Si, wearing all black clothing and his face full of sadness, looked like a ghost as he came into their home and knelt in front of Shiang-Sao and tearfully said, "My father passed away last night."

"What did you say?" Nobody could believe what had happened.

A millionaire had passed away. In Lian-Zi's mind, the palatial building suddenly collapsed in the dust. A cloud of dust rose everywhere. A misty fog enveloped everything as if dusk had fallen.

Zi-Tian had five sons but no daughter. He borrowed Zi-Shan's daughter, Lian-Zi, who was now sixteen years old. She needed to do the daughter's job when Zi-Tian's funeral took place.

Lian-Zi, acting as her uncle's daughter, came to the big house wearing a mourning dress. She waited in the hall before the opening ceremony of the funeral. She didn't know what to do next. She was a little sad because this beautiful house was becoming a sorrowful place. She was surrounded by a big crowd of mourners as her eyes kept searching for her real parents who were busy at the other side of the house. Finally, a Taoist priest came near her and checked on her clothing. Now everything was ready; Zi-Tian was surrounded by all his sons, daughter, grandchildren, and grandchildren-in-law. Everything was perfect, so now the funeral could begin.

First, Zi-Tian's eldest son needed to clean his father's body. And then the daughter put new underclothes on Zi-Tian's body. Now Lian-Zi was expected to perform the daughter's duty. The Taoist priest pointed to her and said, "Daughter, put the clothes on your father's body!"

"No! He wasn't my father. My father is a man who will never die," Lian-Zi said to herself tearfully. She looked for her papa and mama, whose eyes were swollen. They gave her a signal that she must follow the priest's orders. Lian-Zi wanted to cry bitterly.

After continually sobbing in silence, Zi-Tian's wife suddenly cried out. Lian-Zi's tremulous little hands found it difficult to carry the underclothes to her uncle's body.

"You just go through the motions. I will do it properly later," another Taoist priest said.

Missing her uncle's presence, once again Lian-Zi walked to his huge garden. All kinds of gorgeous flowers had faded. The flowing fountain had already become a stagnant cesspool; the side building with its winding corridor was too cold now. At times the wind bellowed out in its deep voice with a tremolo of anger. As she witnessed the death of her uncle's home, Lian-Zi just wanted to persuade her dear parents to return to their crude but sweet home as soon as possible.

Actually, she became busy following the whole process of the funeral ceremony because there were numerous and diverse traditions that needed sons and daughter to perform them.

The funeral host began to describe Zi-Tian's life. "Lee Zi-Tian was born in 1902 into an impoverished family. When he was twelve years old, he moved to Kaohsiung from Penghu to start working in a hard-labor job and then became the head coolie at the age of nineteen. Through his diligent work, by the time he was twenty-four years old, he had rapidly developed a small shipping industry into a big corporation that included fisheries, importing and exporting food, picking coral, and so on. His businesses not only developed good communication between Taiwan and Penghu but it also created a society that promoted economic development in Taiwan. Additionally, while Taiwan was a Japanese colony, Lee Zi-Tian always disbursed a lot of money to the Penghu fellowship.

He was an outstanding citizen of Penghu. He got where he was by working hard. He is a fine example for us."

After that, they went to the memorial park. Lee Zi-Tian's six sons were hand to hand together carrying their father's cemetery tablet as they followed the priests who circled the grave again and again. Even though their steps were the same, their thoughts were different because the inheritance of their father's properties hadn't been settled among them before he passed away. The birds chirped among the trees. The priests grasped the bells to chant and acknowledge the end of Lee Zi-Tian's life.

The Lee family's house in Kaohsiung was considered one of the best buildings in south Taiwan. On a sultry summer afternoon, Lee Lian-Si, who was Lee Zi-Tian's fourth son, looked for the title deed after his father had been dead for one hundred days, but he couldn't find it.

"What are you looking for so hard?" Lian-Wu asked gently.

"There's no use my living here. I want to move out."

"Don't say such a thing!" Lian-Wu was confused about his brother's point as he said, "Even though eldest brother settled down here after moving from Japan, there is still space for you to live here. You don't need to move out."

"Most members of this family, such as Mother, Second Brother, and Third Brother, take me for a fool. I have no reason to stay here." Lian-Si kept looking for the deed.

"Have you been looking for the contract of the number 29 house?" Lian-Wu asked his brother.

"Yes, you know it?" Lian-Si lifted up his head.

"It is—," his younger brother Lian-Wu wished to say something but hesitated.

"Tell me!" Lian-Si ran hurriedly to Lian-Wu.

"I heard that probably Second Brother has sold it."

"I don't get it." Lian-Si flew into a rage. "That house was registered in my name. Why did he do that?"

"You know, when Father was sick, we needed to spend a lot of money."

"What did you say? Oh fuck! When Father was ill, we didn't spend very much to cover the hospital expenses. Anyway, there appears to be no doubt that I am disagreeable in my brothers' eye. I'll have my revenge on them for what they did."

"Aye, there's the rub. Your temperament is so awful that nobody could get along with you. No wonder Mother couldn't love you deeply. Don't bother me about the matter of the property," Lian-Wu said and then angrily walked toward his piano room. Only this music area could smooth his feeling.

Lian-Si often had been told that he was very quick-tempered, but he also had been praised because he never hesitated to do what was right. For example, he was always arguing with his mother about his half-brother, Lee Lian-Yuan, for his family rights.

"All members of this family are snobs except Lian-Wu," Lian-Si thought. But he also couldn't accept this younger brother, Lian-Wu, with his artistic temperament. After his father passed away, Lian-Si really became an orphan.

He considered his position to be very difficult in this family. He needed to arrange his life better. He should find someone to discuss his problem with.

"But domestic shame should not be made public," he said to himself. "Yes, I know! I should visit my uncle, Lee Zi-Shan. Only he understands my family, and he might give me his good opinion." He suddenly remembered Auntie Chu-Su's gallbladder disease and knew he must visit them.

"I am going to Uncle's place," Lian-Si said to his wife, Cai-Lian, who was busy outside doing housework.

"Will you come back for dinner?" Cai-Lian asked worriedly. She knew from his expression that some trouble had happened.

"Where is E-Cai?" He couldn't see their pedicab driver. He didn't answer his wife's question.

"He is driving Mother to the temple this morning."

Lian-Si walked to the end of the lane. He called another pedicab and jumped on it.

"Go to Penghu Society!"

On the way, he heard a voice, "Brother! Brother!"

Lian-Si looked around. He waved excitedly as he recognized who had called him.

"Lian-Shi! Where are you going? You are completely blushing and sweaty." Lian-Shi was his uncle's fourth son.

He told the driver to stop and then moved over as he said to his cousin, "Jump up and take a seat. I'm on my way to your home."

"I just went to Uncle Opium to ask for some opium ashes."

"For what?"

"My mom is still in pain from her disease. The opium ashes can stop the pain."

"She must go to see a doctor. Are opium ashes effective?"

"My papa asked this question, but my mom insisted. She said if she uses the ashes she doesn't need to pay."

"How about our grandmother?"

Lian-Shi shook his head and said, "When her feet hurt, she cries loudly that she wants to go back to Penghu, especially after Uncle passed away."

By now, the smoke coal from Chu-Su's fire filled their noses, and they began to cough; Lian-Shi jumped out of the cart and ran toward his mom as happy as a clam. "Mom! I got the opium ashes. And look! My brother Lian-Si has come to our home."

"Auntie Chu-Su! I heard you are not feeling well."

"Don't worry about it. It is just an old illness." Even as Chu-Su said that, she still couldn't hide the pain on her face.

"Is Uncle Zi-Shan at home?"

"He is doing a morning shift. He will come home after three o'clock," Chu-Su put down her fan and pulled up her sleeve to wipe the sweat from her forehead. Then she said, "Come see Grandma."

Near the window of Grandma's room there were so many things piled up that there was barely room to pass. Because of her useless legs and being hunchbacked, Shiang-Sao looked like the portrait of a bowl looking down on the gloomy room.

"Mother, Lian-Si has come to visit you." Chu-Su stroked Shiang-Sao's hair, then she asked Lian-Si to stay with Shiang-Sao while she went to prepare the dinner.

"My dear grandson, come here, let Grandma touch you." Her forehead covered by a black kerchief, Shiang-sao raised her head and tried to open her muddy eyes, her two hands danced in the air as they sought her grandson.

Shiang-Sao got a grip on Lian-Si's hands.

"Grandma, I am here. I have been so insulted all my life by my bully brothers," Lian-Si complained tearfully.

"There is sibling rivalry again?"

"It is a long story."

"There should be patience among siblings. Everyone must be open-minded."

"They don't act like my siblings. They made a fool of me. I feel like an outsider in this family."

"Don't get angry. Keep your balance. You have a good heart, but you should control your bad temper. Otherwise, you will always be at a disadvantage," Shiang-Sao strongly advised him.

"Only a saint could keep his temper under such irritating circumstances," Lian-Si said. After thinking for a moment, he added, "I want to go to court to sue them for invading and occupying my property."

"You must look before you leap. Let your mother deal with them."

"It is useless. They are a group of bullies, and they are united in fighting me," Lian-Si said. "Grandma, maybe one day you could go to court to help me by testifying on this matter for me."

"Go to court?" Shiang-Sao was used to crying a lot, but now she was crying seriously. "I don't know what evil things I did in my previous life that I keep experiencing so many evil events in this life."

"Grandma, don't cry. I just want to ask for justice."

6-2

The Wishes of Daughters

One August noon, after a breeze of drizzly days had soaked the golden straw in the field, everywhere you could smell the fragrance of land and rice straw.

Zi-Shan rode a bicycle on Shin-Tyon Road through a field of straw on his way from his job at the aluminum company. On the right side, there was a field of harvested rice. On the left, there was a series of Japanese houses that was built during the period of Japan colonization. After the Japanese returned to their own country, these houses were sold several times by the United Society.

Zi-Shan stopped in front of one of these Japanese-style houses. He walked into the courtyard. He furrowed his brow a little when he saw how dirty the area was because he was obsessive about cleanliness.

He didn't enter the house at once. Instead of entering through the front door, Zi-Shan walked to the west side of the house where he could enter his mother's room through her outside door. He could see his dear, cruel mama, faster than if he entered from the front door. But before he entered the room, he heard Mother's grateful voice.

"Mrs. Chang, you don't need to bring a gift to me, your visit is our honor," Shiang-Sao said.

"E-Ma! I will visit you again, take care!" A woman of medium height, a geography teacher at a female high school, just wanted to leave; but she saw Lee Zi-Shan entering, so she said to Shiang-Sao, "Here you are, your son has come home."

"Zi-Shan, come quickly. You need to fully appreciate Mrs. Chang."

Chu-Su came from the kitchen; Zi-Shan came from outside, and they both said to this Chinese woman, "Mrs. Chang, please accept our sincere thanks."

"Don't do that. Actually, I did appreciate your compassion when you protected us against a group of Taiwanese people who chased us after the Japanese left. Otherwise, we would have had a sad life."

"Oh, that was a terrible event. Why can't human beings live in peace together?" Chu-Su said. As they talked about those dark days, Chu-Su's heart still fluttered with fear.

"Mrs. Chang, I will make a house payment to you next week." Zi-Shan gave Mrs. Chang a charming smile.

"Zi-Shan, don't worry about the money. Today I'm here to visit your mother, not for money."

"You gave us a great deal when you sold us this wonderful house for only $20,000. Thank you so much."

"I should say thanks. Now that I have cash, I can deal with my school project more smoothly."

"Where is the location that you and your husband want to found a school?" Chu-Su asked.

"Where we want to build the school is near the Big Bei Lake."

"Founding a school is really a great undertaking!" Zi-Shan said in a respectful posture.

"Yes! There are a multitude of things. Lucky for me, I have several nice friends to help me. The school name we have chosen for the time being is Kaohsiung Private Female Shu-De Junior School."

"Perfect! According to your behavior, your plan will be successful."

"Thank you so much. On the other hand, I have never seen a more warmhearted Taiwanese couple than you are."

The couple and visitor who mutually respected and loved each other walked outside. Suddenly, Mrs. Chang remembered something she had read in the newspaper, and she pulled out the newspaper from her handbag.

"Here is news about your elder brother in the Taiwanese newspaper. Look at this. *'After the millionaire, Lee Zi-Tian, passed away, his children became embroiled in sibling rivalry for his property and are going to sue each other.'*"

"Shame on us! Our family matter is presented to the public. However, I asked some of Penghu's most powerful people to solve this problem. Finally, it is coming to an end. I hope they can stop the quarrel between brothers and let their father rest in peace," Zi-Shan said.

Then he took the newspaper cautiously from Mrs. Chang as he bowed to bid her adieu.

On the other side of the house, Lian-Zi; her sister's daughter, Wan-Jun; and her elder brother's son, E-Lin, returned home after playing water games and catching dragonflies from the so-called pond that was actually a big hole made by a US military bomb during World War Two.

"Auntie, I have caught a dragonfly. If you like, I can give it to you." Jin-Hua wanted to please her auntie.

"Auntie, I have also caught a big one for you." E-Lin wanted to please his auntie too.

"Don't quarrel with each other, otherwise, I will not love you anymore." Although Lian-Zi said that, she was enjoying her nephew and niece's struggle for her favor. She felt like a little mother.

E-Lin was Lian-Zi's eldest brother's son. Lian-Zi's mother, Chu-Su, had been looking after E-Lin and his sister, Jin-Hua, since her sister-in-law passed away. Thinking about her eldest brother, Lian-Zi became angry because he was her hero when she was younger, but now he was becoming a very bad person.

Her eldest brother, Lian-Ren, was a confirmed gambler. His poor wife had needed to work hard to make money, but after they had been married five years, she was killed in a sea accident trying to make more money for their family.

Their parents, Zi-Shan and Chu-Su, thought their gambler son would reform after his wife's death. But he didn't repent his past mistakes, and his behavior became even worse. He always threatened his parents that he would sell his children to pay a gambling debt. Now his parents bore a bitter hatred toward him.

His younger sister, Lian-Zi, realized how repugnant he was. When he appeared at home, the surroundings immediately darkened in his shady presence. Despite Mother's disagreement, he still often came home to look for some food to eat in the kitchen. He dreaded seeing his father, so he would only step in when Father wasn't at home.

One day, in the afternoon when Lian-Zi returned home from school, she saw her eldest brother in the kitchen looking for food again. She checked the time and knew that Father would soon be home. She feared Father would fly into a rage when he saw this situation, so she shouted the first thing that came into her head, "Get out as soon as possible! Father will come back soon."

As long as her parents hated Lian-Ren, Lian-Zi would also dislike him. What gave her the most happiness? Of course, she wished her parents would have longevity so that she could hum her love forever to them. All in all, she adored her parents so much that she couldn't stand the thought of losing them. She feared her parents' disappearance one day. There was a saying, *The sound of a crow means a death will occur*; thus, she hated the sound of crows.

But it happened that after playing for a long time with her nephew and niece around the field and pond, Lian-Zi suddenly heard the sound of a crow. She dropped several finished paper ships and hurried home. She felt relieved when she saw her parents were safe and sound, but suddenly, she suffered from serious stomach pains.

She didn't know how long she had slept and how worried her parents had been when she woke up to the heavy smell of a medicinal herb. She opened her eyes to see Mother beside her. She felt comfortable now.

"Mama," she called lightly from her bed.

"Lian-Zi is awake!" Chu-Su said joyfully.

"The medicine will be finished quickly, but I need more dry straw." Zi-Shan was making medicine for his dear daughter. He was carefully looking at the heating control of the stove since the fire couldn't be too strong or too weak and had to last for three hours. This kind of special cure for someone with a stomachache was a secret recipe that required a lot of patience.

The memory of nameless days, day after day, clung to Chu-Su's heart like moss around an old tree. Her life was a series of undertakings whether inside her soul or in the outside world. For example, her oldest son, Lian-Ren, was a gambling hooligan; her only daughter, Lian-Zi, was a small and sickly girl. Chu-Su not only worried about her children but she also needed to supervise her grandchildren; additionally, her mother-in-law was in pain day and night. Thus her own gallbladder disease was hidden. Nobody knew the mother and grandmother of this family was completely exhausted.

But one afternoon, Chu-Su suddenly passed out on the doorsill while she was helping Lian-Si's wife haggle over prices to buy their new house. As if awakening from a dream after the accident happened, Chu-Su was told by her doctor that she must not work so hard anymore.

"I am in the hospital!" Chu-Su sat up anxiously from her hospital bed when she saw the nurse.

"Auntie, do you feel better? I'm going to give you an injection to help you," Exue, the nurse, said gently.

"Mama, Ms. Exue is especially looking after you," Lian-Li gazed at Exue with great admiration in his heart as he introduced the beautiful nurse to his mother.

"Exue, Exue, oh no," Chu-Su talked to herself, trying not to shiver. "The pumpkin grievance?"

"Mother, are you okay?" Lian-Li asked worriedly.

Chu-Su gradually calmed herself down. Looking at this Exue, who was carefully injecting her, she could see that she was significantly different from that unlucky girl in her hometown, Waian. When she was more conscious of the reality of her situation, she put a smile on her weary face. But then she added, "It is too expensive staying in the hospital so I want to go home."

"When you are better. Otherwise, you need to stay at the hospital," Lian-Li said, and he looked at Exue, hoping she could also advise his mother to stay in the hospital longer.

"The surgery hasn't healed yet, so you must stay here for several days," Exue said; at the same time, she took a three-foot long red rubber tube connected to an inhaler. Although she was busy with her work, she still could feel admiring glances from the patient's son. She was a little bit shy and became somewhat agitated, but somehow she managed to stay calm so she could do her job. She softly said to the patient, "Doctor said that we have to draw out some bile from your gallbladder and reduce your pain."

And then, Exue put the tube into Chu-Su's mouth. Looking like a mother trying to keep her child calm, she said, "I will help you to advance the tube. You should swallow the tube gradually. It will hurt, but you must endure the pain to swallow the whole tube."

Chu-Su almost suffocated from this procedure. She swallowed the tube while in tears.

"I am willing to die of this illness to avoid swallowing this kind of thing again."

Nearly one year later, Lian-Li married Exue. It was true that if there wasn't pain to hollow out the heart, there wouldn't be space to fill it with happiness. Due to Chu-Su's disease, Exue became her daughter-in-law. But Chu-Su hadn't fully recovered from her illness yet.

A cheery wedding was held at the Lee family's house on Shin-Tyan Road. The new couple, Lian-Li and Exue, held a tray of sugar for their departing guests as they said farewell. After being dressed in formal evening attire, Chu-Su now wore casual clothes so she could clean up the house.

A lot of guests congratulated Exue on her happy marriage. They said, "Your groom is handsome and intelligent. Your mother-in-law is a diligent and kind person. You are a lucky woman."

But Exue disliked her mother-in-law going barefoot at the end of the wedding feast to do a cleaning job like a common villager. She looked for her own mother. At that time, a woman wearing splendid jewels approached the newlywed couple; Exue introduced her to the other guests, "This is my mother."

"Although the parents of my son-in-law are Penghu people, their family's financial situation is very good, and one of their houses has been rented by an American. In addition, my son-in-law works in a bank. You know the bank's salary is perfect." Exue's mother was satisfied with her daughter's marriage.

On the other hand, Chu-Su couldn't tell why her heart drooped in silence after she became a mother-in-law. Maybe it was about all the little needs she never asked for so that no one knew or recalled what she needed. She had sung the song of the days and nights. She suddenly felt old and weary.

One day, she walked to Lu Shan's grocery store.

"Sister Shan, recently I have been very tired. I have often dreamed about my parents and my brothers," she said weakly.

"Chu-Su, it is time for you to enjoy life in comfort and happiness after your diligent days and nights."

"Alas! I thought my third son, Lian-Li, was one of the best children who I could depend on, but after he married, he is becoming his wife's son. Now he gives money to me less and less."

"Don't be frustrated! I still believe he is a nice son."

"Yes, it might be that the bigger the hope, the bigger the disappointment."

"Don't worry. You also have a wonderful daughter. You are held in deep affection by Lian-Zi."

"Useless! You know that the daughter goes to others the day she gets married. Yet the daughter-in-law is ours because she married into our family." The atmosphere was too oppressive, so Chu-Su changed the topic. She asked how her sister Shan's business was doing.

"It is not too bad. I do appreciate you. If it hadn't been for Zi-Shan's and your help, we couldn't open this grocery store," Lu-Shan said sincerely.

"Don't say that. We are the same family."

"Auntie Chu-Su, drink some tea." Lu Shan's daughter-in-law, Mei-Qi, brought a pot of tea for Chu-Su.

"Where is Lian-Yuan?" Chu-Su asked.

"He left early this morning for Harmarsu to buy some fresh goods."

"Sister Shan, you are doing better. I knew that Lian-Yuan would be an industrious man, so you don't need to get into a sibling rivalry for property. Depending on ourselves is the most important aspect of a successful lifestyle."

"I really admire Auntie's behavior," Mei-Qi said. "I heard Auntie's forefather was a scholar. No wonder you have a very different personality from others."

Talking about her auntie Chu-Su, Mei-Qi had a lot of things she wanted to express. For example, Chu-Su helped their family through their ups and downs and helped her to find a buyer to buy her own milk. Chu-Su and her husband were the saviors of their lives.

Hearing her family of origin mentioned, Chu-Su became sad. She stood up and looked at the many goods in the store's display window. She told Shan, "One of these days, you will have to prepare thirty gifts for me to send to my Penghu friends and relatives. Even though Zi-Shan has a strong objection to my plan to move the graves of my parents and brothers in Penghu, I've already decided to return to Penghu to deal with this important issue. My Zhu family must continue forever even though there are no longer any males, so I have a responsibility for this family."

"You are still ill. Don't rush into this business of moving graves. It is a big issue."

"I insist on this idea," Chu-Su was holding her stomach and bending over. Then with a sigh, she said, "Let me take a rest first, then I'll shop later."

There was a saying that "the world kissed her soul with its pains asking for its repayment in the form of a kind and pleasant face." Did this describe the life of Chu-Su?

6-3

Reconstructing a Grave

Autumn 1958

Outside spread the sea and night—the infinite solitude of dark fathomless waters—but one could not be quite sure of that in the dismal cabin that reeked with the smell of fish, gasoline, and saltwater. A group of homesick people and a lot of goods were being ferried by the ship, *Tai-Peng-Lun*, from Kaohsiung to Penghu. As a powerful wind of the Taiwan Strait rocked the ocean, the whole ship rolled with a monotonous wail as it swung to and fro.

A wood statuette of Mazu, Goddess of the Sea, was fastened on a bracket against the fore ship partition, in a place of honor. By now Chu-Su, with a heavy heart, couldn't help putting her hands together to pray when she saw Mazu. Mazu, Goddess of the Sea, was also the protective god of fisherman. She looked after all living and dead creatures of the sea everywhere and throughout time.

Chu-Su changed her sitting position and looked at the big bag of gifts she had brought. She and Zi-Shan had had a long quarrel about her taking this trip. She had always been obedient to her husband's wishes, but finally, she had insisted on returning to

Penghu to reconstruct her ancestors' grave. She absolutely needed to do her duty as a daughter because her family had no one else left, male or female, in this world.

Chu-Su was getting sleepy as the ship continued to move slowly and steadily. But she was awoken by a strong sour smell that meant someone was getting seasick. She felt grateful to her parents who had given her the good health to avoid seasickness. She stood up and walked on to the deck for a breath of fresh air. Facing the ocean, she was filled with emotion because the sea triggered so many childhood memories, both happy and sad.

Now the moon appeared in the sky and feebly lit up the surging water. Chu-Su's eyes could not see what lay before her as her mind became a quivering mirror that reflected her many sorrowful memories, such as her brother and friends being killed in shipwrecks. It was so long ago, but there was no limit to the expanse of the unknown underworld where her brother and friends now stood. Now she needed to take a rest. She looked like an eighty-year-old woman as she shakily entered the cabin.

She settled down near the statuette of Mazu, who was said to protect fishermen and sailors. Mazu also had a significant influence on East Asian sea culture, especially in China and Taiwan. It was said that Lin Moniang (Mazu's name when she was a human being) resolutely plunged into the South China Sea to identify with her father who was killed by the sea. So she drowned herself at the age of twenty-seven. Chu-Su knew she didn't have Lin Moniang's great courage and determination even though she loved her father very much as well. Lin-Moniang became a spirit after she died, with the power to rescue thousands and thousands of people lost at sea, yet there were still a lot of sea accidents. Did the Goddess of the Sea also lack great courage sometimes?

At last Chu-Su arrived at the land she missed so much—Waian, Penghu. Chu-Su's tears flowed more and more, expressing both sorrow and joy. She remembered visiting Waian, Penghu, ten years ago when she, Zi-Shan, and her mother-in-law had attended Zi-Shan's brother's wedding. Ten years! What had happened during these ten years in her home country?

She had a strong desire for her dear Zhu family to have a nice place to live. Finally, after a long, hard search, she found a plot in the tomb area between Waian and Neian, a nearby village. In this bleak area, all things seemed rougher and more desolate. The violent sea winds that made village people stronger, made shorter, lower, and fatter plants, especially many kinds of prickly plants that could be found everywhere. As a result, the grave workers' hands were bloodstained as they removed these prickly plants from the new grave site.

"It is a really difficult job." The workers grasped their hoes and complained to Chu-Su.

"Please help me with this. You know I looked hard to find this good location that has such good feng shui."

"Is it acceptable to put several generations into one grave?"

"I am living in Taiwan. I can't visit them very often here. I guess it is fine to let them enjoy family happiness forever rather than living individual lonely afterlives." Chu-Su faced the northern ocean to look out at the boundless waters as if expressing her wish to go to another world.

She had arranged for a gravestone, "The Zhu Family Mausoleum," that would be set near the sea but facing the road. Thus her ancestors would see all the situations of their home country both on water and land.

The mountainless land was surrounded by the sea and smooth hills. It was also the midpoint between Waian and Neian, and the tomb area was near the historical site of Si Islet Western Fort. As a result, Chu-Su met many people as they happened to pass by the new grave site. They could be seen from a long way off, walking through the bare country, outlined and magnified against the high sealine. Fishers with the openness of the great ocean wished her good day as they passed by her. Chu-Su was called a Taiwan-Penghu woman by these friendly folks. She raised her hand in response.

She looked at both land and sea, trying to think of something to talk about with the workers. Suddenly, she saw a person who was holding a water bottle walking toward her. Broad, sunburned face, manly and determined under his bamboo hat, Yang-En had loved her over several decades.

"Chu-Su, please take a rest! It is too hot to work under the big sun," Yang-En advised.

"Don't worry. I am okay. It was hard to come here, but now that I know my dear family will be together, I feel as free as the air I breathe."

"Don't cry again. Your eyes will swell up."

"I do appreciate your help. Otherwise, I couldn't handle this family matter at all."

"Don't say that. Your relatives are my relatives too."

Chu-Su knew Yang-En's mind very well, but she feared him speaking out about their relationship. She rearranged paper money on the grave to avoid looking at him.

Yang-En took the money from his pocket. "This is your money that you always asked someone to bring from Taiwan for me." Then he added, "You'll need to spend a lot of money on the reconstruction of your family grave."

Chu-Su looked disapprovingly at Yang-En as she returned the money to him.

"Chu-Su, don't remain a stranger to me. I always feel like a son-in-law worshipping at your parents' house."

"Your deep affection burdens me. You should be married." Chu-Su ran close to the ocean and started to weep uncontrollably.

"Where can I find a person like you?" He couldn't conceal his love for Chu-Su.

"Gossip is a fearful thing. I can't give you anything. You need to go on with your life." Chu-Su spoke as softly as the sea wind blew. Did Yang-En hear her words?

"I heard that Lian-Yi got married. Is the daughter-in-law okay?" Yang-En asked in a low voice as he poured water into a bowl for Chu-Su.

Chu-Su felt like her heart had been stabbed by a knife. She couldn't even look at Yang-En.

"Zi-Shan is not a fool. I guess he should know who Lian-Yi's father is," Yang-En declared.

Chu-Su couldn't say anything in response to Yang-En. She felt a sharp pain in her stomach. Her words were choked by sobbing. Then suddenly, she felt as if the sky and earth were spinning round as she fainted.

"Ah!" Yang-En reached for Chu-Su as he said, "Chu-Su, I have no idea what I am talking about. Don't worry, my dear."

There was melancholy in the wind and sorrow in the sea at this Waian, Penghu, shore. At another shore in Kaohsiung, a raging family conflict had been ignited by Zi-Tian's son, Lian-Er, who had come back from Japan two years ago and then was elected to serve on the local Alliance for Self-Governance during the period of Japanese colonization.

In fact, even though this alliance hadn't had much effect, it had given the Taiwanese people the chance to participate in Japanese Congress; additionally, it also spoke out against Japan and for the liberation of Taiwan by the Americans. But the Japanese had given up their power too late; Japan's unconditional surrender didn't happen until 1945. Then Chiang Kai-shek's national Chinese government (Kuomintang) came to Taiwan from China after the Communists took over China in 1949.

However, many of the Kuomintang officials wanted to extort money from the Lee family after the newspaper reported on the millionaire, Lee Zi-Tian, when he passed away; his children became embroiled in sibling rivalry as they sued each other for their father's wealth. Unfortunately, Lee Zi-Tian's son, Lian-Er, being a former member of the Alliance for Self-Governance, also came to the attention of Kuomintang. Lian-Er was caught in the glare of a fat-cat government that eyed him like a tiger stalking its prey.

Then one morning, exactly at sunrise, Zi-Tian's concubine, Gao Zhao, carrying a gift, suddenly showed herself at her brother-in-law Lee Zi-Shan's home, which she had always looked down upon and rarely visited before.

Lian-Zi was teaching her nephews to speak the national Chinese language in the front yard. She was studying at high school where she was now taught to be fluent in the Chinese language as if it was a great honor. While she was explaining to her nephews that speaking out in the Taiwanese language would be punished, she saw Gao-Zhao coming to visit them. She spoke fluently in Chinese to tell her mother even though Chu-Su didn't understand the Chinese language.

Then she very politely welcomed their guest in the style of a good student as she continued to speak in Chinese.

Chu-Su had just come home from Penghu several days ago. She was lying down on her bed dispiritedly.

"Chu-Su, are you okay?" Gao-Zhao said.

"This is a rare honor. You are most welcome!" Chu-Su was very surprised by Gao-Zhao's visit.

"We are close relatives, so we don't need polite greetings," Gao-Zhao hurried on to make her point. "I want you and Zi-Shan to help me because my son, Lian-Er, is in trouble."

"What is the problem?"

"Ah, it is a long story." Gao-Zhao breathed a sigh of regret and explained, "Lian-Er was interrogated by the police for over six hours. It is said that some people don't even come back home again after they are interrogated."

"Don't worry. Lian-Er has already come back." Chu-Su comforted her sister-in-law. As they talked about this sensitive topic, they lowered their voices.

"Lian-Er is a lawyer, but it is a hard job at this time. He is often threatened by government officials. I don't know if he gave offense to someone, but we haven't received rent for over half a year since our house was rented by an officer's relative. They even said this house was a public building so they don't need to pay. Government officials are really bullying us!" Gao-Zhao ignored all the pain on Chu-Su's face as she talked quickly and endlessly. She gazed around, and then she whispered in Chu-Su's ear, "It is my feeling that the Japanese ruled better than the Chinese."

"Yes, life is really difficult now," Chu-Su said slowly like a ghost.

"To make a long story short, my main purpose is to ask you to tell the officer that the house is yours, and now you need to use this house because of your son's marriage." Gao-Zhao wanted to make a tool of Chu-Su.

Gao-Zhao hadn't finished her words when Chu-Su suddenly seemed to be under a spell. She had changed into another person whose lips moved crazily and whose eyes stared unseeingly. Gao-Zhao stared at her, frozen with shock and then yelled for help. At the right moment, Zi-Shan came back home from work, and he also brought a psychic to help Chu-Su. Actually, since she had come back from Penghu, Chu-Su's strange behavior had occurred several times.

After each episode, Chu-Su was either sick in bed or wandered around like a lost soul babbling nonsense.

It was said that she had been wrong to construct the new grave for her family.

It was said that her family's ghosts had been released back to this world.

There were many people talking about Chu-Su's situation.

However, on another day, Chu-Su was very quiet, even singing an old song. It seemed like the world had opened its heart of light in the morning. A neighbor, a high-level government executive, warmly invited Chu-Su's newly married third son, Lian-Li, and his wife to go to a movie with him. When Chu-Su saw that Lian-Li didn't want to go, she anxiously urged Lian-Li to accompany his wife to the movie.

"You two should go. Don't refuse the officer's kind invitation!"

"Why did he invite us to go to a movie?" Lian-Li asked his beautiful wife.

"He might appreciate an injection from me."

"I don't want to go. Let Lian-Zi go with you."

"Okay. Watching movies is my favorite activity." Lian-Zi was so excited. She also saw Mother smiling and nodding at her.

The government executive, Exue, and Lian-Zi took the private car of the port bureau chief to the theater to see the movie *The Great Waltz.*

Just when they were deeply involved in the film, they suddenly saw on the right side of the movie screen, these words: "Lian-Zi, your family has an emergency. Please go home as soon as possible."

They ran from the movie theater and rushed to the Kaohsiung Hospital.

"What happened? Is something wrong with my mom?" Lian-Zi cried out as she rushed toward her mother's hospital room. A crowd of nurses stood in the hall where they were sadly discussing her mother. Lian-Zi and Exue waited in the doorway of the hall, shivering and listening, wanting to go to Chu-Su, but afraid to go lest there be some sight there more terrifying than Lian-Zi could bear.

"She was found too late to rescue. We are so sorry!" a nurse said.

Lian-Zi swung around, "What did you say? How is my mother?"

"She passed away before she arrived at the hospital."

Lian-Zi heard a rustle of things behind her sadness of heart, but she couldn't see them. She hoped the thick cloud would melt the rain instead of her tears because she couldn't cry her heart out at this moment.

Zi-Shan's home on Shin-Tyan Road was abuzz with grieving, praying, and supportive relatives and friends.

Lian-Zi wept as she held her mother's body tightly. "Mother, how can you leave me like this?"

Shiang-Sao used to moan in pain, but now she couldn't cry at all because she was so shocked by the sudden death of her daughter-in-law.

Many friends placed their money in front of a picture of Chu-Su that represented her spirit in gratitude for all the help Chu-Su had given them while she was alive.

The Lee family was devastated by the death of Chu-Su. They were also very worried about Lian-Zi's abnormal behavior, but they didn't know what to do about it. First, she fought against priests who wanted to put her dear mother's body in a coffin. Then she refused to let workers place her mother in the ground. Finally, she accepted her father's promise that he would build a small cabin beside her mother's house so that she could stay close to her mother forever.

People can recover from physical injuries, but emotional traumas can stay with them for the rest of their lives; in fact, Zi-Shan felt like he needed to be both father and mother as he tried to comfort his shattered daughter.

There has to be a peaceful place to let people who are enduring a great, bitter loss take a rest. It is as if when a difficult day is done, he or she needs to be like a boat resting on the beach, listening to the dance music of the tide in the evening.

A half a year after her daughter-in-law passed away, Shiang-Sao was again singing the music of the Nanyue program that she had almost forgotten about as her most interesting hobby. But she would be in tears before she could finish the song. Then she had no more tears to shed and no longer had the energy to finish the whole program. Finally, she saw her life reflected in well water, creating a wonderful circle like the moon of her hometown; her life was reflected in well water. At last, she was relieved of the heaviness of her crooked body as it now became a peaceful soft body, easily lying down on the bed.

One misfortune had come on the back of another. In the space of a year, two lovely and important women in Zi-Shan's life had departed, one after another. The priest's bell rang out again in the Lee family home, and it seemed like the language of empty eternity. Zi-Shan held a funerary bamboo streamer as he knelt to pray for his deceased mother and cried silent tears.

After Shiang-Sao passed away, Zi-Shan remembered his little brother, Zi-Song, in Penghu; and now this brother was coming to Kaohsiung. When he arrived at Zi-Shan's house, he talked cheerfully and humorously, in complete disregard of the placement of their mother's coffin in the front hall.

"Are you a heartless animal?" Zi-Shan was very angry with his little brother. "Is it possible that you have no tears when you see that your mother has passed away?"

"Mother's eyes only looked at you. I am nothing."

Zi-Shan slapped Zi-Song hard across the face. Suddenly, his little brother seemed to understand what was happening. He rubbed his red cheeks and quickly walked to their mother's coffin, crying out for her.

Then they were together burning silver joss paper (called *feet paper*) near the feet of their mother in the hope that Mother's soul could use the silver joss paper as money to buy her way to heaven and lit oil lamps (called *feet lamps*) in the same place, in the hope that her soul's path would be brightened. They were performing a ceremony for their mother, hoping she could walk to the land of purity.

Are pain and love only separated by a thin line?

The two grandfathers, Zi-Shan and Zi-Song, held each other and cried.

What is life? Does a life only consist of a passerby stopping for a moment, nodding to the world and then leaving?

"Am I always going to be in a perpetual state of shock in my life?" Zi-Shan thought.

In front of his house on Shin-Tyan Road, Zi-Shan bowed his head as he went down on his knees and took three steps toward his relatives and friends to thank them for coming to celebrate the life of his mother.

It is true; death belongs to life just as much as birth does. Birth and death are both as necessary to life as raising and lowering our feet are to walking.

6-4

An Old Haunt of Childhood

Summer 1978

"*Penghu is surrounded by the sea so fishing is the main economic activity, but there are no paddy fields and, hence, no production of rice or plants here.*" *This comment is printed in the records of Penghu. However, fishermen have to watch the weather while farmers can grow diverse plants for food throughout the seasons.*

"Look at that mother and son who are working in the field," Zi-Shan said to his children, who had accompanied him on his trip to Waian where he grew up. Penghu was a windy place, but stone walls around the fields provided protection against wind. Thus everywhere, one still could see plants, even on barren land. The people of Penghu wisely consulted the farmer's almanac so that they knew what they could grow in each season. "Look! The fields of Waian seemed to be framed side by side, like the bureau drawers in Mother's room, hiding amazing things."

Zi-Shan walked hurriedly to the mother and son. He took one red five-dollar bill from his pocket and said, choking with sobs, "Hi, kid, I want to give you this money so you can go buy a real fish and enjoy it with your mother." He looked at the child as if he was seeing himself when he was a boy, and he saw the woman as if she was his long-suffering mother.

Dreams and visions of home haunted his brain; in the homeland, beloved villagers' faces bent over him. He was in a never-ending hallucination through which apparitions of relatives and friends of his childhood floated.

"Mama, come here quickly!" the child yelled out for his mother to see what Zi-Shan had given him.

"Uncle Zi-Shan, we welcome you and your children to Waian," said the mother respectfully. She was masked, wore a big bamboo hat, and carried a sword.

"You know me?" Slowly Zi-Shan's excited brain was becoming calmer and clearer.

"I'm the daughter-in-law of Wen-Men. The whole village knew that you were coming to Waian."

"Are you Wen-Men's daughter-in-law!? Wen-Men was my fishing friend, but I could never find as much seafood on the beach as him." Zi-Shan was falling back into his memories again. He often acted more strangely and excitedly since he arrived in Waian three days ago.

"My papa said that we don't know what time you will come to our home for dinner," Wen-Men's daughter-in-law said.

"I will come there in a couple of days. I want to take my children to visit my ancestor's place and also see Wenwang Temple's reconstruction. I recently retired from the aluminum company in Kaohsiung."

"Look! This kind of Penghu melon is different from Taiwan. It has ten sides." Lian-Shi took a melon from a bamboo basket and said, "Thus it is called a *big mouth* just like women have."

"That's very funny," said Lian-Zi as she looked at the melon with an amazed expression on her face.

The daughter-in-law of Wen-Men took pride in talking with this group of people that had come from Taiwan. She said to

Zi-Shan, "It is said that you are a wonderful son and you have nice children as well."

"It is very difficult for me to express how I feel, but my children have always been good." Zi-Shan wanted to say more, but he couldn't because it was so hard to explain his feelings in just a few words. Many thoughts of his early childhood came back to him as he passed through the homeland, but they seemed far away, now hidden by his love for his mother and wife.

"Papa, do you want to take a rest?" Lian-Zi saw her father becoming lost in sadness again. She hurried forward to check on him. After her mother passed away, Lian-Zi had been inspired and encouraged by her father. Now she needed to look after Father, who often felt depressed and talked less and less.

"My dear, you are married now. You should care more about your husband's family than your original Lee family." Zi-Shan always warned Lian-Zi not to focus on him.

"Do you want me to forget you and just focus on my husband's family? If so, I wish I had never married!"

"If you were a boy that would be nice, but alas . . ."

By tradition, the wife must pay more attention to her husband's family than to her own. Lian-Zi always protested against this to her father as complete nonsense.

Lian-Zi had lived in constant fear of losing her parents from childhood. As she grew older, even though she became more open-minded and she came to a better understanding of the variability of things in life, she still couldn't stand any heavy wind and rain. Lian-Zi was always filled with emotion when she thought about this issue especially after she had arrived in Waian, Penghu, where her parents had grown up.

Lian-Zi had always been attracted by the beauty of the series of islands that was Penghu, a window facing the sea. Whole ocean-loads of coral were condensed into pure beaches; in front of the Wenwang shrine, often the last stop before leaving home, travelers or fishermen placed their palms together peacefully. Gazing at Penghu's sandy beaches, blue skies, crystal-clear seas, and seashores of stunning natural beauty, Lian-Zi knew that her family's ancestors had lived in this wonderful place; and this was the place that their father had longed for, year after year, day after day.

This summer, to make their father happy and share their memories of their mother, Zi-Shan's children accompanied him on a trip to his hometown. But they did not expect Waian to be such an appealing place. Every evening, the Lee family enjoyed Waian's beautiful sunsets, and this place of their ancestors satisfied the long-held curiosity of Zi-Shan's children about their father's birthplace while the people of Waian finally got to know these Penghu children who had been born in Kaohsiung.

"There, now what did I tell you?" Lian-Zi said teasingly to her second oldest brother, Lian-Yi, who originally didn't want to come here. "You now see that I was right, don't you?"

"Over ten years ago, when I visited here with Mother, I had a terrible experience. There was no power, no water, and no toilets. There were many houseflies when we ate meals. Moreover, it took over twenty-four hours by ship to come here. Even though they have improved things like the Penghu Great Bridge, which was once the longest bridge stretching over the sea in the Far East and we can now take a one-hour bus from Magong to Waian, there is still poor sanitation." But Lian-Yi still preferred material comforts to the scenery of Penghu.

"Although there are some fields that are planted, there is too much empty land. It wastes energy," said Lian-Li, who was Lian-Zi's third oldest brother. He was a bank manager, so he also looked at financial possibilities rather than the beautiful views.

"How about we go swimming tomorrow?" said Lian-Shi, who was Lian-Zi's fourth oldest brother.

There they were—five people of two generations—Zi-Shan and his four children who had come with him. Among the four siblings, the mysteries of Waian, Penghu, made them very curious, but at the same time, gave them great pleasure.

They had been walking for the last hour, and then toward the northwest on the way to the Temple of Kind Navigation, they struggled up a grassy slope and headed into the wind with a lot of grasshoppers hopping in the air. They inhaled the healthy open breeze whistling up the trails to where they were going. Lian-Zi was holding on to Zi-Shan's arm both carefully and happily as they walked ahead of her brothers. It was very rare to see Father smile as he did now because after her mother and grandmother passed away, her father never smiled for a long, long time.

Now Zi-Shan was walking on the fields of his home country, but his heart had remained in Waian all along, so he had a feeling of really being at home at long last. He remembered his hard life with his mother when he was a child, yet he reflected that while suffering was painful, at the same time, it reflected the truth of life.

They arrived at an abandoned garden. Long grass sprawled over the field where enormous guavas had grown when they had been the source of livelihood for the Zhu family for generations.

"This area that was your grandpa Zhu Wang's garden of native guava has now become a field of garbage," Zi-Shan said. He couldn't restrain his melancholy and added to himself, "No living man can control all things because all things are governed by God imperceptibly but inexorably." Yet just as Li Yi-Ren had been helped by Lian-Zi's grandpa, Zhu Wang, then Li Yi-Ren saved Zi-Shan's life. Is God assuring that one good deed leads to another?

On this walking tour, they saw the scenery of Waian village and the local cattle pastures as well as the fake cannon built by the Japanese on the plateau and the oldest lighthouse in the Taiwan area, the Si Islet Lighthouse. Near the lighthouse was the tomb of Anatole Courbet, the French general who led his troops into battle with Penghu in the year 1885 and began the Sino-French War.

As the Lee family members continued their walking tour, they divided into two smaller groups; father and daughter, Zi-Shan and Lian-Zi, walked ahead while her brothers, Lian-Yi, Lian-Li, and Lian-Shi, stopped to talk near a small pond. They knew it was actually a big hole made by a US military bomb during the War World Two. But they didn't know that a lot of villagers, including their grandpa Zhu Wang, had been killed by the bombs on the grassy fields of Waian.

"I think we can agree that our retired father needs to take a long rest," Lian-Li said to his brothers. "Our younger sister, Lian-Zi, is already married, and Father wants to give his property to us."

"Our oldest brother, Lian-Ren, needs money very quickly, so he prefers cash." Lian-Yi longed to be taken seriously by his brothers, so he joined the discussion very carefully.

"So I will ask the bank to make a property assessment of father's three houses. We can divide it into four parts, and then we three will give him his share in the cash," Lian-Li said. Now that Father was living with Lian-Li, he was used to dealing with most things regarding his father.

"Does the property only go to us and not Lian-Zi?" Lian-Yi asked.

"Yes, because Father said that she's married to another family, so she can't have our family's property," Lian-Li answered.

"Really?!" Lian-Yi didn't believe this as he looked at Lian-Zi and their father who were so dependent on each other. Was it true that Father didn't want his property to go to his lovely daughter? After Lian-Yi thought for a while, he asked again, "How about father's pension?"

"I've deposited it in the bank to cover father's living expenses." Lian-Li's face looked like an ominous dark cloud. He didn't have a bomb, but there was still the smell of gunpowder.

The idea of history repeating itself is a profound issue, and philosophers are often perplexed about it, thinking about how everything is experienced over and over again and what this means to humankind. For example, at the time of war or any kind of threat, there are always many words or theories about these situations. Similarly, the brothers were still arguing with each other for their own individual benefit even though there wasn't actually an official war. But there had been an atmosphere of war among the brothers for many years.

"I welcome Father to live in my home," Lian-Shi said to ease the tense situation.

"It is okay. Father is used to living with me. It also gives me an opportunity to look after him," said Lian-Li sincerely. He was considered the best child of their father by Zi-Shan's friends. "Father often said that he wanted to move to Waian after he retired. If so, who could look after him? I think he should stay with me."

Lian-Yi had no idea about this issue of caring for their father. He only cared about whether Father would appoint crafty Lian-Li to handle his property. Would he be fair? How about the bank assessment? Would he play tricks?

In most lives, people argue with each other about their ideas until they grow weary of defending themselves, and their lives come to an end. Just as the world is becoming silent, we can already hear the crying of babies yet to come into this world. These babies will argue about their ideas, thus repeating the cycle.

What on earth is this world coming to?

Indeed, in the hospital, there is not much distance between the delivery room and the morgue. But why do we need to walk for such a long time from one to the other and find it so difficult to take the few steps of life?

In fact, Lian-Li was the most dutiful son in the Lee family, but now that he wore this royal crown, he just wanted to get off the seat of honor because he couldn't handle the heavy burden. Lian-Li had been transformed from a good son responsible for his parents' well-being into a hard-hearted man—at least in the eyes of his younger sister, Lian-Zi.

What was the problem? This is what the problem was:

One day, several years after the Penghu trip, Zi-Shan, in a state of stupor, rang the door of Lian-Li's house where he had lived for over ten years. He couldn't understand that he was now living with his second son, Lian-Yi, so he yelled, "Lian-Li, Exue, open the door and let me sleep in my own room." But his daughter-in-law, Exue, pretending to be a Japanese person, told Zi-Shan that he was at the wrong place because this house was already rented to someone else.

At this time, Lian-Li said nothing because he was lying down on his bed, too tired to get up. Needing to ease the heavy burden of looking after his troublesome, sick father, he had had decided it was time for his brothers to do their duty. He had arranged for Father to live with each son in turn, but it was difficult for his father to remember where he was staying.

"It is very strange. Why didn't Lian-Li tell me that the house was already rented to a Japanese person?" Zi-Shan asked, becoming more and more confused about what was actually happening.

"Old man, we should return home to sleep. It is midnight," said Yang Sang, who was employed by the Lee brothers to look after their sick father because he was getting lost so often.

"Return? Return to where? This is my place!" Zi-Shan struggled to free himself from Yang Sang's hands. He totally forgot what he'd just heard over the intercom.

"This is your third son's place. You are now staying at your second son's place," Yang Sang said patiently even though he yawned continually.

They couldn't enter the house, and Yang Sang held tightly onto Zi-Shan's bag that was full of his clothing. It was already midnight as they walked the streets to his second son's house. Zi-Shan's heart languished in silence and sorrow. He needed so little just to be where he wanted to be, but he could never get what he asked for.

The wind bellowed out in a deep voice with a tremolo of rage. Suddenly, a shadow came running to them from the opposite side of the street, yelling, "Papa! Papa! I am here."

"Lian-Zi, where are you going? My dear, I have looked for you so hard," said Zi-Shan when he realized clearly who it was. He stretched out his hands to hold his daughter as if she were a little child.

"It is not right that a man is not in his bed yet, but you two are still walking the streets. My poor father." Lian-Zi rubbed her father's ice-cold hands and put an overcoat on him. She couldn't say anything more. Her words were choked by sobbing.

"We have been walking for three hours on the street and never stopping. Although your third brother reminded me not to bring your father to his place whenever he wakes up, he wants to go home," Yang Sang complained to Lian-Zi.

"Sure, everyone wants their own place, especially if you are an old man," Lian-Zi said. She was overcome with sadness and crying again.

Zi-Shan was clearly confused as he helplessly followed Yang Sang and Lian-Zi walking to his second son's place. Then suddenly, Zi-Shan remembered something important. His look was very serious, like someone lost in faraway thoughts, as he said, "We must go home as quickly as possible. We need to look after your grandma. We have been away from home such a long time that she will find nobody beside her. It is no good."

When Zi-Shan was very tired, he would become dizzy and act strangely, saying things like "The time is up, I need to work. Where is your mama?" In fact, Grandma and Mother had passed away many years ago.

All things on earth easily decline, but only God can be evergreen. However, who can imagine the suffering of people as they go through birth, aging, sickness, and death? Lian-Zi grasped her angular father and looked up at the sky as she silently and sorrowfully questioned God.

When Zi-Shan had moved in with his second son, Lian-Yi, less than twenty-four hours ago, Lian-Yi had immediately complained about his father's actions. "What a mess! It's not my day. After Father comes here, everything is in disorder."

When Lian-Zi heard her second brother grumbling about their father, she wanted to say to him, "What are you talking about? The cause of the disorder is Father's illness. Let me tell you about a matter of principle: *Neither father nor king can abandon benevolence nor justice to behave likes beasts.* But Lian-Zi didn't say these words. Instead, she begged Lian-Yi to help. "Papa doesn't cause trouble intentionally. Please have patience with him."

Lian-Zi thought that the most important thing was taking good care of their father and helping him through his illness. She didn't want to have frost or snow falling over her father's declining years.

"It was unfair to deal out his wealth first. Now he is useless. As a result, he needs to be taken care of," Lian-Yi complained.

"Please lower your voice. If Father hears you, it will do him no good." Lian-Zi covered her father's ears with her hands to block out the cruel and coldhearted words of his second son.

"Don't worry about him. His brain has died already," Lian-Yi said.

As her brother's mean words merged with the loud barks of a dog outside, Lian-Zi felt that an opposing mind was like a knife with many blades, making her heart bleed like a river running through a snowy land.

Lian-Zi thought that her third brother's place was more suitable for her father because he was used to living there, and

Lian-Li knew much more about Father's habits than anyone else. She decided what she must do—she would beg Lian-Li to let Father return to his home to live. So she phoned him and said, "Brother! Did you know that when Father left the place where he was living for a long time, he felt anxious and unwilling to go to another place? How could he deal with going to a different place while struggling with his extreme illness? So I hope—"

"It is impossible! I am not the only one responsible for Father among all my brothers. Let them share the duty of caring for Father. Otherwise, they are just onlookers telling me what to do. It is unfair!" Lian-Li angrily responded to his younger sister's plea.

"If he can stay with you, in the daytime, he would have Yang Sang to accompany him, and at night he would have his grandsons to look after him," Lian-Zi pointed out to her brother. "We have to have a common consensus to help Father deal with his sickness and enjoy his declining years peacefully. We shouldn't give him a feeling of always being on the run."

"If he comes back here, he will always want to live here and won't want to move to another place. I am sick and tired of my brothers' arguing with everybody as they try to get a word in edgewise. Don't you see I am as sick as a dog?" Lian-Li said angrily and hung up on Lian-Zi.

After she put the phone down, Lian-Zi pondered: What on earth is this world coming to? Our parents willingly diapered us when we were kids, yet we are unwilling to take care of our parents when they need help.

"God! Can you please tell me why our survival is such a crushing burden?"

The conflict among the siblings heightened as they argued about taking responsibility for their father when his illness became more severe. At the same time, dreams and visions of home haunted Zi-Shan's brain. He was in a never-ending hallucination through which floated apparitions of Waian, Penghu. Of course,

Penghu was the island where he was born. While he was taking his last breath, his hometown was attacked by the typhoon Waian and completely destroyed in one day. Undoubtedly, Zi-Shan's weakened condition couldn't endure those tyrannical winds and rains on the island that was as close as flesh and blood to him, and so he stopped struggling with his illness.

When the doctor confirmed that smoking played a major part in the death of Zi-Shan, Lian-Zi felt completely frustrated. She used to buy the leading US brand of cigarettes for her smoke-addicted and unhappy father. How could she blame her brothers for Father's death when she was the chief criminal?

The sorrow of nameless days clung to Lian-Zi's heart like moss around an old tree.

Epilogue

The ship, *Tai-Peng-Lun*, draws alongside the shore of Magong, Penghu, in the summer of 1996. From the ship, Lian-Zi sees the port, as if her eyes could see through the minds of islands and sea. A strong sea breeze kisses Lian-Zi's face, and she feels her ancestors' warm hugs. She appreciates with deep emotion that all her abilities were given to her by her parents, the strength and focus of her father steady as a fixed star, and the maternal pliancy of her mother like the shimmering moon in the well.

At the Wenwang Temple in the village of Waian, where her father's name was carved, there is still the painted sea, wind-sketched outlines, surf swaying constantly while waves curl up to the seashore and an endless stream of pilgrims with unsophisticated reverence.

At the midpoint between Waian and Neian, in the tomb area near the historical site of Si Islet West Fortress, a gravestone "The Zhu Family Mausoleum" still stands against the strong wind in an upright position, perched high on the cliffs above the Taiwan Strait. Lian-Zi thinks of her ancestors' hundred years of trial, from the battles of the Sino-Japanese War to the Penghu of today—the wartime beacon of fire has been extinguished, and the colonial age has passed too, but beloved cultural traditions and family love are still warm and never-ending.

Even though God allows the sufferings of all human beings to go on and on, and the beautiful chrysanthemums have withered, we continue to devote ourselves to moving through the vastness of history from generation to generation.

The ship at Waian Bay contains haunting childhood memories as the Penghu moon in the well lights up many past lives, both happy and sad, under the stars and on the waters.